# Ariel

## DANCING ON TV

Ailish Sinclair

GRAUPIUS

First published in 2025 by Graupius Books

Produced in Scotland

ISBN 978-1-7396159-5-6 Paperback Edition

www.ailishsinclair.com

Ariel: Dancing on TV contains memories of abuse and threat of violence.

For Patti, Ann, Georgina and Janet

# 1

It's the night before I'm due to start at the most prestigious dance school in Scotland, so, of course, my mother tries to kill me.

She's always done horrible things at moments that matter, but up until now, she mainly just used words. Psychological abuse is easier to hide from others. I always told myself that was worse: the secret cruelty.

But I was wrong. This is worse. This means nothing can ever be the same again.

So now, after the stabbing, and the screaming, and the fleeing, and the words – because there's always words – I'm at the top of a tall, dark tower, hiding and waiting. It was the only choice I had, to come here. She knows so little of who I truly am that she would never guess this is where I'd run to.

So, I escaped. I got away from her.

I hate myself for shaking: should be strong! I hate myself for jumping at the sound of a vehicle in the field: should be brave!

Is it him? Or is it her? I lean out, peering between two of the small turrets of the tower, and can just make out the square shape of the familiar 4X4 below.

The sight should make things better, but it doesn't. I want to run and meet him, but I don't. I am immobile as if I've become an inanimate object now, so I just listen. The hollow centre of the tower carries his footsteps to me, bottom to top, round and round and then – finally – his arms are round me.

Jonasz. I press my face into his chest and feel his strength and his gentleness. Just to stand like this is all I need in this moment, but we don't stay this way for long. Because he needs to know what happened. Of course he does. It's just difficult to remember and difficult to speak. My neck is bleeding. He tells me that.

My head feels thick and stupid. I'm in shock. That's what Tomas says when I get into his car. When I see him, Jonasz's father, I only feel embarrassed and ashamed. This is what everyone sees now: Ariel broken and Ariel sad, and I don't want that to be me.

I'm going to report my mother to the police. That's my grand plan, and it's the strongest thing I can do now. Jonasz and Tomas agree with me on this, but they want to go to the hospital first as if that's the main priority. There's a brief argument before I realise that the police can be summoned from the hospital, and maybe that's better anyway. Doctors will write things down and that will be proof.

What a night of proof. Proof that she stabbed me: seven stitches go in. Proof that Jonasz loves me: he doesn't want me to see him cry, but I do. Proof of my total freakdom: doctors and police discover my hand.

"Was this her too?" asks a meaning-to-be-kind doctor, holding my two-fingered hand in his. He's noting how much of the palm is missing as he sees the jagged V shape for the first time, and his professional interest is piqued.

I don't tell him how amazingly strong the hand is or give any indication that it can hold almost anything with ease. I just answer the question he asked: "No, it happened in an accident when I tried to run away, years ago."

It is linked to a pattern of abuse then, they all agree. Labels are handed out like treats at Halloween, sticky and scary, scaly and sharp: neglected, traumatised, victim.

I make an important decision when the doctor asks if I have somewhere safe to go. I'm going home with Jonasz and Tomas, which seems great to begin with because I get to sit by Jonasz in the dark in the back of the 4X4 and hold his hand and calm down and feel a little bit normal again. But it's not normal, and it's not great. It's another one of those things that will never be the same again.

We soon arrive at the Serafin family farmhouse. Janet, Jonasz's mum, is no longer just friendly Janet who smiles at me and suspects things and tries to make awkward encounters easier. This is Janet who's just discovered that her son and I are not the enemies we pretended to be to keep me safe from my mother. She knows it was him that I called when I needed help. Questions hang in the air all around us in Janet's kitchen, for the room is her domain; there's no question about that. She makes cups of tea, darting sideways looks at us as she does so: me on the high stool, Jonasz standing between my legs, hardly having let go of me since he arrived in the tower.

"I'm so glad you came to us," says Janet, again, and then she tries really hard to normalise things: "I know it feels terrible now, Ariel, but this is a turning point for you. The worst is over. And don't you worry about having to go to the castle school tomorrow. I'll phone them in the morning; I'm sure there'll be no problem."

"I'm going," I say, and they all stare at me, the whole family who are now gathered round the big old-fashioned breakfast bar, clutching steaming brown mugs of tea. "To the castle," I clarify in case they thought I was going to walk out of the house or something. "They wait-listed me—"

"I know, love," Janet interrupts.

3

More clarification is needed. "No, you see, one person dropped out, and they arranged my audition last week even though it was the Christmas holidays, and they only take ten students each year, and I'm not going to miss a moment of it and let someone else get my place." Possibly more clarification than was needed. But this matters: "That's what she wanted. I know she intercepted my original application for a September start there. She was trying to sabotage it again."

Janet gets it. They all do.

I explain a bit more anyway. "It's what I do, who I am. No matter what's going on, I can always stand at the barre, and bend and stretch and focus only on that."

"I'll fetch your stuff for you," says Jonasz with a squeeze of my hand.

My stuff! I'd forgotten all about that and... "Caliban!" My dog. He must be terrified with everything that has happened tonight.

"I'll get him too," Jonasz promises. "I know how to break into that house, remember? I know where the hidden key is."

I smile before seeing Janet's face. She is learning new things about her son tonight, and they are only good things, but she doesn't understand that. Jonasz once saved me when I was locked in the house with no food and no heat. My parents went to stay in a hotel to wait out the winter power cut. I was left behind. He came. He found the key. He brought warmth and safety and love. I want to say it, to proclaim the goodness of Jonasz to the room, but Janet changes the subject before I can.

"I'll make up a bed for you," she says.

"She'll sleep with me," says Jonasz, both arms round my back now, pulling me closer.

And the question is given form, as if it's an actual other person in the room, standing there, laughing at the fact I didn't notice that they've been there all along. Everybody is wondering

4

if we've had sex. Well, maybe not six-year-old Jack; I hope not six-year-old Jack. But we haven't. I'm sixteen, and Jonasz is seventeen, and we haven't. One day. One day in the great big forever that is us. But not yet. We decided that long ago. I would like to tell this truth, to say it out loud, but at the same time I don't want to, and it's not like it's anyone else's business anyway, and I don't like being told what to do, so I just say: "I'll sleep on the sofa."

Older brother Janek, usually only grumpy and rude, currently looking like he wants to laugh, speaks up: "You can have my room. I'm back at Uni tomorrow, so it makes sense. Dude," he says to Jonasz. "She'll need her own space."

_ele_

Janek is really tall, and his room, his own space, seems to have been built around the fact. The shelves of books are so high, the chair and desk are set for tall, and even the bed is super long. Was it specially made? I don't know, but it's an easier question to ponder than the others that are spinning through my mind.

Questions: has she been arrested yet? Or did she run away and escape? Is she still out there? Has my father been told and summoned back from offshore? What will he say? And where is Jonasz? His dad went with him to get my things; that's good, because what if she was still there? Stinking of whisky and wielding a knife? I need to wash away that last image of her and its accompanying smell.

I shower and put on a T-shirt and pyjama bottoms that belong to Jonasz. They smell of him too; it's a mix of soap and laundry stuff and something big and strong and expansive like the Aberdeenshire landscape that he spends so much of his time in.

And then he's here and it's such a relief that I cry, which is shameful and embarrassing. Again. He's got a bag of my belongings and says Caliban is downstairs and curled up with the other dogs already.

"Sorry about saying that in front of them all about the sleeping arrangements," he adds. "I just thought it would be better to, you ken..."

"I don't know, I don't ken; you'll have to tell me."

"Ariel," he says, stretching out my name as his smile stretches to one side in embarrassment.

"Say it for me, Jonasz Serafin. It would be better to...?"

I study him as he squirms, each freckle across his nose perfectly placed, his short brown hair messed kind of to one side like his smile. He'd been in bed when I'd called, of course he had. Safe and sound until I burst into his night, all wounded and needy and—

"Snuggle!" he announces, and it comes out so loud that I laugh. "I thought it would be better to snuggle tonight," he explains.

Then kissing Jonasz takes everything else away. For a few moments the whole world is warm and loving and good, how it always should be, how I always want it to be.

And then his mum walks in with towels. And then he goes. And then it proves super surprisingly easy to get to sleep: almost being murdered has to have some benefits, I suppose.

2

I STARE UP AT the castle. Jonasz stares up at the castle. The school is a great big block of a building with lots of narrow, pointed windows and a tall tower at the back. Towers, we know. Towers, we can do. It's the rest of it that's daunting.

Opening the curtains in Janek's room this morning gave me a close-up view of our tower on the hill in the field. It's a monument to some politician of the past. It's where Jonasz and I first met, where we first talked, first kissed, and then, more recently, very recently, where I hid from a would-be murderer.

"Hey," says Jonasz now, leaning on the steering wheel of the 4X4 and turning towards me.

"Hey," I say back. "So what are you doing today?"

"Ploughing."

"Maybe I can come and sit in the tractor with you, instead of... you know..." I gesture at the huge building in front of us.

He leans over and takes both my hands in his. "You're beautiful. You're perfect. And you're brilliant. You'll wow 'em all in there. You've done a term at the college in London; you'll be way better than everyone else."

I shake my head, holding on to his hands. He's the one who's perfect, and: "This is the better school; it's more exclusive, more scary, more..." I look back at the castle. "It's actually pink and sparkly, isn't it?"

"Harled and painted pink," he confirms, peering up through the windscreen. "Windows are made of pink granite, like the statues at the gate."

Right. The Mermaid and the Bear. Jonasz, knowing a lot about local history, told me they were the first inhabitants of the castle. The tale only added to the weirdness of the morning.

"Okay." I open the car door. "Okay." I climb out. The pink gravel shifts a little under my feet as Jonasz hands me out my bag.

"I'll be here at five," he tells me. "Text if the time changes, or if you just want to text me because you miss me so much."

So he gets me to smile as I quake in my boots in front of the castle.

I turn and walk away from him, feet crunching over the gravel. I climb the steps to the huge studded door and look back at him. He waves and starts the engine. I turn back and knock on the door with my left hand; it hardly makes any noise at all on the solid wood. I hear Jonasz drive away and use my right hand to knock instead. When it forms a fist shape you would hardly know that three fingers and three knuckles are missing. The strength in the remaining thumb and little finger is immense after all the years of physio, and I succeed in making a satisfyingly large sound on the black painted door.

There's no sound from within, though, so I try the golden knob and the thick door swings inwards.

I step into the big echoey entrance hall with its black-and-white floor and carved stone angels up by the ceiling. When I came for my audition, I took the wide staircase at the back of the room to an upstairs dance studio, but today all the noise – a steady hum of many voices talking all at once – is coming from a doorway to the left.

I hesitate, reconsidering the 'no gloves' plan. I always wore them at college in London, and people always wondered. I saw their eyes lingering, minds thinking, imagining the horror beneath the gloves. So, here I planned to bare everything from the first, get any shock and disgust over with, and maybe it could be forgotten about? In time? Or not.

I unzip my bag and rummage for the gloves. Everything's so disordered. Jonasz has shoved all sorts of things in here that I don't need.

"You must be Ariel!"

The words put a stop to the search, and I look up to see a large woman approaching at speed.

"Well, look at you," she says, placing one hand on each of my upper arms and staring. I study her too. She looks kind, grandmotherly, not that I really know about such things, but I think she's that. "You ken this," she says, speaking a bit like Jonasz; 'ken' is how he says 'know' too. "You really remind me of Amalphia when she first came here, all big eyes and dark hair, looking about her and not kenning fit to think."

It's a huge compliment. Amalphia Treadwell is a famous actress. She's very beautiful, and she was a student here and at the college I was at in London too, so we do have an educational background in common. I don't believe the stories about her having two husbands. That can't be true; it wouldn't be legal for a start, though the tale did feature in some of my mother's pre-attempted-murder ravings. The words 'perverted' and 'degenerate' did too.

The woman introduces herself as Holly, the housekeeper. "You can come through to see me in the kitchen anytime if you need anything, even just a wee chat." Holly is obviously a big Amalphia Treadwell fan. She tells me that Amalphia is a counsellor at the school and that I'll be seeing her – everybody does – and I'm 'not to be feart' to tell her anything as she's been through all sorts herself.

I want to ask if the two-husbands thing is true, but I don't. Anyway, there's not time. I'm quickly bustled through to the enormous room on the left where all the noise is coming from. It goes quiet. Thirty students and about ten members of staff turn their faces away from their breakfasts to look at me.

Mr. Zolotov, the man who I saw at my audition, the head of the school – famous dancer and possibly one of the two husbands – stands and introduces me. He encourages everyone to welcome me and show me where things are. There's a collective "Hi!" and the eyes return to the breakfasts.

Holly points me to the long first-year table and encourages the eating of toast and bacon and beans and cereal and smoothies and tells me that food can be obtained from the canteen area at the far side of the hall at any time.

I take a piece of toast then glance up at the interested faces of my new classmates. Like Holly, they look friendly too, and I determine to learn all their names quickly and efficiently.

I've sat down beside **Clinton.** He is black and impressively muscular. He shows me his bicep which is how I know this last bit. He tells me that he's the best partner to get in pas de deux, partnering class, as he's the strongest. Mr. Zolotov's son, Alexander, who is away at the dentist this morning, thinks he's the best, but this is not true at all according to Clinton.

"It was him got Chantal expelled," Clinton explains. "You'll need to watch out for him."

"Clinton, that's not true," hisses a bespectacled girl from across the table. "Don't mislead Ariel with gossip on her first day."

"He was involved," counters Clinton. "They was always up to stuff together."

"Chantal wasn't making the required progress," states a bespectacled boy from beside the bespectacled girl, and I think they're actually twins. Their faces are tilted towards Clinton and

10

me in disapproval. Their expressions are really similar looking, and it's a little bit unnerving.

"She fell behind because of all the night-time escapades with Alexander, duh!" says Clinton, then quickly moving on. "We was all told what happened to you—"

"Clinton!" says the female twin, but Clinton holds up a large splayed hand at her as if warding off evil.

"We was also told not to say anything," says Clinton, "but I'm putting it out there, in case you want to talk about it, not that you have to, but you might want to, and that's fine."

He looks at me and smiles. He seems really open and honest and genuine. I smile back because I suddenly know just what to do to put everything on my terms.

"Do you mean what happened to me last night, when my mother tried to kill me?" I ask. "Or do you mean this?" I hold up my hand, splayed as Clinton's was moments earlier, only mine makes a lumpy and purple-lined V shape. "When I fell into a threshing machine as a kid and got three fingers chopped off?"

It's a perfect moment. Everybody's gobsmacked except Clinton who reaches forwards and says: "That's amazing; can I touch it?" and, when I nod, he does.

And no one has ever done exactly this before. Jonasz touches, he holds my hand like there's nothing different. But it is different. It's really different.

And Clinton actually seems impressed by it. "Gives you a really cool look," he says. "A USP. Unique selling point. Dancers need that, to stand out, be spotted, you know."

There's no time to dwell on this unique – really unique – way of looking at my deformity, because breakfast is over and the entire school is moving, like some sort of graceful dancer-y ocean, towards the door. I swim along with them, noticing the grand fireplace and blazing flames within as I ride the current back into the entrance lobby.

# 3

OUR CLASS IS HEADED to the dungeon, a big studio below ground, to take morning class. It's the biggest dance studio in the UK and, like so many things here, it's famous. It once caved in, but was then done up in environmentally friendly ways and has been on TV many times.

The older students set off up the stairs while we first years pile into the elevator.

"Wait! Wait!" A tiny Indian girl arrives, breathless, in muddy running shoes and pink leggings. "I'm ready. I'm ready."

Clinton introduces **Belinda** and tells me that her unique selling point, or USP, is that she never keeps still. She grins and the lift doors close.

By the time we've reached the bottom – just how deep is this studio? – I've met:

**Henry**: bleached blond hair hanging over his eyes, shy looking. USP: only speaks one word at a time. Yes, really. He says "Aye," to confirm this, but I don't think he's Scottish.

**Bubbles**: actually called Serena, but she's bubbly. "I am," she giggles, doing jazz hands, blonde curls bouncing around happily.

**Star** is a Goth girl with really big make-up and really big hair which would never have been allowed at the college in London. She looks gentle behind it all, though.

**Lewis** is a sour-faced boy from Aberdeen. He's very thin with brown hair and rolls his eyes when Clinton states: "Lewis likes to make out he's the bad boy of the group, but he's kidding no one; we all know that's Alexander."

Then there's **Paul** and **Paula**, the twins: dark hair, dark-rimmed spectacles, serious faces.

"And that completes the freak show," says Lewis.

"No," corrects Clinton. "I complete the show. I stand out the most. I'm a tall, tall Englishman in a short Scottish world."

Lewis snorts.

"What?" demands Clinton. "I get admiring looks when I go up the village."

"Right," says Lewis with a snigger. "Admiring."

"Oh, shut up," says Clinton.

"No, you shut up," replies Lewis, but thankfully we've arrived.

The elevator doors slide open and Clinton and Lewis run into the studio and accost our teacher (**Guy**, Australian, sexy and he knows it) with questions about pas de deux partnerings.

I leave them to it, taking the opportunity to stare in wonder at the enormous space while people are otherwise engaged. We're in a room that's the size of a football pitch. I think. Jonasz would know. There's pillars dotted about the place, holding up the ceiling. The smooth whitewashed walls only make the room seem even bigger. I examine a stone plaque on the wall and find images of the Mermaid and the Bear and thistles and a heart.

The words "Well, maybe Ariel should decide!" call me back to the others. Lewis said the words and he says some more now: "I'm a more compatible height."

"But I would be better overall," says Clinton.

"Size isn't everything," says Lewis causing Henry to do some sort of laugh/cough thing. Lewis glares at him and continues:

"It's all moot, anyhow. If Alexander wants her, he'll get her. That's how it works round here."

"No, it isn't," says Guy, turning to me. "Don't worry, Ariel. Mr. Timms will arrange the best pairings this afternoon."

Boys are fighting over me, only in a ballet way, but it's still an entirely new experience. And it's ongoing.

"You could stand by me," says Clinton gesturing to a space at the barre.

"Or you could take Alexander's spot at the front by me," Lewis points out.

"Alexander goes at the back when his dad's teaching," informs Clinton.

"With added slouch," agrees Lewis, and they both laugh.

Everyone is at the barre, neatly in place, except me. I'm supposed to make this choice that will offend someone, but two boys are basically telling me what to do which makes the decision easy.

"Could I squeeze in here?" I ask Belinda and Star.

I can and I do, and then class begins, and it's awesome in oh-so-many ways. It's hard. I struggle to keep up at times, and I struggle with the very concept that I struggle to keep up. It's never happened before, though I've always wanted it to: I'm being properly stretched in this properly difficult class. The choreography in the centre is hard to pick up, and the jumpy allegro routines are fast and exhausting.

This school is different to anything I've ever known. I was always the best, in my local ballet classes as a kid, and in the top first-year class at the college. I can no longer say that.

Everybody is good here, really good. Clinton's power is incredible; he fills the underground studio with it. I want to watch them all: Henry's purity of line, his face almost angelic at times; the way Bubbles embodies the music, flowing and frothy and,

I guess, bubbly; and then the twins who are so similar to each other, like perfect corps de ballet dancers.

Everyone is, in fact, utterly perfect, utterly mesmerising, but I can't pause to watch. I'm still struggling. Guy corrects so much about me: my shoulders, my arms; he encourages me to use more energy, to fill the space. Who does he think I am? Clinton?

I feel the shift of life again: everything different, nothing the same, ever. I'm going to improve here, and fast. I have to. It's going to be amazing. These people are amazing. We reach the end of class with a very stretchy curtsey/bow révérence, and my muscles are in shaky spasm with the exertion of it all.

And then it's like a celebration. "Good class, good class!" We all high five each other, chanting the words. It isn't till after the high five that I realise I used my right hand for it, and no one reacted or commented.

"That was the best class I've ever had," I tell them all.

"Aren't you the sweetest?" says Guy who gets into the elevator with us.

And I think about the other big difference here: the clothes. Once the knitted ballet warm-ups got peeled off, the other students became a rainbow of colour to my very plain black leotard and pink ballet tights. That was how we had to be at the college: generic ballet girls and boys, all. Here there's colours and tie dye, and football teams, and stars and stripes and even a unicorn. Bubbles has a lilac leotard with a sparkly unicorn. I wonder where she got it.

I would love to be colourful like the others but... An uncomfortable subject surfaces in my mind: money. I don't have any and can't buy new stuff, and I have nobody that I can ask for any. The Serafin family are doing an embarrassing amount of looking after and feeding and driving me around as it is.

But, as the elevator doors open to the foyer, I wonder if the problem is about to be clarified. I somehow doubt, solved. I doubt anything good will come from what I'm seeing here.

My father is in the entrance hall with Holly. He looks round as we all pour out of the lift. Black-and-white floor below him, stone angels overhead, he doesn't smile. He just stands there, unshaven, freshly summoned from his oil rig in his working jeans, and he glares.

# 4

"I'LL SHOW YOU THROUGH to the office," Holly says to me, and to him, my father. "Get Aleks," she adds with a sideways glace at Guy, and he heads up the stairs.

She leads us up a dark corridor behind the dining hall, chatting all the time, about the weather, and how was his flight? Was it stormy at sea? Would he like a cup of tea? He would not. She tells us to sit, and we do.

The office is big and sunny and filled with books and papers and pens and lots of dance photos. Holly steps out of the room to hurry Aleks, Mr. Zolotov, along and I'm left alone with my father who continues to glare at me.

I study the family photos on Mr. Zolotov's desk and think about family: my father is Scottish but very properly spoken. Not like Jonasz. Jonasz's father is Polish and a kind person, like Jonasz, but not like my father. Jonasz and I both have English mothers, but they are nothing alike.

My father speaks, his voice cold and monotonous and proper as he tells me what to do: "You will drop these ridiculous charges at once. You'll contact the police right now, on this phone here," – he points at the old-fashioned black telephone on the desk – "and change your statement."

I examine some of the dance photos on the wall. I recognise Amalphia Treadwell in one of them.

"Are you listening to me, Ariel?" my father continues. "Your mother is in a terrible state. This nonsense stops now."

"She tried to kill me." I look at him to see what he thinks about this.

He shakes his head. "She had a little too much to drink. Things got a little bit out of hand. There's no need to make a fuss."

I've heard these words before. They are his go-to words whenever she does anything abusive that he can't ignore. It's as if he hopes that by saying, 'little bit,' he can lessen what's happened; you know, make it 'not a crime.'

I point at the stitched up part of my neck. "This is where she stuck me with the knife," I tell him. "I moved fast else it would have gone right in." He'd said the charges were ridiculous. I know it's ridiculous to think that maybe all that's needed here is more clarification, but I provide it anyway: "And I would be dead."

He's furious. He loses it. He has me by the two sides of my crossover cardigan, almost lifting me out of my chair. "You will toe the line if you want to keep coming to this place, missy. You will drop those charges—"

Everything suddenly happens so fast that I don't quite know how, but I've been let go and Mr. Zolotov is standing between me and my father. Mr. Zolotov is taller than my father. My father is looking up at him now, not quite so furious and glary anymore.

Mr. Zolotov's Ukrainian accent is strong and his tone deep as he says: "No person is ever to behave to another person this way in my school. No man should ever behave this way to a woman."

My father sneers and looks past Mr. Zolotov to me. "She's not a woman, she's a stupid little girl who—"

18

"I have witnessed an assault," says the head of the school. "Before I call the police, you have something supportive to say to your daughter?"

My parent makes several false starts. Most of them begin with: "Well..." It's difficult for him. New territory. He huffs and puffs and finally manages: "Well, if you think I'm still paying for all this finery, you've got another think coming."

Mr. Zolotov, still standing between us: "Then you have no business being here, and you will leave." He says it in a way that cannot be disobeyed.

So my father leaves.

Mr. Zolotov sits down in the chair beside mine. "You are not to worry about your place here; it is assured, and we will sort the money for your fees. Would you like me to contact the police for what has happened here today?" He says happened like 'heppened.' It's kind of nice. I shake my head because: enough charges and police and shouting and horribleness.

"I will write up a report of the incident," the teacher tells me. "It will serve as evidence if you ever need it. But you are shaken. We need sweet tea, and maybe cake, yes?"

It seems such an odd thing for this handsome and important man to say that, in spite of everything, I laugh. I had a poster of him on my bedroom wall when I was younger. The picture was from when he was much younger. My mother made me take it down; she said it was indecent due to the wearing of tights. And here he is in real life, now, offering me cake. He's not in tights, though; he's wearing black jeans.

We go through to the kitchen, and it's a proper historical-looking castle kitchen, like we've stepped into another time. We haven't really, of course; there's a modern cooker and kettle under the huge fireplace archway. Mr. Zolotov puts the kettle on and urges me to sit at the long table.

19

"Ach, it's wee Ariel!" says Holly, as she comes into the room, and she squeezes my shoulders before proceeding to put cake and biscuits out on the table, and there we all sit.

I'm not stupid. I know glances have been exchanged, and they must both know my recent history and be feeling sorry for me, and I don't like it. I don't like the pity. And I'm fine anyway. I don't need the pity.

"I'm missing contemporary class," I say.

It's not a good start to my first day, and it's not who I want to be: almost missing the first day completely because I was almost killed by my mother, then actually missing classes because I was actually assaulted by my father.

"Everybody misses parts of the curriculum in their first week," Mr. Zolotov tells me. "The school doctor sees each new student and also you can speak to a counsellor if you like. Amalphia is in this afternoon."

"Well, that's a good idea," says Holly. "You can have a good wee natter; it disna have to be about the serious stuff, but it's good to ken you've got someone to speak to, someone who's not a teacher, or a cook, especially if it's the teaching or cooking you want to complain aboot!"

It's arranged, and after pas de deux class I'll get to meet the great Amalphia Treadwell. I won't ask if she has two husbands. I'll just wonder.

# 5

I DON'T HAVE TO wonder about the husbands for long. After the cake in the kitchen, I go through to the dining hall and sit with a mug of tomato soup as prescribed by Holly. Then various waves of people flood into the hall. Third years. Second years. My class pile their plates high. I'm a little surprised at the food-lovingness of them. People nibbled on apples and bits of cheese at the college. This is different, again, and I like it.

Heads turn as an assortment of children and Amalphia Treadwell – yes, it's really her – arrive in the doorway. The older children head straight to the canteen area to get food. The smallest, a tiny dark-haired girl in a blue tutu and ballet shoes, goes straight to the teachers' table with Amalphia and sits by Mr. Zolotov. Amalphia kisses Mr. Zolotov, like really kisses him, for a really long amount of time.

"It's true," Clinton whispers really loudly in my ear.

"What?" I ask.

"What you're thinking. What you're wondering about. Well, it is!" These last three words are said to the twins, as if they had complained.

"It is," they confirm, as one.

"It's actually pretty cool," says Star.

"Polyamory," says Henry.

"Oh, yes," adds Bubbles, smiling with enthusiasm. "They all teach here sometimes; you'll meet them all."

All? Exactly how many—

"More to the immediate point," says Lewis, with a smirk. "Who's going to tell Alexander?"

"Tell him what?" I ask.

"That he's no longer the best in the class," declares Clinton. "I get to tell him, I call it, it's going to be me."

And then a boy sits down in front of me, and I can't believe that I didn't notice him come in with the others. I never knew it was possible for someone to be this good looking. His dark blond hair seems to do that shampoo-advert thing, to sway gracefully to the side in slow motion as he moves his head. It seems as if there's romantic and dramatic music playing like in a film, but that's stupid; there can't be. This is no film. This is Mr. Zolotov when young, a boy from a bedroom wall. This has to be Alexander.

Alexander looks at me with his big brown eyes. Alexander smiles at me, and a spark of white light glints from his perfect teeth. And then he speaks. To me.

"So," he says. "Is it true?"

True? I blush all over. Does he know what I was wondering about his parents? Is he asking for my assessment of that? Or is it about what happened to me, the things that everyone knew about earlier? I don't know which is worse, but I don't want him to be asking about either of these things.

He must sense a question in my silence, and he offers the needed clarity: "Does my new partner have better extension than me?" He flashes that sparkly smile again. It's infectious. I find myself grinning back, like an idiot.

"Who told you?" demands Clinton.

"Guy."

"Oh," says Clinton, disappointed. "Well, it's true. But the partner thing's not decided. Timms is going to see about it this afternoon."

Alexander smiles again, full of beautiful confidence, and I feel a need to put something right here. Maybe there's some sort of sheen of newness or novelty about me today, but they all seem to think I'm way better than I am.

"I've hardly done any partner work," I tell them. "We only did shoulder lifts and simple promenades at the college. So, maybe you should be competing to, like, not get me as a partner?"

"Pas de deux virgin?" says Lewis. "We all want you, baby. Mould you to our way of doing things, isn't it?"

"Ignore him," advises Paula, needlessly.

I am ignoring Lewis. It's the fact that Alexander is still looking at me that is taking up all my attention. I know I haven't taken my hand, that hand, out from under the table since he sat down, and it's become an issue. He wasn't here for the grand gesture earlier. I can't do it again. And I really don't want to see his beautiful face look horrified or disgusted or freaked out in any way.

"So, have you got the cottage that's just been done up?" Paula asks, which is distracting but also confusing.

"Oh, it's just lovely," informs Bubbles. "They've done it in seascape colours, all aquamarines and purples. I could share with you if you don't want to be alone?"

"Thanks a lot, Serena," says Paula. "Then I'd be on my own."

"Yes, but after what Ariel's been through—"

I interrupt: "I'm not staying here; I'm staying at my boyfriend's house."

They're all immediately fascinated. What's he like? What's his name? How old is he? Is he a dancer too? They are far more interested in Jonasz than he seems to be in them later in the car on the way back to his parents' house.

He starts off really concerned when I first run out to him and climb in beside him at the end of the day. There are lots of hugs

23

and kisses; he'd been feeling that he shouldn't have driven off and left me in the morning, after all that had happened.

"Was your neck all right, Ariel?" he asks now as we drive off. "I was worried about you dancing with the injury."

"It hasn't hurt at all," I say truthfully, putting a hand up to my stitches, having forgotten that they'd been fully visible all day, and using the sun visor mirror to examine them. "Not even in pas de deux, and it was so difficult. But fantastic. Alexander is such an amazing partner. Mr. Timms said we should just stay together for now as we're working well."

The tale of Alexander's helpfulness, how he'd guided me and explained things and caught me when I over balanced, doesn't appear to impress Jonasz. He's very quiet through it. So I don't mention that Alexander held my hand like there was nothing different, how he hadn't flinched, hadn't seemed to be trying not to flinch even. The fact that all the touching, the holding, the lifting, the balancing and the intertwining of legs and arms had been super intense also seems best left out of the conversation. It had been strangely sexy when it shouldn't have been. I'm just not used to it and, like my father's visit, it's a nothing, and hardly worthy of thought or mention.

Where Jonasz and I find common ground is in my counselling session with Amalphia. "She was really nice, normal, you know?" I tell him. "She spilled hot chocolate down her front."

"Aye? And is it true about the two husbands?"

"Yes. At least, I think so; the others said it was, but they used the word all, as in: I'll meet them all, as in I'll meet them all, as they all teach at the castle sometimes."

"And did she help you? Did you talk about what happened?"

"No, we just chatted about pas de deux and the castle and you. I told her about you."

"Why, is she on the look-out for hubbie number three? Four?"

"Jonasz!"

But we're laughing, and that's good. We're not surround-ed by the bad things as the headlights illuminate the tall tower on the hill and we arrive home, to Jonasz's home, to be engulfed in dinner smells and more queries of well-being, and the sound of the television and an excited mass of ginger fur and excitement. Caliban is glad to see me and happy and tail-waggy, and I love him so much.

Amalphia had mentioned, as I was leaving her small office earlier in the day, that reaction to trauma can be delayed, and that I could go to any of the teachers or Holly at any time if I was struggling. She'd said they'd all been through some shit – she'd actually said that word – and that they would all understand.

I don't talk about any of that now in the happy house of Serafins. I smile and laugh with them through dinner, and the happiness continues as we all sit down in front of the TV afterwards.

I don't like that the police liaison officer interrupts the happy, relaxed time. I listen as she tells me that charges have been brought against my mother, but I don't ask any questions. I don't want to think about any of that.

Later, by myself in the bath, I just float, thinking of noth-ing but the warmth and the comfort and the quiet.

"It's nice being just through the wall from each other," says Jonasz later as we kiss goodnight before going to our separate beds, him to his, me to Janek's.

And I look out at the tower again before I close the cur-tains, its silhouette stark against large silver clouds that are lit from behind by the moon. Thoughts flow through my mind. Simple thoughts. Basic ones. All that a tired mind like mine can manage.

We used to meet in the tower. We used to be alone there. Alone together. Sometimes we even lay down and went to sleep there for short whiles.

Now we're here. Surrounded by people. Nice people. Good people. But we're not alone together. We never go to sleep together. There's a wall between us now. And that feels like a deeper thought than I can cope with. A 'nothing will ever be the same again' type of thought. So I turn away from the luminous clouds and dark tower and get into the long bed.

Jonasz was right in what he said: it is nice being here. And that's all I want now. Only nice. Only good. Forever and ever and ever.

# 6

ON MY SECOND DAY at the castle, Alexander offers to stay late with me and practise the complex piece we're working on in pas de deux. I text Jonasz to let him know, not foreseeing the concern the decision will cause.

Alexander and I dance for two hours straight that evening with no one else there to take turns and observe and discuss. It's just us and the music, us and Alexander's movie-star smile. Alexander's long legs and arms are much stronger than they look, so we do lift after lift, and turn after turn, until there's more blisters than skin on my feet.

I can barely walk out to the 4X4 when it's over. My legs were sore when I woke up this morning after only one day at the castle. Of course they were. In sixteen years of walking and dancing about this planet, they've never been worked so hard, but the extra evening practice has pushed everything past normal limits of strain and pain. So I hobble over to the car; I limp across the gravel and pull myself up into the passenger seat.

"Has this Alexander guy hurt you?" demands Jonasz.

"No, of course not."

"He must have been too rough; look at the state of you. Where is he?"

"Jonasz," I say, putting my hand on his arm to still him as he seems ready to shoot out of the car on some sort of seek-and-destroy mission. "I'm sore from all the new classes, is all. It'll soon fade. I need the pas de deux help, believe me; they've all done so much more than me."

He touches my face and his voice softens. "You sure you're okay?"

"I'm sure."

I get the feeling that he's not convinced, but we set off up the dark driveway between the trees, pausing to check for traffic at the end of the road. Jonasz only passed his driving test a few months ago, but he's so confident and strong operating the large vehicle. I tell him so, and his shoulders relax a bit.

"I like watching you drive," I say.

He takes my hand in his. "We never got to be like this before," he points out. "Everything's different now. We could go out somewhere together at the weekend. Fit d'you think?"

It's a new thought, and a slightly unsettling one, but he's right. The time of our relationship being a big secret is over. We don't have to pretend to loathe one another so that she won't find out. She's gone, out of the equation, out of my life, and we're free to be us.

"Where would we go?" I ask, intrigued by the idea.

"Anywhere you like. Dinner? Dancing? Or maybe you've had enough dancing... Let's go somewhere on Saturday. If you're not practising with romantic-music boy, that is."

"We have class on Saturday morning, but that's all for the weekend. And I found out about the music."

It had been a mistake to tell Jonasz that rousing music seemed to play whenever Alexander approached, but hopefully I could undo any harm done now. "He has headphones in a lot of the time, little buds, you know? He pulls them out of his ears and leaves the music playing when he's talking to people, so I wasn't imagining it. He showed me tonight; it was the soundtrack to Amalphia's latest film. It was her singing."

"So he's walking round listening to his mum sing? Is he gay?"

"No," I say at once, feeling totally sure of it somehow.

"Oh? How d'you know?"

"I don't," I admit. "I'm not good at assessing people like that, but what does it matter, anyway?"

"It doesn't," he says which is a good clarification. "I'm just saying. Listening to show tunes? Close with his mum?"

Now I'm cross. "You're stereotyping. And you're close with your mum."

"Aye, fitever."

'Fitever' is how people say 'whatever' up here, but Jonasz saying it now is a shock. It's what he often used to say to me when we encountered each other in front of her, to feign indifference and dislike, even hatred, to stop her putting bars on my windows or one of those security monitor things round my ankle. I take my hand back. And we're quiet for the rest of the drive. Then the tower appears on the horizon.

"Ariel, I'm sorry," he says. "I'm affa worried for you, and it's turning me into a right idiot."

"You don't have to worry about me," I assure him. "I'm fine."

—ele—

I have to explain myself all over again in the big old farmhouse. Janet is concerned on two counts: my soreness, soon explained; and then, oddly, she's worried about what I eat.

"Are you on some special dancer's diet?" she asks. "I wondered if that's why you had dinner at the castle tonight."

"No, I was doing extra practice," I explain. "I eat anything. The turkey shapes last night were great."

"She really does eat anything," says Jonasz as if it's a matter of pride. "I often took stuff from the chipper up to the tower, and she ate it all."

29

"Oh," says Janet, frowning. "But what sort of things did you have for dinner at home?"

"Sandwiches," I tell her, again not foreseeing concern, not in a sandwich.

"Your parents ate sandwiches for dinner?"

"No. I made them their meal and then took a sandwich to my room."

"You made the dinner?"

I can't seem to say anything without causing upset. "I like cooking," I explain because I do. It was actually one of the better times of day in that house. They had their drinks. I had a recipe and ingredients and was left in peace to make the best of them, and then I got to be alone in my room, only coming back down to do the dishes. I try to tell it in an upbeat way, but Janet is open-mouthed.

"Ariel, that's terrible," she says. "I feel responsible. You see, I always suspected something was off. I should have spoken out before."

I shake my head because it's not true. None of it was Janet's fault. And the cooking was nothing. Slaps were something. Words were more. But not the cooking. Unless it was lunch for her friends and I did it wrong, or didn't do it at all because she hadn't told me to do it but insisted she had.

But on normal evenings, I used to look out the kitchen window at the tower while I was cutting and chopping and stirring. Sometimes the sky was all pink and mellow, and it made me feel that way too. Sometimes I made something extra to take to Jonasz later.

"Ariel's food's amazing," he says now. "She used to bring me bits. It's like real posh-restaurant stuff."

"I'd love to make a meal for you all," I offer, keen to keep the subject happy. "I can make anything you like if I have a recipe."

But it's not allowed, not yet anyway. I am to do nothing until I'm well settled in and recovered. But I help Jonasz pack the dishwasher. I help Jack with his homework, and that raises yet more concerns for Janet.

"Are you taking academic subjects at the castle too, Ariel?'

"No, well, drama," I say, not sure if that counts as academic, though we will be studying Shakespeare at some point.

"But you're only sixteen, and so bright."

"Mum, it's like vocational college," says Jonasz. "You can go at sixteen."

"There isn't time for anything else," I explain. "Not if you want to get good enough at ballet."

"But what if you were injured?" asks Janet. "Surely you should have something to fall back on?"

"I left school at sixteen too," says Jonasz, and that ends the conversation, if not the atmosphere of disapproval.

Finally we all go to bed on the same side of the tower, the brighter and better side, the opposite side to where I'm used to being. I look out the bedroom window at the tall shape, its turrets just visible in the dark of the January night. Everything behind it is pitch black and invisible as if there's actually nothing there. That house, those bad times; it's like they don't exist anymore. The moon begins to emerge from behind a cloud, and I don't want it to illuminate things that I'm pretending are gone. I don't want it to inspire difficult-to-deal-with thoughts either about 'walls between' and the aloneness or togetherness of Jonasz and me.

The curtains close over the night-time scene with a satisfying swish, and then there's just the blissful nothing of blank, dreamless sleep.

# 7

By Friday morning, my legs are feeling a lot better, though my arms and hands still ache from the new partner work, but I'm excited for our weekly class with Mr. Zolotov. He's the man that made this school what it is. He's supposed to be an inspiring teacher – many of his past students have gone on to great things – and with what happened earlier in the week, in his office with my father, I'm expecting him to be nice to me. You know: kind, easygoing, letting me settle in.

There he is in his signature black, all handsome and lean and amazing.

And then he's horrible to me! Unbelievably mean! I'm not imagining it; he really is picking on me more than anyone else. It's all about my extension, the stretch of my aching arms and legs. It could be longer apparently, the extension. It could express so much more. Like what? The futility of attempting to make my limbs longer than they are? He is frustrated with me, and cross. It makes me frustrated and cross too, and I fling myself around the room in a rage of turning leaps – grand jetés – when we reach that part, the grand allegro part of class.

"Ah, the bars, they begin to break," he says, presumably referencing the strange little speech he gave during the slow and painful adage section of the day. He'd made us stand there, keeping our left legs out to the side at full height while he talked about me having built a cage around myself. I mean, what the actual—? "You are being smaller than you have to be," he says now. "But this will change. I understand that you are partnering Alexander in pas de deux?"

I nod, still breathless from the raging leaps.

"Soon there are to be exciting challenges in that area," he continues. "For you all. Make sure to stretch before your next class." And off he goes, heading out the door.

"What challenges?" I ask, loudly, angered by this new unfairness, at the half-said comment, the almost-reveal, then everything just left hanging like that.

The Great Aleksandr Zolotov halts. He turns and looks at me in surprise, I assume because he's not used to being questioned. His mouth twitches and then breaks into a smile which makes him look younger and so like Alexander. "Is huge secret," he says. "I will be in much trouble if I tell before I am permitted." And he's gone.

"Great guy, my dad," says Alexander at my shoulder. "Don't you think?"

"Hmm..." I say.

Everyone else is abuzz. What was the exciting thing Mr. Zolotov was talking about? Could it be a show? A performance? A guest teacher? Famous names are bounced round the sunny walls and mirrors of the upstairs studio, which though normal sized seems small after a week in the dungeon. Apparently Mr. Zolotov doesn't teach down there if he can help it. He also doesn't allow students to use it without supervision. Alexander and I used this studio for our evening practice; it has good views over the surrounding forest, the trees looking particularly mysterious all lit up by lights from the castle in the evening.

"You were so brave to ask him about it, Ariel," says Bubbles. "Especially when he was being a bit, well..."

"A bit of a tosser?" says Alexander.

I'm the only one that laughs. The rest of our classmates continue the deliberations of what could be going to happen. A TV show of some sort? A reality one? Or a dancing game show? A documentary? Maybe a film's going to be made at the castle? With all Amalphia's contacts, you never know... During the deliberations, black tights go on top of pink ones, and black socks are added for contemporary.

Contemporary is good. Contemporary is nice. No one shouts or tells me my limbs should be any longer than they are.

Then lunch is lasagne, and it's so good. It seems like I haven't really tasted food properly in a while, or maybe I haven't felt anything properly since the 'almost murder' night. Dismissing the odd thought, I ask the others: "Is he often like that? Mr. Zolotov? Picking on one person?"

"Honour!" says Henry, looking straight at me from under his bright blond hair and nodding. I can't ask him for clarification because I've learned that he really does only say one word at a time, and at least a couple of hours will go by before he says another.

"Yeah, totally," agrees Star. "He sees potential in you, and he'll push you till it's released. He was hardest on Henry back at the start of last term."

Henry nods, proud.

"Or," sides Alexander, "he's just an enormous walking ego who enjoys feeling important."

"Ooh, does somebody have daddy issues?" says Lewis with a laugh.

Alexander shakes his head. "I live with him and know him better than you."

"We need you to listen at keyholes for us, Alexander," says Belinda. "Find out what is to occur."

And we're back on the subject of the upcoming 'challenges.'

_ℓℓ_

I learn that Friday afternoons are easy and relaxed at the castle: there's Pilates, drama and swimming. I get out of swimming with my lack-of-swimsuit situation which is a relief because, though everyone was fine with my hand, I don't feel ready to bare the scarred skin of my legs and arms. The large purple band across my thigh is going to stand out in the tights-less setting of swimming like a grotesque garter. Aileen, the second years' ballet teacher, and also a trained lifeguard who supervises swimming, is not pleased but says I can be let off this once.

Afterwards, I head towards the front door of the castle, and Jonasz, to travel home.

"Come on, he's here!" Clinton calls to everyone. "You've kept him hidden all week, sweetie; we want a look."

The entire class stands at the castle door to ogle my boyfriend. At any other school, this behaviour would have been bullying, done for purposes of cruelty and taunting, but here it's just friendly and funny.

I laugh as I run over to the car and get in to the front seat beside Jonasz. "They all want to see you," I explain.

He turns and gives them a wave and a smile. "Which one's Alexander?" he asks.

"Blond boy at the end."

He squints to see. The class are backlit in front of the large arched door; they can probably see us better than we can see them.

We set off, trundling towards the gap in the trees, but then Jonasz brakes and stops, looking in his rear-view mirror. "Someone's coming," he says.

35

It's Clinton; he's running across the gravel, waving his arms in the air as if something's wrong. I wind the window down as he reaches us.

"Henry said two words!" he tells us. "Two words, one right after the other."

"That's awesome," I say. "What were they?"

"Oh, well..." Clinton looks doubtfully across at Jonasz, and I introduce them. "It was about you, Jonasz," he admits. "Henry gets these instant crushes when he sees people for the first time sometimes; last year it was on Alexander, but that fizzled out."

"What did he say, Clinton?" I demand.

"Two words." He pauses, possibly for dramatic effect as discussed in drama earlier. "Farm. Porn." He gestures at Jonasz in his chequered shirt and working boots. "Farm porn."

"Bit much, isn't it?" says Jonasz as we drive away.

So I tell him of Henry's one-word dialogue, and about drama and Pilates, and the exciting and unknown challenges that lie ahead, and Mr. Zolotov's meanness and Henry's one word about that.

"Told you you'd be the best in there," he says, pausing at the end of the road, between the statues of the Mermaid and the Bear, not for dramatic effect but for a kiss, and not just any kiss, a triple kiss like we did when we were younger: forehead, nose, mouth.

It's sweet, and I smile, and it's like I feel an emotion properly for the first time in a while. I think it's my love for Jonasz. Or his for me. We're alone together for this short time. Between places. Instead of a wall between. And it's nice. And it's good. And then we drive home.

8

SATURDAY LUNCH AT THE castle is Shepherd's Pie, and it's lovely, so warming and satisfying. I could get used to eating food that I didn't have to prepare. It feels relaxing and luxurious somehow, even though the dining hall is much louder and noisier than usual. Amalphia teaches weekly children's classes on a Saturday, and the room is full of their waiting families.

I recall how I'd begged to be allowed to attend those classes when I was younger. I knew they'd be better than the dance school I was at, but no: it was not permitted. Too good for me, my mother had said. Yet, here I am.

I'm just finished my meal when Henry calls over from where he's standing, beside the long Gothic windows: "Farm Porn!"

I smile at him and grab my bag, but I'm not at all sure I like Jonasz being referred to this way, and they're all doing it now, using the words like a nickname. There's nothing of porn about Jonasz; he's totally lovely, though, I think as I climb into the car and kiss him. Then, another thought comes: Henry's probably still watching from the dining room windows – we're not properly alone in this moment – so I cut the kiss short.

—ell—

We spend the afternoon at a tractor centre, examining each and every vehicle, Jonasz fantasising about which model he will own one day. I like the blue one with the flashy looking lights and sit in it with him while he tries out every feature and stick and pedal.

"You're right, Ariel," he says. "This is the best one."

The owner of the place is impressed with all the questions and knowledge and tells Jonasz there's a job there if he wants it. Jonasz doesn't want it. He's a man of the soil and the outside; he needs to be driving the tractors, not selling them.

"We're going out for supper," he tells me as we head back to his house in the car.

"Ooh, where to?"

He won't say but tells me jeans are fine to wear. I sense that he's a little nervous, so I am too. There's a feeling of something not quite right about the evening, and I'd rather stay at home and have Janet's potato waffles and tinned spaghetti, but I don't say it. I can tell that Jonasz is excited as well as nervous.

It's dark when we head out; the moon has risen full and orangey red behind the tower. We drive through the village and up a bumpy farm track, and he still won't tell me where we're going, but it's seems unlikely that it's to a pub or a restaurant.

Butterflies dance about in my middle as we reach a large converted barn with lots of other cars parked outside it. They glint in the reddish moonlight as if they're on fire which does not feel like a good omen.

As soon as Jonasz opens the smoked glass door of the barn place, I know exactly where we are, and I quake inside. Twenty or so faces turn to us and, without looking away from them, I reach into my bag. Thankfully, the gloves are there, right on top and easily slipped on before anyone sees.

We're at a Young Farmers gathering. Jonasz knows everyone. He comes here often. I know most of these people from the local secondary school we all attended, so it's like stepping back into a very familiar and totally abhorrent past life.

Everyone's pleased to see Jonasz. Everyone stares at me. I remember Scott, Jonasz's cheery best friend. I think he was the only person who knew about us back then. In the past. Before. In the present, we sit down at a table with just him. Maybe it won't be so bad.

"So, Ariel," says Scott. "You a famous ballerina yet?"

I smile and shake my head, uncomfortably aware of the table of big-haired girls next to us, and the fact that they're all staring and listening.

"She's working on it," Jonasz replies. "Already the best dancer at the castle."

"I'm really not," I say. "I'm only a first year."

"I do like a modest quine," says Scott.

"Well, get your own," says Jonasz and they get up and leave, laughing, to fetch drinks and food.

And they don't come back. They stand up at the bar with a bunch of other boys who keep darting looks back at me. Maybe Jonasz hasn't seen them for a while and has lots to catch up on. Maybe the food is taking a while.

The girls at the next table are whispering, sniggering too, as if we're still at school. I snigger on the inside at their hair. Hello! Are we in an eighties movie?

Time passes so slowly that it's almost like we've stepped into another dimension. The hands of the clock on the wall hardly move. I count the bottles above the bar. I take out my phone and look at it, but it also shows me how slowly time seems to be passing. I listen to small explosive laughs from nearby. I need the loo, and there must be one here, and maybe it'll break the ice.

"Excuse me, can you tell me where the toilets are?" I ask the collective of perms and peroxide, accidently inhaling some of the hairspray mist that surrounds them.

They look astonished to be asked. I remember one of them, Katy, very clearly and expect her to come out with a torrent of abuse. I recall her lifting up my skirt at school one day to show my thigh. She'd shouted: "Freak parts! Buy one, get one free!"

Tonight she just says: "They're through that door there, Ariel. You canna miss 'em."

Turns out, I can miss them. Off the large bar and dining area of this converted barn is a long corridor with many new wooden doors, all unmarked. I open each one, in search of the toilets. There's a cupboard, a kitchen, a room with a freezer and a lot of beer and crisps in it, and then a door that leads directly to the outside. I retrace my steps, but by the time I locate the bathroom, which has a small corridor into it, Katy and her crew are already in there.

I hover round the corner from them, unseen, unsure what I should do. They're chatting loudly, and – surprise, surprise – it's all about me.

The first voice is Katy's and it's loud, echoey with bathroom acoustics: "Can you believe Jonasz fancies that?"

"He doesn't, Katy," says one of the other girls. "He likes you, it's easy to see. He must just feel sorry for her."

Girl number three chimes in. "Aye, Katy slow danced wi' him at Christmas. Three songs. I dinna even believe Ariel's mother tried to kill her. She's just makin' that up for attention. Maxine's a real fine woman to speak to, and even if she did do it, who could blame her?"

There's a group cackle. Maybe they're dancing round a cauldron in there.

"She's such a little freak." That's Katy again. "Hiding it under her gloves, did you see it when she came in? The Claw!"

"So, is Jonasz a good kisser?" one of the girls asks.

Katy is very definite with her answer: "Oh aye, he knows fit he's doing."

Unsure no more, I walk back along the corridor and take the door to the outside. It's cold which is refreshing. It's dark so I'm invisible. The moon looks down and doesn't judge, merely lighting the way for me. I know it's not that far back to Janet and Tomas's house, but I wish I could walk even further, all the way home to the castle.

By the time I reach the proper road, the moon has gone behind a cloud, a puffy cotton-wool ball of a cloud which is now lit up all round the edges. There is no silver lining down here on the ground, though, only a damaged girl, a girl out of place, a girl shining her phone light on the road.

A car approaches from behind, and I step up onto the grassy verge to let it pass.

The car stops and the window rolls down. "Ariel!" It's Jonasz.

I resume my walk along the road.

He gets out of the car and runs after me. "Ariel, get in the car!"

"No." I shake his hand off my arm and keep walking.

"Fit happened? I don't understand."

I turn and examine him in the phone light and can see that he's looking totally exasperated with me.

"Go back to your night out," I say.

"Our night out, Ariel. Or it was supposed to be."

"Well, now it doesn't have to be. You're off the hook. Free as a bird."

"Let's get back in the car and talk about it there."

When it becomes plain this is not going to happen, he returns to the car and follows me in it, which is really aggravating. When

41

hail stones begin to pelt, he pulls out alongside me. "Please? Now?"

I get in. Girl defeated. But we don't talk. I go straight to bed when we arrive back at his house. We don't kiss goodnight like usual, and I actually feel glad of the wall between us. And then I feel sad, really sad, properly sad, about both the wall and the gladness, and it's all too confusing. So I just try to empty my mind and sleep. And it feels like that keeps me busy all night long.

# 9

SUNDAY. WORD OF THE day: awkward.

"Are you okay?" asks Jonasz as his family buzz around us in the kitchen getting toast and jam.

I didn't sleep much so I'm really tired. Words from the evening played in my head all night, and I'm confused. His question is too large, so I just look at him to try and see the truth of everything in his face. He looks all earnest and concerned. It's not his fault if it's true that he doesn't fancy me like the girls implied last night. If he just felt sorry for me all those years. What does it mean, though? That he's a good person? I can't really judge him for that, can I? But what if he really did kiss Katy like she said? What then? I feel too tired and muddled to work it all out.

"We always go out to a carvery for Sunday lunch," he tells me as I look at him. "As a family." He grimaces as if I might disapprove or something. "You don't have to come. You don't have to go out at all if you don't want, or you and me can go somewhere else by ourselves?"

I turn away from him and lean against the kitchen sink, looking out the window at the tower. It feels mocking today, taunting and pointing from almost every window of this house, dark and damp and cold. Was I part of some dark and deformed adventure to Jonasz? Has the magic gone now that we don't have to meet in a Gothic tower? I immediately feel bad for

43

thinking that because I know really that it's not true. I know that my tiredness and the unpleasantness from last night are influencing my feelings today.

"The carvery is good," I say.

It is. Sort of. The lighting is dim, and we all sit in a booth with padded seats and little curtains, partially obscuring us from the other diners.

I do some colouring-in with Jack. We use wax crayons to turn the pictures of dancing food bizarre colours, and the little boy laughs.

"Why have you got gloves on, Ariel?" Jack asks, wide-eyed, innocent, honest.

"Well, you know how my hand is strange?"

He nods. "You fell in our thresher."

I nod too, aware that the other three are listening intently, but I'm only going to reply with honesty to the child who asked. "Seeing my hand sometimes upsets people, and makes them uncomfortable. So I only take my gloves off when I know everyone is okay with the way I am."

"I'm okay with you," says Jack. "I love you, Ariel."

"I love you too, Jack," I say, wanting to cry. It's the first time anyone has said those words to me. Ever.

A visit to the pub toilet causes unfortunate memories of my almost-visit to the one in the barn last night. Jonasz is waiting for me when I come out, and we stand together on the plush carpet of the carvery hallway.

"Did they mess with you?" he asks. "The quines, last night? I ken you all went to the toilet together."

We didn't, of course, but I realise now that the girls thought I was in there, and were saying all that stuff for my benefit. "Oh," I say and pause, for dramatic thought rather than effect. "They put on a bit of a performance, you know, bitched about me for me to hear."

"You should have told me."

"Why?"

"I would have done something about it."

I shrug. What could he have done? What happened, happened.

"Please tell me these things, Ariel," he says. "I want to know."

That can't be true. He'd be happier not knowing this stuff, surely? "Well, now you do," I say simply.

I was right. He doesn't look happy at all. Jonasz looks downright miserable. I did that to him. And I hate that.

"I want to do everything right for you," he says. "But I seem to be doing everything wrong."

I shake my head. And I want to tell him more, like how I don't seem to be feeling things normally or be able to think about things properly, but it sounds so stupid in my head that I don't say it aloud.

"I want pudding," I say, that being a nice, simple thought. "Let's get pudding."

He smiles and takes my hand, and we walk back through to the table where desserts have just arrived. I pick at a chocolate cheesecake for the rest of the meal, not seeming to be able to taste it properly, but at least Jonasz smiled. And that was good.

Back at the Serafins' house, I plead exhaustion – it's not untrue – and go to bed without dinner.

"You know you can speak to us at any time, Ariel?" says Tomas as I head up the stairs. He reminds me a little of Mr. Zolotov, tall and heroic, his Polish accent charming somehow, but I know I can't actually speak to him or any of them.

I want silence. Peace. To be alone in my, Janek's, room. Emptiness lies with me in the long bed as I hug my gloved hands to my chest and stare up at the sloping ceiling of the old house. I haven't shut the curtains, and the moon is creating an amazing tower shadow on the wall. It moves round the bedroom during the evening, growing taller as it progresses. When it reaches the bed, I get up, empty in various ways, hungry and thirsty, and creep down the stairs.

It's happening again. I'm paused in my journey of basic human need to listen to people talk about me. This is so much worse, though, because I always thought that Janet liked me.

"She's a deeply troubled girl, Tom," she says now.

"She has been through much."

"I know, and I feel for her, but I'm worried for my own three. There's Jonasz; all this secrecy for years. That's not healthy, and we don't really know all he's had to deal with. You saw today what a creature of moods she is. And are they all besotted with her? Janek gave up his room quick as a flash. Jack saying he loves her. But it's Jonasz that's the biggest concern; if it wasn't for her, would he be applying to universities? Is he only staying here to look after her? Ruining his life to deal with a traumatised child? He's too young to—"

"I don't think—" begins Tomas, but I don't let him finish.

I stomp down the rest of the stairs, and they stop talking. Unfortunately they're in the kitchen where I have to go, but I refuse to let that change my mission. A glass of water is not too much to ask. It comes out of the taps and is free. Me taking it won't ruin anyone's life. I march straight past the two of them as they stand at the breakfast-bar thing in the middle of the room.

"I'm just getting a glass of water," I say, wanting that to be quite clear.

"We thought you were sleeping, Ariel, dear," says Janet, that last word grating now that I know it's insincere.

I look straight at her and say: "Nope."

She looks round the kitchen, looking for a way to make things right. "You didn't have any dinner, love. Would you like me to make you some toast? Or there's a couple of leftover burgers..."

"Nope." I turn, and on the slidy kitchen floor it's a bit dramatic, almost like a dance move, and then I flounce off upstairs.

I don't feel so flouncy back in the room with the shadow of the tower slanting across the floor, but there's clarity to be gained in lying awake all night in the silver light of the moon.

The great spotlight in the sky highlights everything that's wrong and pushes me to fix it. I can do it. I am strong; I've always had to be. My thoughts are finally clear, if only on this one thing.

My love for Jonasz is enormous; I can feel it pulsating in my heart, but it hurts now, so much, after everything that's been said, with everything that I now know. But I can do right by him like he's always done right by me. That's what has to happen now; it's all I can let happen.

So, I decide: tomorrow is going to be easy, simple and straightforward. Bring it on.

IN THE WEAK WATERY sunlight of the winter morning, I feel a bit weak and watery myself. I close my eyes, feigning sleep for much of the drive to the castle, frustrated by my lack of driving abilities and car and house and money. Oh, to be independent and free of the guilt of relying on other people!

"I'm sorry about this, you having to drive me," I say to Jonasz.

He smiles, and even though this is a terrible morning, I still like to see it. His smile makes me feel soft inside somehow, like it takes away all the badness from the recent few days.

"Thought you were asleep," he says. "And I always love driving you."

So I watch him drive. Something I always love. For the last time? Probably. And then we're there.

There. Here. In front of the pink walls and sparkling windows of the castle. I try to summon last night's moon-fuelled strength to do what has to be done, and fail. I end up pulling Jonasz to me and kissing him, really kissing him, and then kissing him again in a desperate fashion, inhaling his salty, fresh-air scent, and touching the sexy roughness of his unshaven chin.

"Is everything okay?" he says, frowny.

"I love you, Jonasz."

"Now, I'm really worried."

"Why? I've said it before."

Jonasz is an honest boy. Jonasz only says things that he means. "I ken," he says. "But this is different. Something's wrong."

I nod. I can't speak. I get out and run towards the castle door as everything bad builds up inside me, creating an inner storm of sadness and rage and grief. I hear the car, and Jonasz, draw away from the castle, away from me, and I pull my gloves off, flinging them to the ground and stamping them into the gravel.

"Ariel!"

The male voice comes from behind, from the direction of the trees, and for a moment I think it's Jonasz come back to say something very important, something that would take all the rest away. What Katy said, what his mum said; these things would fade to nothing and be fixed in the bright light of something bigger. But no, the 4X4 is just disappearing into the track between the tall pine trees.

It's Alexander who's running towards me, Alexander who's saying, "Hey," as his movie-star smile fades and his shampoo-advert hair moves gracefully in the breeze. The soundtrack emanating from below his hoodie today is appropriately sad and dramatic. He takes my hands in his, and it's good that it's him who's here because he can help.

"I need to speak to someone," I tell him. "Mr. Zolotov or Amalphia or Holly."

"You're upset," he says, taking my hand. "It's Amalphia you need. Come on."

He's pulling me toward the trees, and away from the castle. It makes no sense. "Alexander! Where are we going?"

"My house. I just came from there." He stops and looks a bit embarrassed. "I eat my meals at the castle, but I still live at home."

Of course. That's where he'd come from, out of the trees. I did know that Mr. Zolotov's house was nearby.

"Amalphia's just having breakfast," he tells me. "She'll be pleased to see you."

"Oh. No. I don't want to bother her in her home."

We're at the start of the forest now, beside a narrow pathway that leads into it.

Alexander looks at me. "Didn't she give you the speech? Anytime, anywhere, anything?"

"Well, yes." But being a burden to people in their homes is something I want to stop doing.

"She'll be upset if you don't go to her with this, not if you do."

So now I'm flying through a magical fairyland, fairy-tale prince at my side. There's lichen-covered trees and a dark pool, then a little bridge, and now we're walking through a pretty garden with more big trees and a swing.

Up the path we go, and there's a boy who looks a lot like Alexander sitting on the steps of a three-storey house.

"Woah," he says, standing up as we approach. He looks at me, and I notice he's got rounder cheeks than Alexander, so a bit younger, maybe.

"This is Ariel," Alexander explains to him.

"You're like, really hot," the boy tells me, and for some strange reason I feel the prick of tears behind my eyes.

"Lexi," chides Alexander, then turning to me. "My brother, Alexei."

We walk pass Alexei and into a bright sitting room where an old-fashioned stove glows warmly, but we don't pause there. We hurry up a hallway and into a big kitchen with stone tiles on the floor and a massive table in the middle of the room.

I smell coffee and toast, and then Amalphia emerges from a door at the side carrying an enormous chocolate cake.

"I feel a bit caught," she says, laughing and laying the cake on the table.

"Ariel needs to speak to you," Alexander tells her.

"Okay," she says, then really studying my face. "Us girls will have breakfast together."

"What, I've to go back to the castle for mine?" moans Alexander.

"Yes," she says, smiling as she does so. Movie-star smiles are obviously a trend in this family, an inherited trait perhaps.

"Are you having that cake for breakfast?" Alexander asks her.

She smiles again. "It's my birthday."

"That was two days ago," he points out.

"It's my birthday week," she counters, and he leaves, laughing, and closing the door behind him.

She indicates that I should sit and then cuts us both a piece of the cake, glancing at me as she does. "Sorry if you felt I was staring at you," she says. "I'm autistic, and it takes me a little longer than other people to assess what's going on with someone from their facial expressions. I didn't mean to make you uncomfortable."

This is news. Amalphia Treadwell is autistic? But she's so normal, not to mention successful. She can only be a little bit autistic, surely? And then I hate myself for that thought. People have said things like it to me, that I'm not really disabled. I can walk and talk. I've got all my limbs. Like it's not a thing. But it is a thing. Sometimes it's a really huge thing.

I need to get straight to the point, though. I can't make chit-chat today. I can't eat cake. "Is there any way I can stay at the castle?" I ask her. "Live there, I mean?"

"Of course," she says. "I think there's a spare cottage if you'd like to be alone, or you can bunk with whoever Chantal was sharing with. Holly lives down there too to keep an eye on everyone."

Worries come out as I watch her start to eat her cake. "But there's a question of who's paying for my course now, after everything. Will that be a problem?"

"That's never an issue at the castle," she assures me. "Aleks always get funding."

"I just can't live there anymore," I tell her, somehow following her lead and taking a forkful of cake. It's so good.

"You're staying at your boyfriend's house at the moment, aren't you?"

I nod, mouth full of cake.

"That's a big step," she says, "living with someone for the first time."

"We're not really living together," I explain. "I sleep in his brother's bedroom."

"Still, you had it foisted on you before you would have chosen it."

We both eat more cake. It has four layers of icing and is topped with cherries and cream.

"Do you have stuff to pick up?" she asks.

I do. I forgot about that.

"We can go and get it this morning if you like?" she suggests. "You can skip class, and we'll get you all settled in and sorted out?"

"Yes." That gets it over with quickly, right now, today.

Amalphia glances down at herself. "Am I likely to be asked in, do you think? If so, I'll go and change."

"I only have one suitcase; it's still packed. I can just run in and get it." There hadn't really been anywhere to put things. The drawers and cupboard were still full of Janek's clothes.

"Great," she says. "I better just tell Aleks." She proceeds to type a lengthy text, and it's only then that I notice she's still in pyjamas: red tartan trousers, fleecy teddy top.

While she's typing, a man comes into the room. He smiles at me in greeting and goes and puts the kettle on.

"Oh, Will, could you make us a flask of sweet tea?" Amalphia asks, pausing mid-text and looking round at him.

"No probs," he says and clatters around in a cupboard till he finds a flask.

Amalphia introduces us. "Will: husband. Ariel: student and friend of Alexander's."

We say hi to each other, and I notice that he's less theatrical and movie-star-ish than the rest of the family. Short brown hair. Down to earth. Kind of like an older version of Jonasz. Amalphia tells him that we're going to get my things.

"Do you want me to come with you?" he offers.

"It's only one suitcase; I think we'll manage," she says, walking through to a porch. I get up and follow her. "I'll take your jacket, though," she calls back, pulling on a green waxed jacket like Jonasz wears sometimes. "And your car," she says, finding the keys in the jacket pocket. "It's a farm we're going to, isn't it?" she asks me and I nod.

# 11

WE GET INTO A 4X4. It's green like Jonasz's but quite a bit older, possibly a classic car. I know he would be interested in this one, wanting to know all about the engine and chassis and model. He may see it when we get there, or he may not. The other end of this drive is full of unknowns. I don't know how it will go, but I know I can't be cowardly. That's not an option that I will allow myself.

The journey itself is simple. We talk about the landmarks and villages and farms that we pass, exchanging knowledge on the everyday. Then the Serafins' big farmhouse is before us far too quickly. And I don't feel ready. But I make myself move. I make myself speak.

"I'll just run in and get my case," I tell Amalphia, but then find that this part is not that simple.

I can't just run in. It's not my home. I find myself knocking on the red painted door and cringing, wondering whether maybe everyone's out, but the door might be un-locked and I could—

The door opens. "Ariel!" says Janet. "You don't have to knock, dear. This is your home."

"No, it isn't."

Her face lines up with worry. "Did you forget something? Are you not well?"

I stand up tall, facing her on the doorstep. "I'm here to get my things. I'm moving into the castle."

"Oh." She steps aside and allows me access to the house.

I run straight up the stairs to Janek's room, zip the case closed over my clothes, and hurry back down to where Janet's still standing near the front door.

"Ariel, is this about last night? Because if it is, I really want to say that I didn't mean—"

"It's not," I say at once, then wanting to be only truthful, I add: "I mean, it did clarify the situation for me. Thank you for having me this week. It was good of you, but it's time I left." There. That's done. And now: "I have to speak to Jonasz. Where is he?"

"Up in the top field. They're trying to get the early ploughing done before lambing starts."

I pick up my case and walk outside. "I won't keep him long."

"That's not what I meant either," she says, following, actually wringing her hands before grabbing my arm. "Oh! Is that Amalphia Treadwell?"

"Yes." I glance over to where Amalphia is sitting in the car fiddling with the radio. "She's not expecting to be asked in," I explain to Janet. "She's in her pyjamas."

"But it would be rude not to say anything to her..." Janet takes my case and starts towards the car.

"I just have to speak to Jonasz," I call out to Amalphia, who's now rolling down her window. "I won't be long."

"Take as long as you want," says Janet in a dreamy voice, moving zombie-like towards Amalphia.

I leave them to it and take the track to the higher fields. I soon see the old tractor, the one they're thinking of replacing, and I know that's where he is. I march on up the side of the half-ploughed field, resolute one minute, quaking the next.

Each footstep towards the encounter is brave. Each footstep is me not turning and running away.

He sees me and waves, and turns the tractor my way.

It's not only Jonasz that gets out of the cab of the vehicle when it stops. Caliban flies at me, a blur of excited Irish setter, jumping about and licking and yelping in delight, and I feel terrible. I've hardly paid him any attention this week, and I'd completely forgotten him in this decision. I have no idea how keeping a dog at the castle will go.

I order Caliban to sit and he does, pressing his body against my legs, probably not intending to lend me his strength, but he does anyway. I keep my hand, that hand, on top of his soft head.

"Everything all right?" says Jonasz, like he knows it's not.

Still, I hesitate. I reach for hope before I do the inevitable.

"Jonasz, if it wasn't for me, would you be here?"

"You what?" he says, standing there all beautiful and perfect in his old blue boiler suit.

"If I wasn't around, would you be doing something other than farming? Like university? Or other jobs?"

He stiffens, his demeanour changing completely. "Is farming not good enough for you, Ariel?"

"That's not what I mean," I say, the words coming out too loud, or maybe just loud enough to express the stupidity of such an idea. "And you know it." There's no way he really thinks that of me.

"Aye," he admits, his eyes shiny. "But you are here to dump me, right?"

I hate that word – dump – and it's not the right word. My chest hurts deep inside as I say the right words. "I'm here to tell you I'm moving into the castle. You're free to live your life any way you like from now on. You rescued me, and I..." I have to rescue him now. From me. But I don't think I should say it. I don't think I can anyway. My throat feels like it's swelling up, and I can't talk anymore.

We stare at each other in the field, brown chocolatey furrows all around, furrows that Jonasz made, deep and wholesome and good like him. There's no bedroom wall between us now, but it feels like there's an enormous one here anyway. A great, thick, medieval one, like there is in parts of the castle. One that stops you hearing anything, or seeing what's going on, or feeling anything properly.

Caliban fidgets, looking up at me, and I take him by the collar.

"Dinna take him as well," says Jonasz, sounding like his throat might be swollen too. "He's happy here. He likes the other dogs and the space, and he comes out wi' me in the tractor. A ballet school is no place for him." He orders Caliban into the tractor cab and closes the door over him, then looks back round at me. "I'll take good care of him," he says and then runs his hands back across his head and stands there like that, in some weird defensive position with his elbows pointing forward, breathing fast as if he's breathless. "Dinna take him," he says, like it's the worst thing I could do now.

I don't demand that he give me my dog back because everything he said was true. Caliban is better off here. Jonasz will look after him well, of course he will.

There's only one thing left to say, one word, and it sounds hollow and small under the large sky, in front of the man of the soil and the land. "Goodbye," I say. It comes out so quietly, like I've forgotten how to speak.

Jonasz's perfect face twitches but he doesn't look at me. "Aye, fitever, Ariel." Moving fast, he opens the cab door, swings up into it, and drives away.

I don't want to watch him getting further and further away, so I turn and immediately see the grey roof of my parents' house just down below the hill. I walk towards it and take hold of a fence post, remembering things, not recent and dramatic things, but smaller incidents, daily words of hate and derision. I have to walk away from it. It's the easier thing I can do here, turning my back on that house and leaving the place behind forever.

To walk down the field and away from Jonasz, forever, is a task that will have me fall to the ground. My legs are shaking and weak at the thought.

To walk away from the house is good. It looks so wrong anyway, so out of place, all modern and flat and white in the natural landscape. I can leave it behind now. Dump it in the past. I shouldn't have thought that word: dump. I force my thoughts back to: out of place. I was out of place there, in that house. I'm not out of place in the castle.

Walking is hard. Seeing is hard. It's because I'm crying, properly crying, not just slightly or maybe crying. I aim myself in the direction of the waiting 4X4 that Jonasz would have been interested to see.

Amalphia gets out of the car and runs towards me, her long dark hair doing the shampoo-advert thing like Alexander's. I notice Janet speaking at the side of us but don't hear what she's saying.

Amalphia smells of chocolate cake and vinegary crisps. She holds me till I can walk, and then I get into the car with her and we drive away.

# 12

I GET TO THAT point where breath comes in desperate gasps between sobs, and Amalphia pulls the car over. She gives me a tissue and I hold on to it, crumpling it up in my hands as I try to breathe. She then gives me a blue plastic cup of tea.

"Go on," she says. "Will's tea tastes vile, but it helps."

That's so stupid. How can tea help me now? I sip it anyway, and it's really strong and a bit like syrup. I wince but take a proper gulp. It's hot and it burns, but it's a relief to feel something else other than this swollen pain inside that won't let me stop crying.

"Did you break up with your boyfriend, Ariel?"

I nod, somehow glugging the tea now. She pours more.

"It's a very particular type of agony," she says. "I went through some traumatic things when I was younger, events that other people look at and say: wow, that was truly terrible. But breaking up with someone you love? It's worse than the rest. For me it was, anyway."

She's right. This is so much worse than nearly being murdered. Losing Jonasz is worse than losing fingers too. He's the biggest thing that will ever be missing now. His loss will leave the biggest scar. I squeeze my eyes shut, because, no, I don't want to think of him; it's too much.

"I'm going to go all counsellor-y on you now with some facts," Amalphia says. She proceeds to tell me that there are

59

three aspects of life that need to be working for a person to be truly happy. Relationships: oh dear. Home: bam! And career or vocation. "You've got the last one down," she says. "Aleks and Guy are delighted with you in class. So you're not in such a bad way as you might think. You can cope as long as all three elements aren't in disarray. You're also fitting in well and making new friends." Astonishingly, this is also true. She goes on. "Friendship is a precious thing, just as important as any other relationship, and the castle's about to be your new home. We have quite a family thing going there; I think it'll be good for you."

I almost want to laugh at this. My new home? Forget new. The castle will be the only home I've ever had. The Serafins' house is a happy home, yes, but it was never mine. My parents' house was just that: their house. My presence in it was barely tolerated, really only resented.

Soon, we're driving off again, and I realise that I didn't see the tower as we passed, and it's long gone now. I may never see it again. High up in that tower, there's a loose brick, and behind the brick, hidden like we were, are the words *Ariel and Jonasz Forever*. Jonasz wrote it in thick black pen two years ago because that's what we were meant to be. Forever. After everything. After all. In the end. Not like the popular kids at school, all romantic with one person one week, then off with someone else the next. We weren't like that. After all the bad stuff was over, we were meant to still be there, still together and still in love.

My reaction to the brick memory causes Amalphia to go to the village pub rather than straight back to the castle.

We sit on a sofa in front of a log fire. The pub landlady asks if I'm Amalphia's daughter and says we look alike. We eat thick vegetable soup. Amalphia does her best to keep up a one-sided conversation as I stare into the orange and black of the fire. I feel a bit sleepy, a bit relaxed. I'm like a computer resetting after a crash. I tell Amalphia this thought and apologise for the fact that she's basically had to talk to herself for an hour.

"I once stayed in that quiet, shocked state for a whole day post-break up," she tells me. "My best friend was stuck beside me on a train for the entire day. Oh! That reminds me, I'd better text him; he arrives tonight." She types on her phone and then goes on: "Once we reached London, I sort of snapped out of it, felt like I wanted to get on with things." She pauses, examining my face as she thinks. "There's actually something very exciting for you to be getting on with," she says, flashing that trademark family smile at me. "It's a secret, though I imagine it'll get announced tomorrow, so what harm could there be in me telling you now?"

I listen. And she's right. This news is exciting. It is distracting. It will keep us all very busy with little time to dwell or think. Part of me perks up in anticipation, not just for the upcoming event but about sharing the information with the others too. It'll get us off the subject of my latest misery, but I feel I should tell them the basics of that too. They are my new friends, after all, maybe even sort of my new family.

# 13

LUNCH IS OVER BY the time we get back to the castle. The big hall is entirely empty of people, making me notice just how huge it is. The wood-lined roof is incredibly high, pitched to a point in the middle. The narrow windows are a bit like longer versions of the ones in the tower. I falter a little.

Holly marches towards us from the direction of the kitchen. "You've a visitor," she tells me.

"Who is it?" I demand, instantly wary, instantly cross. "If it's my father again, I don't want to see him."

It's not my father. A tall and rather severe-looking woman with short grey hair is following behind Holly. I suspect she's the promised social worker and decide to tell her nothing. She took her time coming. Where was she last week?

"Oh, Ariel," she says, and then she starts to cry. "You're such a pretty girl, a dainty little doll." Odd, very odd. "I'm Patti," she explains as if it should mean something to me. "Your grandmother." And she's trying to hug me which is strange in two ways because: I don't know her, like not at all, and I thought both my grandmothers were dead.

We sit down beside the large fire, Patti and me, on a sofa. Amalphia says she'll be in her office if I need her. Holly says the same about the kitchen. I suspect they'll be waiting nearby in case this person resembles my other family members in any way.

The Mermaid and the Bear look down from a stone crest over the fireplace, and it feels as if they're watching over me too.

"I'm so sorry," Patti – my grandmother? – tells me. "It's all my fault. I spoil her, you see. It's why she is the way she is."

During another one-sided conversation, I learn that this woman is my mother's mother. I learn that my mother, Maxine, was attacked by a dog, an Irish setter named Caliban, when she was a small child. She had to have many surgeries, and then her guilt-ridden parents spoilt her rotten, literally, to the point of actually being rotten. The Calibans that we'd had, the current one being number three, were a reminder to Patti: you have to be nice to me; remember what you let happen to me. Photos of the dogs were sent through the post sometimes. It does sound like the sort of thing Maxine would do.

"Why are you here?" I ask, because, really, why now, after all this time?

She looks a bit like she might cry again. "Because I can be?" she says. "She never let me near you before. And because I thought you might need some family now? And I would like to help; if there's any way at all I can help, please tell me."

I don't know if there is any way she can help. "I'm here now," I tell her. "Moving in, I mean. I split up with my boyfriend, and I can't live there anymore."

"Aren't you a bit young to have a boyfriend?"

"No."

"Forgive me, Ariel," she says, smoothing down her grey tartan skirt. "I'm completely out of touch with teenagers, so I hope the things I've brought you are not totally wrong. I accepted a lot of help from shop assistants in the choosing."

The gifts she hands me are overwhelming. First there's a sparkly new phone and tablet, all on some unlimited tariff she's arranged. She hopes I'll call her on the phone if I need anything. Then there's a huge bag of dancewear; seriously, there

63

must be about a hundred items in there: leotards and tights and warm-ups in every colour imaginable, T-shirts and trackies and socks. She didn't know my shoe size, else there would have been more. But she knew I was small. My picture's been in the paper many times over the years for dance-related things and more recently...

"For murderous reasons," I finish for her.

She leans over and takes my hands, surprisingly not crying or looking like she's going to cry at the sight of the mangled one. "Your mother is claiming mental illness as the reason for the attack. It's probably not true, knowing her, but she's been moved somewhere appropriate and very secure. And don't worry about your father; I'll make sure he behaves when it comes to paying for your dancing. The only reason the government aren't covering it is because of his earnings and assets. I'm not always the tearful old woman you see before you today; he's quite frightened of me."

Holly brings tea and chocolate biscuits, and the atmosphere lightens. My grandmother, or Fairy Godmother as she's starting to seem, gives me an envelope of money, a startling amount of money, for anything extra I might need, and takes my bank details so she can give me a startlingly huge allowance every month.

I walk my new grandmother to the big front door of the castle to say goodbye. I hug her back this time and can tell that she's pleased. But it's all really weird, so I ask: "Are you sure you're not just spoiling one girl to try and make up for spoiling the other?"

"You're a very intelligent little thing, aren't you?" she says with some dryness. "But, no. This is hardly spoiling, Ariel. You need resources behind you to do well in your training here; this school is known to be rigorous. I would love to be part of your life in whatever way you find acceptable. I would love to have you stay with me in the holidays, or even at weekends?" All dryness gone, her voice is now hopeful. "In fact, that's going to be my next project: doing up a room for you, so it's there if you ever want it. I've rattled around in that big old house by myself for far too long."

I watch her drive away in a fancy white Mercedes. I exert mental discipline to avoid thinking about the boy who would be interested to know all the details about the car, and then I slowly close the thick, studded door of my first home.

# 14

DISCIPLINE! DISCIPLINE IS THE word of the day. Discipline is the answer to all my problems. It's something I know well. I used to come home from school and do ballet for exactly one hour, all the time I was permitted, but I made the best of every opportunity to stretch and strengthen and perfect. I did Pilates in the bath and grand jetés in the park; I slept in the butterfly position and completed homework while sat on the floor in the box splits. It's how I got good enough to come here. It's how I coped with my life.

So: no thinking about certain people and events. It's a rule, and it's how I will go on. It's my new 'wall between.' It helps that there's so much new everywhere to focus on.

I choose the freshly done-up cottage that I can have all to myself. Of course I do. Who would pick the spare bed in Bubbles and Paula's untidy lodging? There are knickers and socks and leotards in various stages of laundry everywhere, even in the kitchen sink. Holly is most annoyed when we discover that. Students get their clothes washed for them; there's no need to hand wash things at all.

The interior of my cottage is blue and purple and all the colours in between, even the appliances. I have a kitchen the colour of cornflowers and a kettle that lights up bright blue when it's on. I make sweet tea to drink as I unpack my old stuff and my new.

There are two bedrooms upstairs. I put my things in the purple one that faces the woods, the window showing a solid block of pine trees and nothing else. It feels safe somehow. I feel warm and protected amid the soft lilac blankets and cushions with the forest all around me outside.

I do use the other bedroom, though, the stormy blue one. I shut stuff away in it: the clothes I was wearing when something I won't think about happened, and also my old phone. I was never allowed to have a mobile of my own, so it's actually Jonasz's old one that he gave me. Errant thought. I look out at the trees and realise that there's so much more than a wall between us now. There's a dark green forest and miles and miles of grey stony road. I slam the small drawer shut and then close that bedroom door over it all, over the past. Over him. Forever.

I eat more chocolate cake and drink hot chocolate in what I've just learned is actually called 'the great hall.' I like the words, the name of the huge room. It's so much better than just 'dining hall.' The great hall of the castle. The dungeon of the castle. The tower of— Discipline! No tower-related thoughts. But my new home is grand and special, and so are my new family.

My class gather round when they arrive in the hall, full of concern, stopping to ask if I'm okay before going to get food.

"We was all really worried about what had happened to you, Ariel," says Clinton. "What with you not showing up to class."

Alexander gives me a small smile, not a movie-star one, and I take it to mean that he didn't say anything to anyone about this morning.

"I broke up with my boyfriend," I tell them, just providing information, just saying words, not thinking about the event itself, or him. "And I've moved in here."

Henry hugs me; it's sudden and tight. I hug him back, inhaling his soapy, vanilla scent. I urge them all to get food, and then more bits of the day get told as everyone trickles back to the table with plates and trays.

The girls want to know all about my cottage. There's an awkward moment when Bubbles repeats her offer of moving in with me, but Paula saves things by saying that I probably need time to myself after everything. I tell them about the blue light-up kettle and the mugs with sea creatures on them and say they can visit anytime.

Clinton notices the new phone on the table, and having thought I would have almost no contacts in it, I immediately have many. It gets passed to the second and third year tables too, which seems strange as I don't know any of them.

"Oh, but you will," Clinton assures me. "Soon enough we'll all be doing activities, you know, workshops and stuff, together. You need to add everyone to your social medias too."

I'm not on social media. I never have been. The thought of seeing people from my old school horrified me too much, but now, everything is different. I will have at least thirty instant friends/followers. I let Clinton take control of the phone when it comes back, and he starts setting up accounts for me. Profile pictures will be taken later, outside or in the studio. Cool stuff, fun stuff: my life now.

"I have gossip," I tell them. "Well, news." I lower my voice. "Amalphia told me what's going to be happening here, but you mustn't tell anyone, and you'll all have to act surprised when we're told, which will probably be tomorrow."

So I detail the upcoming national competition for young dancers that Amalphia told me about. It's based around partner and group work, and it's all going to be televised: auditions are going to be in front of a celebrity panel, the semi-final is to be in London, and then the final is to be a big and grand occasion at the castle itself.

"The preparations for the competition here at this school are going to be filmed in a programme called *Castle Dancers*," I tell my new friends. "We're all going to be on TV right from the start."

Discussion about who might be on the celebrity panel begins at once. Amalphia? Mr. Zolotov? Will? Crispin Truelove, famous actor and friend of Amalphia? Only Alexander seems less than excited by the news.

"Did you ask her about it? Is that why she told you?" he asks me now.

"No, she just came out with it. I think it was like something good for me to focus on?"

"Oh, right," he says, and I can tell he's a bit put out, like maybe upset she didn't tell him first. "It'll be something to do with Justin," he adds, sounding quite bored with it all. "He's going to be staying with us for a while."

"Justin Bevan?" shrieks Bubbles. "The TV producer? I knew he was connected to the castle in some way, but this is big!"

Everyone's phones come out. I see them light up at the other tables too, screens blinking with a chain of news that I started. I did something that, strictly speaking, I shouldn't have. I shared a secret, and people listened. It's different and new. And I really, really like it.

# 15

"IT'S ALL RIGHT, MY darlings, I am here! You're safe now."
So says the newly arrived man with a cheeky look on his face
at the end of breakfast time in the great hall.

He's the TV producer. Everyone's been whispering about
the fact he's at the teachers' table and hoping he might give
a bit of a speech. He is actually doing so with a microphone,
so his voice blasts out into every corner of the room.

"I know what it's like, you see," he goes on. "I went here.
I was one of the very first, and..." There's a pause before he
says, darkly: "I remember. It's all: ballet, ballet, ballet, haggis,
ballet, ballet – ooh, a man in a kilt! – ballet, ballet... You
think you're heading to contemporary for a bit of a reprieve,
and then it snows, and the teacher can't get here, and you
can't get out, and Aleks declares: we will do extra ballet!"

Everyone laughs, well, not quite everyone, not Mr. Zolotov, though he does sort of join in by standing and saying:
"Ballet in the dungeon for all classes this morning!" He
takes the microphone away from the producer before he can
retort.

We make our way down to the dungeon in batches, in the
elevator, to find a large crew of TV people setting up cameras
and fluffy microphones and huge lights on legs in the big
studio. The air buzzes with their chatter. It makes it difficult
to hear Mr. Zolotov's instructions to us.

We all make mistakes during barre, and our teacher cuts the lesson short after one distracted adagio exercise (slow and painful unfolding of legs) and one disastrous allegro (fast and fiddly jumps) saying the main thing is that we are all well warmed-up and ready for the day.

We scatter ourselves over the floor of the massive studio in various stretching and resting positions to listen to the 'news.' It's not exactly what I thought it was going to be. I mean, it is really, but the competition is choreographic in nature. And I've never done anything like that. I'm only just getting used to pas de deux, and this could be combinations of dancers in any number, as the producer, Justin Bevan, says: "Pas de trois, pas de quatre, pas de... ten, whatever that's called. What?" he says sharply to his assistant, a small man who's constantly scribbling into a notebook. "Oh, dix. Nigel says it's pas de dix."

The name of the national competition is *Ballerina Ballerino*, but it is not just for ballet; all and any forms of dance are welcome, the more innovative and exciting the better. Justin tells us that there have been teaser adverts about it on television already, but the name is just being announced today, along with the connection to the castle, and Amalphia, and the secondary series, *Castle Dancers*. It's the first episode of that second series that is being filmed here at the castle this week.

"Where is Phi?" Justin says, looking around. "We want her on camera from the off. Fame it up a bit, you know? Here, Nigel, take my phone and text her to get her arse down here pronto. In the meantime, let's start with Aleks at the piano – sex things up from the start too – and you lot," he says, turning to us students: "Get going with your own stuff. Let your creativity fly. Try out new partners. Don't just stick to people from your own class. Mix it up; enjoy a dance orgy, if you will."

Everyone jumps right into the middle of Mr. Zolotov's improvised music, everyone except me, that is, but Alexander's there at my side, so it's not so bad.

"How about we do this?" he says, suggesting a high lift. We do it. "And this?" A fish dive. I've never done one before but somehow I'm perfectly balanced over Alexander's thigh, my feet pulled back round his shoulder.

"Now me?" asks Clinton, and the lift I do with him is so high that I feel slightly dizzy when returned to the ground.

Henry's there and we spin and spin, and it would be fun if it weren't so embarrassing. I'm only doing what others suggest. I have nothing to contribute. I'm like a wee puppet, being pulled and lifted and spun.

I try to express the problem to Alexander as the music gets faster.

"Just move," he advises. "Don't think about it."

But if I don't think, I can't move. I don't work like that, I don't think.

"I'm sensing drama here," says Justin as he arrives beside us, followed closely by Nigel and the notebook, and a woman with a large portable camera.

"I've never done choreography before," I tell the producer. "I've only just started learning pas de deux."

"It's all a journey, darling," he says, then doing a double take. He's seen my hand, but he's not horrified; if anything, he's excited. "You're Ariel. Oh yes, this is good. Stick to her," he orders the camera woman. "Nigel! Write this down: oh the pain of youth, the sighing sadness... no, cut that. Start again: a young woman, beautiful, talented, just starting out in her dancing life, is suddenly the victim of a crime so terrible, so heinous, that it cannot be detailed for legal reasons."

"Justin, what are you doing?" Amalphia, newly appeared with two little girls in tow, is cross. Good. So am I.

"I'm finding the story, Phi," Justin tells her. "What are you doing? Hello, angels!" The little girls hug him.

"Find it among the older students, Just," she says. "And it was patently obvious that this polite and reverential text was not sent by you."

"Well, of course not; Nigel did it for me, apparently not very convincingly. Nigel! It's eleven o' clock! My tea? And make sure to get it right this time. I don't want half a lemon in it."

Nigel scuttles away, pulling his phone from his pocket as he goes.

Alexander and I perform a supported turn, all his idea. It's not good.

Amalphia continues her interrogation of Justin, which is good. "You can't speak to people like that," she tells him.

"Keep your hair on," retorts Justin. "He's on his socials moaning about my mistreatment of him to zillions of followers every day. They're champing at the bit to see it on the telly."

She doesn't look convinced, and continues: "And you can't follow the students about doing some sort of creepy voiceover."

"I have to get something down, sweets. The actual voiceover guy is an imbecile. He did that football reality thing? People know him; they like his voice? But the truth is he can barely say hello unless someone writes it on a piece of paper for him."

They wander off, but one of the little girls, the older one, blonde curls like Bubbles, stays and watches us, not that there's much to see. I feel limp and useless, just a cog in other people's creations.

"It will be okay," the girl says to me as I stand still in frustration. "You will win in the end."

"My sister, Faye," explains Alexander. "She's the deep and insightful one of the family. And she tends to be right in her predictions."

"Alexander and I actually have no biological link," the little girl tells me. "Justin's my father and Amalphia's my mother, but Alexander is still my favourite brother."

"I'd better be," he says and picks her up, swinging her round in the air, making her giggle and scream.

And then it's my turn to be swung around and lifted again. I don't giggle or scream, but I do wonder: Amalphia's not Alexander's mother? I look over at Mr. Zolotov, surely, definitely, no question, his father. And Justin? Amalphia and Justin? I would have said Justin was gay. I feel really sure of it, not that I'm good at telling; hadn't I said that only the other day? To Jonasz? It takes a lot of discipline to stop that thought train which was keen to run on to: is Jonasz living his best life now without me? And what will that look like? And what will he do? He'll be amazing. I know that. How could he be anything else?

Enough. Enough now. In fact: enough of boys. "How about a female ensemble?" I suggest, finally having an idea of my own.

Bubbles, Belinda, Star and I attempt a modern version of the *Dance of the Little Swans* from *Swan Lake*, and Mr. Zolotov adjusts his piano playing especially for us. It's not our own choreography, but at least I came up with something.

# 16

AFTER A LONG DAY of proving that I have no choreographic ability at all, and having the fact constantly captured on camera, I am in no mood for Alexander's whispered plan. The secrecy element has some appeal, though, so after dinner, I go up to one of the first-floor studios with him to discuss it further.

He thinks we should do a pas de deux of our own, but tell no one else about it. All practice will be in secret, in the evenings, off camera, so when it comes to the auditions our piece will be a complete surprise. He thinks it might give us an edge over the other competitors if the TV audience is already bored of seeing their stuff in rehearsals before the auditions.

I like the idea, but: "Are you expecting me to choreograph some of it?"

"Only if you want," he says. "I don't have anything myself yet. I need to lie in bed and listen to music and think about it."

"We could give it a try," I agree, making to leave. "Let me know when you've got something."

"Wait, Ariel. I've been wanting to say this since you got here, but there's never been a good moment. I know what it's like, you see."

He pauses, and I lean back against the barre, waiting to hear what it is that he thinks he knows.

"To have your mother try to kill you," he says.

I stare at him, awaiting an explanation.

"I was eight," he tells me. "And she wasn't really my mother, but I thought she was. She was going to throw me off a cliff to get back at my father for something. Amalphia saved me. And then she made everything all right for me after that too."

"Alexander, I'd no idea." I rub his arm, and then hug him, hearing a rousing melody from those ever-present earbuds.

"Yeah," he says. "I should warn you: I'm seriously messed in the head from it all."

Am I messed in the head too? Is that what he means when he says he knows what it's like? Maybe I am. It's all very recent for me, hasn't had time to settle into my head properly, but I guess it could make a mess when it does. I want to ask him questions about what he's said, about what happened to him, but I don't. I wouldn't want to be questioned about mine. The police interview experience was bad enough. I just want it all to be over, cut away and gone.

"Anyway," he says, like someone backing away from something uncomfortable. "Just thought I'd say, so you know."

"Do the others know?"

"Don't think so. My real mum died at the same time, on the same day, but we can't have the Zolotov name dragged through the mud, so it was all hushed up. But speaking of the others, the rest of the class: we've to go and meet them now. For a surprise."

The surprise involves Alexander and me putting on coats and going outside into the freezing January evening of Aberdeenshire where it's dark and the air is smokey from the fire in the great hall.

It obviously snowed while we were filming in the dungeon, but here in this place that is something that manages to be really pretty. The castle is dusted with white, so are the tall trees, and it's in among them that we go, up a narrow path, not the one to Amalphia's house, or the one to the student cottages either. We're going somewhere else.

The path leads uphill, and it's not long before we hear laughter and talking, and we step out into a large forest glade. It's like a fairy tale. This whole place is like one giant fairy tale. There's great big standing stones, in a circle like the ones on the Serafins' land. Those were knocked down long ago, but Tomas and Jonasz and Janek put them back. Discipline. Discipline.

Alexander tells me these ones are called *Amalphia's Stones*, on account of how much she loves them. There's candles in jars everywhere, lighting the place up in the snow, casting long flickering shadows of people and stones. All our classmates are there within the circle of stones, and they have presents for me.

"To welcome you to the castle," explains Bubbles. Her gift is the unicorn leotard she was wearing on that first day. "You said you liked it. And it's only been worn that once, and I washed it really carefully for you."

I thank her, amazed that someone I hardly know would be so thoughtful.

Henry gives me a heart-shaped stone, wordlessly. I kiss it to thank him rather than speaking. He seems pleased.

Clinton gives me a pair of the longest legwarmers I've ever seen. They're red, knitted and bright against the snowy background. "Never worn them," he tells me. "Too small for me. Thought they would suit you."

Star gives me some eyeliner, also unused, and likely to remain so. I was never allowed to wear make-up so never got into the habit.

Lewis has made me a playlist to inspire choreography which I can download later.

Belinda hands me a book that she loves; I think it's a romance.

The twins hold out a hardback notebook and pens.

"I got Amalphia to bake that for you," says Alexander, pointing at an enormous chocolate cake sitting on a big flat stone. "It's why she was late this morning."

"Thank you all so much," I say, close to crying. "I feel so... welcomed."

Someone puts on music, someone else pours fizzy apple juice into plastic champagne glasses, and we all eat cake and dance and climb on the snow-covered stones until we're cold and damp and shivering.

I invite them all back to mine which is surreal. I have a house, a whole little house of my own, to invite people to. We drink hot chocolate and watch the large flat-screen television in the living room, all snuggled round on the sofa and chairs.

There's no judgement, not even when I say I've hardly ever watched TV in my life. They all have recommendations for the best things to watch and films that I absolutely must see.

Paul explains how to use each of the various television services the castle is subscribed to in such meticulous detail that Star bursts out with frustration: "Enough already! It's intuitive. Ariel will work it out."

Alexander gifts us all with the password to watch age-censored content. It's 'AmalphiaLovesCake' and there's more laughter and more happiness, on what is possibly the weirdest night of my life.

It's only later that a dent in the happy bubble appears. After everyone has left and before I head upstairs to the soft and cosy purple bedroom, I see the plastic champagne glasses in the kitchen bin. I remember a glass of the real stuff, because I may not have done many things, but alcohol was always allowed, encouraged even, before, in that out-of-place house by the hill. The champagne was at Christmas, and I threw it in Jonasz's face as part of our pretence that we hated each other.

Do we hate each other now? No. I don't. But I won't think about it.

I walk upstairs and get ready for bed while listening to Lewis's playlist but I find no inspiration there.

Sleep finally comes, but sleep doesn't obey my new rules; it is an undisciplined disaster. I see Jonasz's face and Jonasz's eyes in my dreams.

"I love you." That's my voice, of course, all pitiful and pathetic in the dark as it echoes round the steps of the night-time tower.

"Aye, fitever Ariel."

# 17

I LOOK AT MYSELF in the mirror of the dungeon in frustration and stamp my foot. The mobile camera points my way. It follows me everywhere until Amalphia come in. Then Justin signals the camera woman, and she moves off to film different dancers all over the huge studio.

My humiliation is fascinating, apparently, and the week wears on. Every day: look at Ariel; she can't do anything. Every night: Jonasz and the tower, Jonasz and the tower. There's no discipline in dreams, no escape or peace, no rest.

Choreography has spread through the castle like an infectious disease. Every teacher is contaminated. Elderly Mr. Timms still teaches his traditional pas de deux pieces, but he asks us to think of variants, to make changes that show off our best talents: Alexander's flexibility, Clinton's strength.

My reflection looks back at me, blank, no more idea than I about what my best talent is. Following instruction? Learning the choreography of others?

In the past, in my small bedroom in the house of Maxine, I made myself learn a new dance amalgamation from the internet every night. It had to be something small that didn't travel much, but it means that now my brain is quick at picking things up. That, I can do. So can everybody else, of course. And they all have so much more training than me.

Discussion of my one weekly ballet class provoked shock. How did I get good enough? Strong enough? Alone, that's how. The internet, that's how. No other interests, no other inspiration allowed.

I kick the mirror in the upstairs studio, hoping the camera didn't capture the event.

And then it's Friday, and Justin Bevan and his cameras are leaving for the weekend. Let's clink champagne glasses to that!

———ele———

The first episode of *Castle Dancers* is to be aired on Saturday night after the main *Ballerina Ballerino* show. I do not share the excitement and enthusiasm of my classmates about the TV programmes. I believe I pretty much know what's coming, but invite everyone to my cottage to watch together anyway.

The first show, the main one, does not feature any students from the castle. We see Mr. Zolotov and Amalphia in the dungeon studio. They speak about the importance of encouraging the arts and dance and giving young people opportunities. Then there's lots of short segments from other schools and colleges across the country.

It's the second show that I'm nervous about, *Castle Dancers*, and it follows straight after the first one. The initial part of it is much better than anticipated because it's not about any of us. I sit closely packed between Henry and Alexander on my sofa and admire beautiful views of the castle, some of them from the air, and the voiceover talks about the building's rich history. The old ballet footage of Mr. Zolotov is impressive, as are the clips from Amalphia's films. Crispin Truelove is in one of them, fuelling the idea that he might be involved in this project at some point.

But here it comes; I'm filled with dread and doom, like an echo from a tower-filled dream. The TV screen fills with Justin telling us all about the competition that first morning. I take some small satisfaction from the fact that nobody looks surprised by the news. I'm also very glad of the new dancewear that my grandmother gave me. At least I look colourful and bright like everyone else. I texted her earlier to tell her about the show. The next five minutes make me regret that. Deeply.

Some of us have been selected for a public vote. Our names light up, big and colourful, on the screen beside close-ups of our faces. There I am. Little Ariel. Shown to be little in every way: so little experience, so little ability, so little and sad, so little and sweet. The voiceover man says I've been turned this and way and that by life; there's a quick montage of various boys turning me in supported pirouettes. He goes on to say that I'm now the focus of a police investigation, a victim of violence, a broken little girl. I recognise some of Justin's earlier notes among the narrative. Nigel obviously got it down word for word, though the word 'alleged' has been placed before the word 'crime.' And I don't like that. I don't like any of it.

I detest the image of myself as a sweet little ballet girl with a neat little bun and perfectly pointed feet. I've no make-up on, no individuality. I'm just so nothingy. I'm shown kicking the mirror, and then the credits roll.

"Great honour," says Henry at once.

"I disagree," I tell him.

"The viewers will be interested in you now," says Paula.

"Invested," adds Paul.

"The audience gets to vote," Alexander reminds me. "You'll win it this week, for sure. You'll get the celebrity coaching session. It's nothing to be scared of, don't worry."

Great. I'm obviously looking pathetic and scared.

"It's with Will," he tells me. "He's cool, and he understands choreography better than anyone. Believe me, this was a good start. Look what they did to me. I don't even have a name. I'm just 'the son of the Great Aleksandr Zolotov,' like a footnote or something."

Alexander had been shown to be full of creative talent and to have amazing technique. Those actual words – creative and amazing – were said by the narrator about him, so I don't think his experience compares to mine, not this time.

"Where do you get your hair cut?" I ask Star, having admired how her short and wild style came over on the screen.

"Do it myself," she tells me. "Belinda helps with the back."

"Could you do anything with mine?" I pull my long mane out to the side and let it fall.

"Of course," she says, delighted. "I have hair-styling magazines and everything."

"No way; don't cut your beautiful hair," is Alexander's input on the subject.

I don't listen to him. Paula suggests that a spontaneous haircut might not be a good idea if it's just in reaction to the show. She advises me to sit with the idea and see how I feel about it in a few days, or to just get a trim for now. I don't listen to her either.

We all agree to meet back at my cottage for the later update show, and then everyone heads out into the snowy night.

Star and Belinda's cottage is furnished in green and a bit smaller than mine. I look at the pictures in the hairdressing magazines and quickly find a style that I like. Star tells me it's a classic pixie cut; she finds another photo of a model from the 60s with it, showing the hair tapering at the neck, and framing the face.

"Are you a hundred percent sure?" she says, holding out my pony tail.

I nod and my long hair is gone in seconds, leaving my head feeling light and free.

Star then snips and snips until she's satisfied.

Belinda says that the cut suits me. "You look ethereal," she says. "Like a fairy. That's what your name means, isn't it? From *The Tempest*?"

"No," I correct. "Shakespeare's Ariel was a spirit and a slave." Alongside Caliban, the beast.

A mirror is produced. The change is bigger even than I'd hoped. The old Ariel is no more. A new one is sitting in her place, stylish and independent, brave and strong.

"I think you'd look good with highlights too," says Star, rummaging through a bag of many coloured tints.

While waiting for the bleach to work, I text Patti, my Fairy Grandmother, to apologise for the awfulness of the show.

"You were beautiful, my darling," she replies. "They're focusing on you for a reason, you know." Hmm.

I now have golden darts in my hair, here and there and everywhere, but I can't decide what colour they should be. Pink? Blue? Purple? Not orange. Not green. So, I choose the first three – pink, blue and purple – and they're scattered about through my hair, bright marks in the dark. I love it so much. I'm uncertain about the matching make-up that Belinda produces but agree to it, knowing it'll just wash off, but then I love it too. She does it subtly, not like Star's dark lines, and it makes me look a lot more grown-up.

"I feel so much more confident," I tell them. "It's like I can go and watch whatever they put on the update show without caring now. That boring little ballet girl doesn't exist anymore."

"Oh, she was never boring," says Belinda.

"She's just been coloured-in a bit now," adds Star.

Air currents move my hair when we step outside. I like that it's not tied in place, that I'm not tied in place. Instant transformation is possible.

"Wow!" says Alexander, who's already waiting outside my cottage. "It's super cool. Can I touch it?"

He holds out a tentative hand. I nod, giving permission, and he runs gentle fingers through my hair and over my ear. My skin tingles, the contact feeling intimate and sexy, a bit like those first days of pas de deux with him.

"It's so soft," he says. "You look beautiful, Ariel."

But, later, much later, Jonasz still rules the dreamy deep of the night. I see his face first, and it's perfect. Everything about him is perfect, and I feel my love for him so strongly it seems like I might burst or burn up with it or something. His voice is loud and clear in the nightmare that follows, in the dark of the tower, and still ringing in my head when I wake, and it's certainly not burning with love. It's only dismissive: "Aye, Ariel, fitever. I dinna care."

# 18

MY FRIENDS WERE PROVED right, and the audience of *Castle Dancers* voted for me as the dancer most in need of a celebrity coaching session. Alexander was right about the details of that too: the coaching is to be provided by Will Hearst, Amalphia's husband, someone I had not realised was a celebrity until the update show did a bit about him. He founded the contemporary dance company Emotzia, and has danced with many great ballet companies around the world and is a highly renowned choreographer and teacher.

Things I know about Will: he makes really sweet tea, and he reminds me of my ex-boyfriend. Things that should be focused on to differentiate him from the not-to-be-thought-about ex-boyfriend: Will is older, quite a bit older, in his thirties, I think; Will is a dancer so as different as different can be; Will is married to Amalphia so open to really unorthodox arrangements whereas farmers are orthodox and narrow minded. Everybody knows that. Right? Wrong, so wrong, but I try to convince myself of it anyway.

So, Monday morning, right after class, I head upstairs for the coaching session and learn something else about Will, something quite interesting: he doesn't get on with Justin Bevan.

"All of it should be filmed," says Justin in an argumentative voice to Will, then switching to sweet for me: "Hello, sweetie, you just warm up over there while we hash out some details."

The studio is bright and sunny as I bend and stretch at the barre and look out the window over the forest. I see the path that leads to the stone circle, and the sun warms my face, making the situation seem less intimidating somehow.

Will tells Justin how it's going to be: "Cameras off and pointed at the floor."

"For how long?" Justin's face reddens in annoyance.

"As long as we need." Will's got a London-y type of accent, another difference from Jonasz.

"No, Hearst, no," says Justin. "You just need to get on with your choreography and ignore the cameras. We'll edit it all to make it right."

"Shall I text Malph and get her up here?"

"She will take my side," says Justin.

"You sure about that?" replies Will.

They face off with a silent stare. I almost expect them to start circling each other and stamping the ground. The sunlight fades as clouds gather in the sky outside.

It's Justin who finally backs down. "Fine, but be as quick as you can with whatever preamble you've got planned."

"Point 'em at the floor, then."

"Oh, come on!"

The cameras get pointed at the floor, Justin sits down on a chair at the side of the studio with his arms folded, and Will turns to me, smiling.

"There's something I want to do first," Will explains. "Not everyone is a choreographer. Some of the greatest dancers in the world have no choreographic ability at all. So please don't worry about it. It doesn't matter a bit for your career, but for the sake of this..." He waves a hand at Justin and the cameras. "I'm going to teach you something I came up with at the weekend. The subject is what it's like to choreograph for the first time. Learn it, and then if nothing comes to you later, you can just do this instead. Pressure removed."

What he demonstrates is simple and beautiful. Walk forwards and think. Walk backwards and think. Spin across the floor, stretch up, stretch down.

I copy him: I hold my head, I hold my knees, I sit on the floor then spring up and copy the complex piece of choreography that finishes Will's piece. No one will believe it came out of me. I could probably simplify it in front of the cameras, though.

Once the piece is learned, Will turns to me. "Now, all this stuff I'm about to say about the deepest and the darkest? It's not for everyone. It might not be for you at all. Rather than go into something uncomfortable in front of this lot..." He gestures at the cameras again. "You can just do what we've practised. If you want."

"Now?" says an impatient Justin, oddly not objecting to the fact that I'm basically being allowed to cheat.

Will nods, and the cameras raise their heads from the floor, big black guns with only one target. But Will is right: the pressure is off now I have a routine to fall back on. So, I relax a bit and listen as he says that the best art often comes from the deepest, darkest memories you've got inside, the most painful emotions you've ever experienced. I've heard things like this before, in improvisation class at college. I realise I've even done things like this before; I just hadn't thought of it as choreography.

Will continues: "You might not be able to put your feelings into words, but you can compose movement about more or less anything."

I think about it. My mother trying to kill me would surely be the darkest thing I have in my past, except I don't believe it is. It was an ending to all the rest, an escape, and not something I want to put into dance, not today anyway, and definitely not in front of the cameras.

"It might be something you don't even want to think about," Will says, and I begin to get an idea.

I know exactly what I don't want to think about. I try hard not to think about it all day long, but it has me at night. Could I let it out like this? Would that work? Would it even make acceptable choreography? There's only one way to find out.

I sit on the floor, broken and sad, heart and head full of the tower, the great dark tower. I spiral upwards like its steps and envisage meeting Jonasz at the top, and he's full of anger and disdain like he is in my dreams, like he never was in real life. That anger, that disdain, that loss of love, sends me back down, all the way to the bottom of the tower to sit on the floor, destroyed and desolate. I repeat the choreography and watch myself in the mirror. It is not what I want it to be at all.

"It needs to be bigger," I tell Will.

He shows me ways to widen my stance and how to breathe into the movement, to inflate the space I occupy, but it's still not right. It's suddenly so obvious what needs to happen here.

"I need more people," I say. "I want my whole class in on this."

Nigel is sent to pull them all out of contemporary, and they soon fill the studio with their excitement. They're perfect, and between us we make a big thick tower with waving turrets at the top. Boys on the outside, girls inside, we climb on each other and make it higher.

"We could throw you up inside and catch you," suggests Clinton.

We do it. It works. Will shows us other throws, and they get practised too.

Ideas flow fast as we all separate out and play the doomed couple at the top of the tower: five pairs, all performing quite traditional pas de deux. It's the tragedy of Jonasz and me, but I'm not dealing with it alone anymore. We're all in it together.

We mix up the partners. I choose Clinton because I can call the shots here today, and he's the biggest and strongest and partnering him is an incredible experience that stops me from thinking too much about what we're depicting. Plus, he can raise me the highest, right to the top of any tower.

"So I got my pas de dix in the end," says Justin at the end of the session. "And what a stunning promo shot your ten-person structure is going to make. It could well go on to win."

It seems bizarre to me that the others are so grateful to be included.

"I needed you," I tell them. "It was rubbish without you."

I thank Will, and he thanks me right back: "Great session. And it was all you."

Justin approaches, Nigel at his side, notebook at the ready. "Sweetness," he says to me. "The new hair – very chic, by the way – is it a rebellion against your dark past?"

"Bevan!" says Will.

"No," I say, though maybe it is, a rejection of it at least. I suspect it will be proclaimed as such to the nation on Saturday. Aye, fitever. I dinna care.

# 19

"WE NEED TO DO research," says Alexander, quietly at the lunch table. "For our own thing."

"Oh, the pas de deux?" I ask. "Have you choreographed it?"

He shakes his head. "I need you to see some places from my dark past." He grins. "But it'll have to be late on, when everyone thinks we're in bed. Are you up for that?"

"Yes!" I say at once, way too loudly, and everyone turns to look at us.

It's been a while since I've snuck out at night to meet a boy in a dark place, or so it feels. Really it's only been a couple of weeks which seems almost unbelievable. But it's true. My wall of discipline crumbles, the wall that exists between Jonasz and me, and the memory that comes is so clear: Jonasz arriving at the top of the tower on that terrible night. His face. His arms. His warmth. The safety of him. The worry of him, the concern. That was love in his face. I'm sure of it. And I miss him so much that I get that burning-up feeling again, like I'm going to burst out with it all, and—

"You can't go out your front door, though," Alexander says.

For a moment I'm disoriented and don't know what he's talking about. The door of the tower? With Jonasz?

"Holly might see you go by," he adds.

And I'm back at the table in the great hall. Without Jonasz. Never to be with Jonasz again.

Alexander is still speaking: "I'll come round the back and throw a stone at your window, like in the movies."

The image is funny, and good for me to focus on. We both laugh, prompting Star to ask what we're up to.

"Nothing at all," says Alexander giving her the movie-star smile.

He's such a movie-star boy, and I'm going to meet him in the middle of the night, me, little Ariel who everyone used to despise. But I'm bigger now: accepted and liked, with colourful hair which I'm not quite used to; the short hairstyle keeps shocking me in the mirror.

In afternoon pas de deux, Mr. Timms wants to see the tower choreography from the morning. We dance through it, and he loves it, and then I tell the background story: what the house I lived in was like, a somewhat edited version; meeting Jonasz in the tower, and how we became friends, then more than friends. I tell everyone how the tower was the only place that felt like home, sometimes, when Jonasz was there.

My sadness must show through what I thought was a disciplined and factual telling of the tale because I get a group hug. It's like a cuddly version of the choreographed tower. Maybe that should be in our piece too? The hug? We absorb a collective embrace into the choreography, to show that new love from friends can help with a lost love from the past.

"Not necessarily lost forever," says Bubbles. "You were the one who ended it. I think he still loves you."

"Don't go all romantic and stupid on her," snarls Lewis.

"It is lost forever," I say firmly, regretting going into so much detail about what had happened. "That's what the pas de deux is, before the group throw at the end: doomed love, finished love, maybe not love at all anyway." I'm babbling, and feeling cross with Bubbles for making daft suggestions.

Mr. Timms is full of suggestions too, albeit only choreographic ones, but I don't want those either.

"We need to practise by ourselves with no teachers," I say. "I want this to be ours alone."

"It is yours, Ariel," says Paula.

"Your idea," agrees Paul.

"No, it's everybody's," I insist. "You've all been such good friends to me, welcoming me, from the moment I arrived... It's about that too: friendship. We're making this together."

<hr>

We're a cosy little group at dinnertime in the great hall. The cosiness continues on into my cottage as we all gather there in the evening to share ideas about the tower piece.

As everyone leaves afterwards, Alexander gives me a meaningful movie-star look, and I walk up my stairs to lie on my bed, fully dressed.

It's tempting to look out the window and watch for him coming, but that would spoil the stone-throwing thing. When it finally happens, it's a much smaller noise than expected, just a tiny 'tink' sound against the glass. But there he is, looking up, all big-eyed, from the snowy ground.

I pull on my new purple jacket and woolly hat, internet purchases made possible by my Fairy Grandmother, and climb half out of the window.

Alexander clambers up on the coal bunker, handily situated below, and helps me jump down onto it. Its lid cracks and caves in, and we leap onto the ground, laughing but trying to be quiet.

"So, where we going?" I ask in a loud whisper.

"To the cliff where I was nearly killed."

The night suddenly feels less fun. My cheeks sting in the frosty air. It must be well down into minus temperatures now;

the snow is crunchy, its top layer frozen hard, and what's it going to be like by the sea? In the dark? Properly dangerous, that's what. Sheep fall off cliffs and get washed away sometimes when the weather's bad. I've been told stories of such events, but – discipline! – I shouldn't think about that.

"It's okay," says Alexander, in a reassuring tone. "I nicked my cousin's keys. We can go down under the castle and through the tunnel there."

"The cliff is indoors?"

"Yeah, kind of. In a cave."

I'm not sure this sounds much better, but the fun element of the night returns as we crawl commando-style past Holly's cottage to avoid detection. We run round by the trees to the back door of the castle.

Alexander removes a large ring of keys from his jacket pocket and jangles them in the moonlight. We stifle our laughter as he unlocks the door in three places with three different keys.

All is silent within. I think we're up near the castle kitchen.

"Right," says the movie-star boy, walking forward and stopping, as if in choreographed thought like Will demonstrated the other day. "There's something I need to find out first."

We sneak along the dark corridor, past the kitchen and many other rooms until we wind round to Mr. Zolotov's office. It's locked. Alexander tries about twenty keys till he finds the one that fits the lock, and that one he removes from the ring and puts in his pocket.

"For another time," he whispers.

We retrace our steps, going past the kitchen again. There's more key fumbling, and then we gain access to a room that has steps down into it and strange green lighting.

It's spooky. Alexander flicks the lights on and off from by the door for added effect.

"See that angel?" he says, indicating a stone carving on the wall. "It's pointing to an entry point to the tunnel system, like a secret message. There's a bunch of those angels hereabouts."

I look up at the pointing angel and then down at the floor of the room. Part of it is made of glass, and it's from there that the green light glows.

"You can walk on it," he tells me, making sure the door to the corridor is properly shut. "It's reinforced glass."

I stare down into the space below the glass floor and see barrels, kegs, bottles of beer on a wall... Are we in a pirate movie or a drinking song?

"Old smuggling stuff," Alexander explains, unlocking a wooden-framed door in the glass.

He expects me to follow him into a damp, scary, probably spider-infested, dangerous dungeon place? The darker part of this fairy tale? No problem. I step right in.

# 20

THE WOODEN STEPS ARE a little rickety, but we're soon on the stone floor below the castle and heading off into a passageway to the left. So far, so good. So far, no spiders. We come to a really thick door, like a grid of metal. The start of a narrow stairway is visible beyond it.

"Ross doesn't have a key to this," Alexander complains, tapping the ring of keys round one of the square gaps in the door, causing clattering metallic echoes. "But I'll find a way in one day."

We retrace our steps to the green-lit area under the glass floor, and Alexander fires up his phone torch and points it towards a pitch black tunnel. A sound of howling wind emanates from it. At least, I think it's howling wind.

"That's where we're going," he tells me of the tunnel. "You ready?"

So I hold hands with a movie-star boy and walk forward into perils unknown. These are not walls that we're walking between, well, they are, just not walls made by people. There's no bricks with forever words behind them here, no cement or building codes and safety rules that have been adhered to.

Alexander's phone lights up the two sides of rock face, so dark that they're almost black, and I see that they're shiny and wet in places.

"You okay?" he asks, squeezing my hand.

"Yes," I say, defensive for a moment before admitting: "It's kind of scary. And smelly." That last part's new. I catch a whiff of... I don't know what? Decaying seaweed?

"The sea," he says. "That means we're nearly at, yeah, here it is. We'll do this bit another day. See the boulder?"

There is a big round rock embedded in the left wall. It's really wide and taller than us. I let go Alexander's hand and lay both of mine on the boulder as if it might ground me into this strange experience.

"There's a really cool room in there," he tells me. "It leads through to another tunnel that goes right to my house. We're not allowed into it, of course. It's right under the stone circle; the chamber is its earthly counterpart."

"That's really weird," I say, because it is.

"Yeah, well, my family are a bit weird. Haven't you noticed?"

"They all seem really nice."

"Even my father?"

"Well..." He hadn't been nice to me in class, but he did stand between me and my own father which was kind of heroic. But it doesn't seem the right time to mention that. This is Alexander's deal, his dark past, not mine.

He laughs, lifting the mood, though only slightly, and takes my hand again as we continue on past the big rock and onto less stable ground.

The floor slopes downwards. The smell increases. I miss my footing and almost fall, but Alexander catches me.

"Do you come here a lot?" I ask, because: really? Does he?

"No." That's a bit of a relief. "I've been quite a few times, though. Look up."

By the light of the phone, I can see the height of the roof which looks like it might be open to the sky. It's jagged and craggy and dangerous looking; we're like small bugs under a big stone. Small bugs that could easily be squished by falling rocks, and judging by the state of the path we're on, that happens a lot, the falling of rocks, not the squishing of people. Hopefully.

On we go. Down we go. We have to clamber over a pile of fallen rubble and then, finally, we reach some sort of destination and exit the tunnel onto a flat rock floor.

I follow the light of the phone with my eyes as Alexander moves it around the space. We are in a large cave. The rocks are pink, but a darker pink than the granite of the castle. The cave roof is high, cracked all over and domed, and there's a roaring sound, a splashing; the sea is nearby.

"We're going round there," he says, pointing the light to the end of a rock wall.

As we walk along, I see the end of the floor too: it drops off and disappears a little way beyond the wall.

"It's okay," he reassures me. "It's safe enough. It's only when the sea's rough that waves splash up into this bit. They shoot out the top too. Looks like smoke when that happens."

Memory stirs, and I recall another story told by a boy who knows a lot of local history, geography, everything really. "Are we inside the Deil's Lum?" I ask.

"Yes!" Alexander seems delighted that I know this, as we edge round the corner of the wall and into a smaller space.

The Deil's Lum, the Devil's Chimney: the entrance to hell. That's where we are.

"This is where Fake Mum made me stand," he tells me. "Right here with her, waiting for my dad. She'd taken my brothers and sisters too, but she left them back round there. They were just little." His voice is different, strained, back in the bad moment of the past. "Look." He shines his light down, and I see the sea and rocks, all dark below, but lapping only, no fierce waves tonight, no devil's smoke.

Alexander sits down and lets his legs hang over the edge. I join him, the cliff feeling quite solid. I almost make a quip about how we should have brought a picnic, but that would be wrong on the site of such a terrible event.

"Tell me yours," he says. "Your dark stuff. If you want. I don't mean to be all: me, me, me."

"There's really not much to tell. She was drunk and lunged at me with a knife. Got me in the neck, but not deeply enough to do any lasting harm. Night before I came here. She was trying to sabotage this, couldn't bear anything going well for me."

He nods emphatically. "They didn't see us as people in our own right. We were only a playing piece in some agenda of their own."

"Yes!" I say, too loudly for the second time that day, or night, because he's so exactly right. "She didn't think I had feelings, or maybe she did, but she loved to hurt them. Every day, telling me how shit I was, everything I did. If I tried anything different with my clothes or hair, she'd mock me, so I stopped. I know what she'd say about this." I pull my hat off and put on a posh voice to imitate Maxine: "A right pig's breakfast!"

"They're the real devils," he says. "It's good that they're locked away. Simone – that's Fake Mum – she tried to make me into some sort of ballet prize for my father. She trained me so badly that Amalphia had to undo it all and start all over again."

"You're amazing now," I remind him. "They all told me you were the best in the class on my first day," I say, aware that this is not exactly what they told me, not all of it anyway, but that bit is true. He is the best in the class, by far. "You said Amalphia saved you, when you told me about this before. Did you mean on that day?"

His gaze is really intense, and for a moment I wonder if I've been too personal or probed too deeply, but then he nods. "Yeah, Amalphia appeared round there, with Michelle, my actual Real Mum," he says, pointing back to the cave wall we've just come round. "Real and Fake got in a fight and nearly pulled me off here. Amalphia grabbed me. They fell. Real died. Fake lived."

I put my hand on his arm. "I'm really glad she saved you, Alexander."

"I'm really glad your devil was a bad aim with a knife."

There's just his great big eyes, so deep and dark, and his hand doing that thing through my hair again, but then the ground below us starts to crumble, little stones moving underneath, and it feels like we're about to fall.

We scramble back as Alexander shouts. The shout, the swear, echoes and repeats in the cave; three times it shouts back at us, the children of devils, as we clutch each other on the cliff, here in this cave of devils.

"I shouldn't have brought you here, Ariel. I'm sorry."

"You couldn't know that was going to happen," I say, standing, pulling at him to do the same and to move back, right back away from the edge.

He's frozen, still sitting, staring out into the abyss towards the sea, looking into the dark. Looking for what? Ghosts of the past? His real mother? Or the fake one?

It's all become too creepy, and I find myself shouting his name. "Alexander!" Again and again.

He finally moves. He stands and lets himself be pulled back round the wall, back towards the tunnel, but then he stops.

"Alexander, we have to go," I tell him.

He smiles. "You look so like her."

"Who? The devil? Your devil? The real mum? The fake one? Who?"

"No." He laughs. "Amalphia."

# 21

"LADIES FIRST," SAYS ALEXANDER, holding out a chivalrous arm to help me up the rickety steps and back through the glass floor into the castle.

I don't need help, but I think he needs to feel he's helping to lessen the guilt about what almost just happened to us. We almost went the way of his real mother, over the cliff, into the sea, and onto the rocks.

I ascend the small wooden stairway and come up into the green-lit room to discover that Mr. Zolotov is descending the stone steps by the main door of the room.

"Good evening, Ariel," he says, face impassive.

"Hello, Mr. Zolotov," I say, not knowing what else to say, actually needing that help from Alexander now.

My partner in crime rises gracefully out of the floor and smiles. "How did you find us?" he asks his father.

"There is snow," replies Mr. Zolotov in his deep voice. "You have left many foot prints." The teacher then turns, goes back up the steps and out the main door of the room.

We follow. We all walk along the corridor to the back door of the castle and then out into the snow where we turn and walk back through the dark towards the cottages. Little lights at the side of the path show the way.

Is no one going to speak? Should I? I'll say goodnight at my door, I decide. They're not coming in. If Mr. Zolotov wants to reprimand us he should do so now, not keep us waiting like this. Is that his game?

But it's Alexander who starts the conversation as we approach my cottage. "We'll make sure there's no snow next time," he says to me.

"If you want to spend time with Ariel," replies Mr. Zolotov, "you should invite her to your home where it is warm and safe."

Alexander looks at me in question. "Sunday lunch?"

"Sure," I say, then adding my own planned, "Goodnight," and going into my cottage and closing the door, and then locking it too. Whatever weird thing they have going on between the two of them can stay out there with them.

Unfortunately I have locked myself in with my own weird thing. Maybe it got set free in the cave when I talked about it. Maybe it was just waiting to jump out at me, biding its time until I was relaxed and settled in my new home. Or did I actually dance Jonasz out of the way by giving him and the tower a place in the daytime, making space in my dreams for her, my very own devil, from my very own dark past?

The dream I have that night is an exact depiction of a day that really happened, a day from when I was twelve years old. It was shortly before I decided to run away, so the thresher incident had not happened. I had all my fingers. My skin was unmarked, my legs and arms, pristine and pale. I feel myself reaching back in time to tell young me: you look great. Don't believe her; she's a devil.

Everything about the day is augmented in the vision: the deep blue of the sky, the warmth of the sun, the kindness of my mother's face, my own naivety: this past me actually believes it is the long-wished-for moment.

She is being nice. She gives me some old clothes and sandals of hers and tells me I can wear them for a day out. I put on the short denim skirt and matching jacket and do up the small golden buckles on the high-heeled sandals. I pair them with knee socks, but I forgive my old self for this as she is only twelve.

Out we go into the world. We go to shops that she likes, a café that she likes, a garden centre she likes. She's still all smiles, no snipes to be heard. Has it finally happened? Does she finally like me? Dare I think, love me? Will I hear that word? Love?

We meet a girl from school who tells me I look really grown-up in the clothes and shoes. "Doesn't Ariel look cool?" she says to my mother, my devil, Maxine.

Maxine says nothing, but the day has changed. The sky is dark, dark grey. Pink lightning shoots between black clouds as we drive home. I'm not sure if that really happened or if my dream mind is adding cinematic effects.

We get back to the house of Maxine where I go to my room, the smallest room, and sit on my bed, the one that sometimes collapses in the middle of the night. Maxine will go on to replace this bed with a nice new divan on the day I leave for college in London, to make the room fit for visitors to sleep in. But on that day, in reality and in the dream, the old bed stays in one piece as I sit on it. It's not the collapse of furniture I'm anticipating anyway. It's something else. An eruption. I know bottles are being opened. Glasses filled. It'll soon be time.

The moment arrives. The door flies open. Her face is red and pointed and furious.

"You!" The word is long and loud, and it smells of whisky. "You are never to do that to me again. Your father saw you when you came in. Said you looked like a prostitute in those heels and that short skirt. You walked around showing your bottom to the whole world all day."

The bed doesn't collapse when she hits me, but I do. The force of the slap knocks me to the floor. It makes the air in the room darker and filled with purple sparks.

After she leaves, I wish, not for the first time, that the bedroom door had a lock. I want to take the clothes off. I need to take the clothes off. But he might be sent. He might come in. He won't knock. They never knock. I opt for just climbing into bed and changing into pyjamas really fast under the covers. He might rip the covers off when he arrives.

He does rip the covers off, but he doesn't hit me. I'm glad for that. He gives a speech that she has scripted for him, like Nigel with his notebook, but also not like Nigel who is just a person doing a job. My father tells me I have to learn to respect myself and my body and my family, like they're being good parents giving good advice to an errant daughter. It's what they pretend to be in front of other people, what they let them see. No, it's more than that: they actually think they are better than other people. That makes me angrier than any of the rest of it. It's the great big lie that they parade about to the whole world, and it's far worse than showing your bottom to the whole world. Which I don't think I actually did anyway.

My father recites the house rule before he goes: "You mustn't upset your mother."

In the dream, I look out the window at the tower on the hill and wonder what it's like inside, and if it's even possible to go inside. I bet it is. And I bet it's a better place than this house.

# 22

I WAKE UP RELIEVED to be in a better place now, though the emotions of the dream linger. I drink tea then put on my coat and head out early to catch Alexander on the woodland path. He always seems to come to school that way; he never arrives with his dad in the car. It's less snowy in the thick of the woods, but I can make out footprints on the ground; I can see exactly how we were found last night.

I lean back against a gnarly old tree, a silver birch, I think.

"Hey," says Alexander when he sees me. "Don't worry; you're not in trouble."

"Yes, I got that impression last night," I tell him. "Are you? In trouble?"

"Bit," he says. "Told not to lead you astray."

"I led myself astray long ago," I assure him. "Alexander, you know your piece, the secret pas de deux that you're choreographing?"

"Our piece."

"Right," I say, hoping that's true. "Is it about your devil?"

"Yeah, or what lay behind it, behind her actions."

"Can it be about mine too? Because, I think I could do that. I think I could choreograph that."

———ere———

I'm excited to get working on the new pas de deux, but Alexander refuses to start until we've finished our research, which will undoubtedly involve more weirdness, and he also insists on it all staying secret. I quite like the secret part, the idea of springing it on everybody at the auditions in ten days' time. I hope we can make something good in just ten days, though. The tower pas de dix improves every day, but that's with ten students inputting suggestions.

Henry is a bird flying off the top of the tower. It works so well, his wordless inspiration. It symbolises freedom but also, I tell him: there were often crows on and in the tower, so it's very real.

The cameras love it. Nigel scribbles away about young girls soaring high after their troubles, or seeking the great heights of fame and fortune from the depths of despair; which should it be? Which is it?

Justin eyes me beadily. "Ariel, what does the tower symbolise for you? Is there any deep hidden meaning that we're missing?"

"No," I tell him. "Not back then, anyway. This work now, is really about friendship. I've never experienced it like this before. I was always the freak." I hold up my right hand. It hasn't been mentioned on the show yet, and I want to be the one to bring it up; I don't want the voiceover man to do it. "Here, I'm accepted," I explain.

Henry grabs me and holds me tight. Justin loves it. The words, the hand and the hug appear in the adverts leading up to Saturday's show.

"Third years are fuming," says Alexander at Saturday lunch. "They thought they'd win this thing with no real competition from anyone else, and then they got no airtime on the show at all last week, and our class is gonna ace it this week too. Everyone knows it."

Now that he mentions it, I do notice some unfriendly glances from the older students' table. For a second it reminds me of other unfriendly school times, but it isn't the same. This is because we're doing well, not because we're looked down upon. It's professional jealousy, so kind of like an achievement or a milestone.

"They need to work on their own stuff 'stead of shooting daggers at us, isn't it?" retorts Clinton, shooting daggers right back at them as he eats.

"They'll be going off on tour soon anyway," says Paul, then explaining further for my benefit, I think. "The third year class becomes a touring company for their last term, every year. It's meant to be a great experience."

I did know about this; I once taught myself one of the touring company's pieces in my bedroom at home while watching it on the internet.

"Animal therapy," says Henry, out of the blue and with no context, pointing at me and smiling as if in encouragement.

My mind does a quick flick through of what this could be about? Henry's nice, so he's not saying I'm an animal. Is it something about the third years? Is it a band? A film? A book? A dance company?

"That might be a good idea for you, Ariel, if you like animals," says Star. "Henry's been going for months; he really loves it."

Alexander provides the needed clarity: "My cousin's farm up the road has an Animal Assisted Therapy unit. You get to pet pigs and feed lambs, that sort of thing. Supposed to be calming or something." He lowers his voice to a warm whisper in my ear. "If you go up to the farm with Henry this afternoon, I'll meet you there. We can go do research."

—ell—

So, Saturday afternoon finds Henry and me strolling along a country lane in silence. It's actually quite freeing not to have to make conversation. We point things out to one another: a hawk hovering high in the sky, a buzzard, a car coming far too fast round a corner, and then we're there.

Inside the entrance of the farm sits a bright blue tractor. My heart beats fast. The vehicle looks exactly like the one Jonasz and I looked at in the tractor centre that day. Henry pats my shoulder, bringing me back to the now, and we walk round the back of the farm buildings. They're not as tidy as other farm buildings I have known. The ground's a lot muddier, and there's straw underfoot all over the place, and the smell of cow dung is really strong. Comparisons don't help, so I force myself to stop. Wall of discipline: activated.

There are no pigs to pet. There's goats, one of whom chews my sleeve, and there's a pair of very large and very friendly turkeys; their plumage is colourful and ornate, and they follow us everywhere. I hold a lamb that was rejected by its mother. It's this lost little baby that I want to pet, to comfort. The dark-haired farmer introduces himself as Ross and gives me a bottle of milk to feed my woolly new friend.

"You Alexander's wee pal?" he asks, and I nod, staying quiet like Henry. "You should come up with him one day, not as part of this; you could go horse riding then." It seems a bit rude that Henry's not being offered the same, so I say nothing, amazed at how fast the lamb is sucking down the milk.

Ross doesn't let the horse idea drop, though, and, once the bottle of milk is empty, he sends me up the track to see them. Henry is sent to groom donkeys that I would have liked to have seen too.

I haven't reached the horses, though I can see several large-looking specimens in a field with various colourful jumps, when a four-wheeled motorbike appears over the horizon of the track. It's moving so fast that the wheels lose all contact with the ground as it travels over the crest of the hill. I scramble up onto the verge and sit on the wall, the dry stane dyke, to let the noisy, dangerously driven vehicle pass.

It doesn't pass. It stops. The driver lifts the visor of his helmet and his movie-star eyes smile as he offers me a helmet too.

"Alexander!"

"You coming?" he asks. "We'll have to be quick to get you back before Henry knows you're gone."

"Research?"

"Yep."

"Super creepy again?"

"Yep."

I take the helmet, pull it on and climb up behind him, then I hold on very tight, tighter than I've ever held on to anyone or anything ever. My presence aboard the bike does not make Alexander drive more carefully. We turn and head back up the way he came, bouncing over the top of the hill – that's painful – through a wide gate that's open, and then down another long grassy field.

There's minor terror in the fast and unexpected journey, but it's also pas de deux style sexy. Our bodies are pressed together, my arms round him, the engine buzzing below. We're surrounded by a green-and-brown agricultural landscape, though there's still some snow to be seen on the distant hills.

The romantic atmosphere built up in the field quickly dissipates when we arrive at our destination: a rundown little house with boarded-up windows.

"We get in round the back," he tells me. "It's easy."

Tall dead thistles and nettles from the year before bend underfoot and tug at our clothes as we head round the side of the building. Alexander pulls down a propped-up board and gives me a leg up into a glass-less window. My foot lands in a kitchen sink, and I jump down onto the floor as he scrambles through after me.

"This is where I lived when I first came to Scotland," he says. "With Fake Mum and Real Mum. I was eight, and they wanted me to spy on Amalphia's family for them."

"Shit," I say, because it obviously was.

"Backfired on them," he tells me. "She welcomed me, Amalphia did. First time I ever felt accepted for who I was; I didn't have to try to be the way someone else wanted me to be."

"I get that. I really do." I remember meeting Jonasz and arranging a time to meet him again, and that I was really late, but he didn't mind. He wasn't cross, he was just so glad that I had managed to come, so pleased to see me, and—

"I know you do," says Alexander. "I know you understand." And on goes the phone light.

We walk up a damp-smelling hall and past lots of peeling wallpaper towards what I think is the front door, but it's a hole in the broken-looking floor that we're going down into. Of course it is.

# 23

THERE'S A FOLDING METAL ladder which Alexander slides open with a crashing sound. He assures me it's safe – no cliffs this time – and down we go.

There are two rooms in the basement of the house. The first is cave-like with an earthen floor, and it leads to the second which is full of boxes and some old chairs and has toilet facilities. There's an actual toilet sitting there, plumbed in, at the side of the room.

"Weird, right?" he says.

"Right."

"Just wait." He pulls a rug out of the way, and we're looking at a big round door on the floor; it's wooden with metal decorations and hinges.

Alexander heaves at a metal ring on the floor-door in vain for a moment – I wonder if I should help – and then the door shifts fast, flying round and knocking us both over.

"Sorry about that," he says as I leap up, embarrassed to have ended up lying on top of him. "But this is the really weird part now."

His phone illuminates a stone staircase that spirals down from this room and looks damp and dark and full of danger.

"Another seaside expedition?" I ask.

He laughs. "No. This goes down to the chamber behind the boulder we saw the other night, the room below the stone circle.

I was never in it as a kid when we lived here; I didn't know about it then; Ross showed it to me later on. Amalphia tore him a new one about that when she found out, I can tell you. But it was a special place to my Real Mum and her family, our family. I'm descended from the Mermaid and the Bear; did you know that?"

"The Mermaid and the Bear?"

"The Manteiths of the castle? Real Mum was one. Ross is related too. We're all a bit cr-a-a-zy!" The extended word echoes a bit in the dark underground room.

So down I go into yet another scary and strange hole in the ground with Alexander, the 'crazy' movie-star boy.

Round plastic lights in the walls come on as we walk. "Motion activated," he tells me. "Ross put those in a few years back."

Soon we reach the bottom of the steps and walk through a short brick-walled corridor.

"My house is up there," Alexander says, pointing to an opening on the left. "Key to our basement never seems to be nickable, though. I suspect Papa Zolotov wears it round his neck."

The door we come to is a bit like the front door of the castle, Gothic shaped with metal studs. It opens without a squeak, or any other anticipated spooky noise, and we walk along a stone passageway, reminiscent of the tunnel from earlier in the week. And then the place does remind me a little of the stone circle. Up above, the tunnel of trees opens into a glade; down here, the stone passage opens into a big oval stone room. The curving walls are made up of grey slabs like flat boulders that flicker in the phone light, nothing motion activated down here.

"Help me light the candles," requests Alexander. "You get the full effect then."

The space brightens as we go round the many little alcoves, lighting big thick white candles as we go.

"They're proper church candles," he tells me, going on to explain that this was a post-reformation Catholic chapel.

It's all very strange. I feel the faint warmth from a candle as I stand near it. All the alcoves have carvings over them: angels, hearts, hands, crests. Is something religious going on here today? Are we going to get down on our knees and pray?

"Cool, isn't it?" remarks Alexander, not getting down on his knees. "Real Mum loved this chamber. It was important to her. Ross thinks she played music down here; the walls make it sound good, or something? Like a speaker? I think Amalphia visits too sometimes, probably to meditate. She does that up there too." He points at the ceiling, which is made up of many long thin stones. "In the stone circle," he adds.

"How can you know that's where we really are, that the stones are directly up there?"

"They are," he says. "Ross told me."

"But has anyone checked? Drilled through or something?"

"It's the chamber under the stones," he says like it can't be argued with. "Also called *The Womb of the Earth Mother*. There's a picture of it in my house. Hardly anyone has ever been down here, seriously, no one knows about it."

"Then I'm very honoured," I tell him, feeling like I might have riled him a bit with my questions. "What does it have to do with our dance, though?"

"Atmosphere," he says. "And, you know, Real Mum liked it, and my father keeps me away from it, or he thinks he does."

He shows me the boulder that we saw the night before. "Takes at least two men to shift it. I did it once with Ross, and we lit a fire in here to freshen the air of the place."

Alexander looks a lot younger in the soft light of the candles among the odd flat stones, and I think I'm on his father's side in this. There's a vulnerability to my movie-star friend that he doesn't mean to show, and I don't think all this weird stuff is helping him.

"Henry's bound to have noticed I'm gone by now," I say.

It works. We blow out the candles and hot-foot it out of there: through the tunnel and the Gothic door, along the passageway and back up the steps.

We leave the round door in the basement open for Ross to get later, climb up the ladder, out the window and dash over the field on the bike. The sexiness is totally gone. Everything feels a bit desperate now.

I run back down the track, passing the blue tractor that's now ploughing up a field to the left amid a cloud of seagulls, back through the farmyard to where Henry is sitting on a wooden fence, smiling at me, looking very cool in his skinny jeans and big farmer-y boots.

"Alexander okay?" he asks.

"Yes," I admit.

Henry places his hands over his heart and leans his head to the side.

"No," I say, because: no, it's not like that. My cheeks warm, though, but I don't think Henry notices.

# 24

SOME OF OUR WALK back to the castle is accompanied by the sound of a four-wheeled motorbike in the distance. The countryside is peaceful and bird-filled no more. And by the time we walk back into the great hall, Alexander is sitting at the first year table with hot chocolate and cake.

"You two took your time," he says. "What you been up to?"

"I got to feed a lamb," I answer truthfully.

"Everyone else is swimming," he tells us, and Henry goes to join them.

Maybe we should too. Maybe I should get this last reveal over? Before Aileen, in her life-guard role, combusts with rage and forces me to wear one of the spare swimsuits. I tell Alexander about it, them, my scars, and pull up a sleeve to show a minor one.

"You don't need to worry about that here," he says. "Amalphia bares hers; she even posed nude once. Look, I'll show you." He scrolls through his phone pictures.

"You have a naked picture of your mum on your phone?"

"She's not my mum," he reminds me.

And the photo he shows me is not indecent; Amalphia is tastefully posed, sitting, legs drawn up. The scars are really obvious in the picture.

"She was injured here when the dungeon caved in," says Alexander.

There's lots of marks on her legs and arms, but it's the large 'W' on her thigh that upsets me. How did that happen in an accident? I shiver. Poor Amalphia. Then I hate myself for the pity. I never want it, and I bet she doesn't either.

"My family are kinda big on the nudity," he says. "I'll show you the photo over their bed tomorrow. When you come to lunch," he reminds me, noticing my blank look. Among all the weird and disturbing things, I had forgotten that – oh, so normal – invitation.

"Anyway, we can't go swimming," he states, and I feel a bit defiant. If I want to go swimming, I will go swimming, but then he explains: "We can do our last bit of research this afternoon and start the choreography tomorrow after lunch. There's a dance studio in my house."

I do want to get going with that, so I join Alexander in creeping along the back part of the corridor system by the kitchens to Mr. Zolotov's office. He unlocks it with the key he stole the other night, we dart in, and he relocks the door behind us.

"My father's real old school," he tells me. "He keeps hard-copy files of everything, and I swiped these earlier."

His hand is full of yet more little keys. They're for the filing cabinets that sit at the back of the office, near the window. He opens one and then closes it again. "I want mine, and I want Amalphia's, and I want Simone's, you know, Fake Mum's. Do you want to see yours? Woah, Bubbles's file is almost as fat as mine. Henry's is not bad either..."

"No, and no," I say, pointing at our classmates folders in case he was going to look inside. "Our own, yes."

Amalphia's is not there. Fake Mum's is not there.

We sit cross-legged on the floor with our own records. We open the files together, visit them together, these pieces of paper that could contain the scariest places we've been this week. I look up from the lengthy doctor's note about the threshing machine accident because Alexander is incensed.

"He didn't want me to come here!" he tells me, holding up a paper from his file. "It's on my audition form. He couldn't tell me himself, of course, massive melt that he is. But listen to this: 'Alexander would benefit by attending another school, one unconnected with his family, maybe somewhere he could continue his academic studies too as I'm not convinced his heart belongs to ballet. However, he lacks the maturity to be away from home—'" He cuts off and spends a few moments swearing and calling his father names.

I locate my own audition form to see what Mr. Zolotov had to say about me. It's not so bad. 'Technically, a good little dancer, very precise, lacks confidence in presentation. I think she would do well here.'

The other pages hold my devil. I know it and return to them. "Social worker saying she'll be to see me soon," I say, holding out the letter.

"They're all a giant waste of space too," growls Alexander, still angry. "I've seen tons of them over the years."

I flick past the police liaison letter, detailing where my mother is now; I don't want to know. It's back to the medical stuff I go, not sure why there's quite so much of it. My hand, blah, blah. Attempted murder; I know all that too. And then I come to something I didn't know but should have. Why did no one tell me? And if all these professional people knew, why did no one help me? I'm furious.

"My mother is an alcoholic," I tell Alexander. "Doctors wrote about it. Teachers knew. They suspected she was abusive, but felt they didn't have enough evidence to report it."

Alexander supports me with an empathetic swear, and I remember some things that should have been clues. An art teacher with kind eyes, no disdain like the others, and her question: is

117

everything all right at home, Ariel? My old ballet teacher after a Christmas party: does your mother often drink that much?

"Why didn't I know?" I say now.

Why didn't I? The drinking: every day, every night. It just seemed normal. When anything went wrong for me outside of the house I would be given a drink too. Period causing writhing agony? She would say: "Have a glass of wine and go to your bedroom. No need to bring me into your drama." Beaten up at school? That deserved a whisky. Someone died? Drinks all round, and an excuse for her to shout for days, to tear into: my clothes, my hair, my face, my body. I thought that was how people grieved.

I am so messed up. I have no idea how normal people, decent people, conduct their lives.

"Enough?" suggests Alexander, watching me, distracted from his own file. "We've got our devils now. Let me show you where we're going to put them."

It's perfect, in so many ways, perfect. Everyone else will be presenting their audition pieces in the small theatre where it's all dark and plain. Ours will stand out and be so different, as long as we're permitted to deviate from form like this.

We will be. Justin will love the drama and surprise of it. Alexander is very sure about that.

Our devils are going to dance on a marble floor of black and white. Carved angels are going to look down from above, see every move the devils make, and document their every crime, and watch over us, and make all things right. Somehow. After all. In the end.

# 25

THE PICTURE ABOVE THE bed in the big white bedroom in Alexander's house is the most erotic thing I've ever seen in my life. Again, like the picture in Alexander's phone, it's not indecent – nobody's bits are showing – but it's so intimate. Such closeness is revealed, and, of course, there's three of them: Amalphia, Mr. Zolotov and Will. They're smiling at something, some personal joke known only to them.

I knew Mr. Zolotov was handsome, but I never really saw him as sexy before. And Will: he's all Jonasz, Jonasz, Jonasz. I try to silence that thought by looking at Amalphia and spend three seconds being sexually confused before looking back at the image of Will. I wonder if Jonasz is all muscly like that under his clothes? I don't know because we never had normal boyfriend/girlfriend stuff. Not until those last few days, and then I couldn't really do normal. But I bet he is, muscly and beautiful like that, I mean.

"Too weird?" says Alexander, misreading my face.

"No," I say, because it's my old life that was weird, not this. People being happy together is not the weird thing.

"Come on, I'll show you the Mermaid and the Bear's bed."

We go upstairs, and it is a bit weird, mainly because there's a bald man reading a book in the four poster bed.

"Oh," says Alexander. "Kian. I didn't know you were here; I was just gonna show Ariel the bed."

"It's a grand old thing," says Kian, apparently not minding the interruption to his reading, and he points out the carvings of the historical characters on the back panels of the bed.

"That was Justin's partner," Alexander tells me, as we head back down to lunch. "He's having cancer treatment; his hair fell out."

So maybe having sadness and weirdness as a part of life is, in fact, normal.

We go through to the kitchen and Justin is there with everyone else. He seems different here, in Amalphia's house, quieter and less theatrical.

"Don't think I don't know you two are up to something," he says to us. "But I suspect it's going to make good telly, so I'm saying nothing." He turns away from us and fusses over a tray of food for Kian before disappearing upstairs with it.

Alexander's family is so big. Faye, I know. Faye, I've met. She's happy and bright and sits on the other side of Alexander from me at the table. Little Anna, I saw on that first day at the castle. She's dressed in a tutu again and performs an astonishingly perfect series of chaîné turns across the room before climbing onto Mr. Zolotov's lap. Chaînés are an advanced step. I don't think I knew them till I was at least fifteen. How old is Anna? Three or four at most, I think. Then there's Alexei, or Lexi as Alexander calls him, who looks so like Alexander, and is just a little younger than us; he seems cool and laid back, though he blushes whenever I speak to him.

The twins are twelve, and Alexander introduces them as "eggheads."

"We're academically motivated," translates Sophia while her brother, David, just smiles. They're not really similar to each other like Paul and Paula. Sophia has a look of Will, while David, like little sister Anna, is more like Amalphia.

The meal is lavish. There's so much food, such much lovely gravy-laden goodness, and it's all so delicious. Amalphia gives me one of her special smiles when I say this, which is good because she has been looking a bit sad. I think it's because Will is not here.

I know there have been complaints made about the castle students getting preferential treatment in *Ballerina Ballerino*, and Will is spending the next week travelling around the country giving workshops in other schools that are entering students into the competition. There was a big deal made of the fact on the previous evening's show. I was quite glad because it meant less time spent on my 'dramatic new look' and 'dramatic old life,' though I liked seeing us all working on the tower piece together.

"He will cope, Malphia," says Mr. Zolotov now. "You should not worry about Will." He looks worried, or cross, or something, though.

"I know," she says. "But the accompanying show is about the castle. It's called *Castle Dancers*. Of course you're going to see the students being helped by their teachers. Justin is sacrificing Will to public demand, and it's not fair, and I can't say anything, because..." She gestures upwards at the ceiling. "And, of course, I don't want to say anything, because..." The gesture is repeated. "And all that stuff about deprived areas and failing schools? I suspect Will is going to be made to walk down dark alleyways at night and be chased by wolves and vampires all in the name of 'good telly.' I'm fed up of the words 'good telly.'"

"The vampires are a concern," says Mr. Zolotov, grim for a moment before his face breaks into an Alexander-type smile.

Amalphia lightens up too, and the two of them cover the table with bowls of ice cream and sprinkles and hot fudge sauce.

I feel the absence of Will as well. I feel it like the absence of Jonasz, or maybe I'm feeling it instead of the absence of Jonasz

121

because I don't want to feel that. It's sad and wrong that a person is missing, though, an integral part of the family.

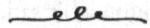

It's happier after lunch when we go upstairs to the top floor of the house where there's a dance studio that has views across to the stone circle. Will's bedroom is up here too, but I've never seen this place, let alone him in it, so his absence is not an issue to me anymore.

Lexi joins us with his guitar after checking that it won't bother Kian, and we get started. It's exciting to have live music; this element will be another surprise for the audience, and I can tell that Lexi is a talented musician. He's going to compose something just for us so we will have an original song too.

I warm up to the music, and the boys talk about timing and then agree that a lot of minor chords are needed. They talk about keywords for the lyrics: hate, beaten down, tied up. Do I have any to add?

I think for a moment. I contribute 'trapped' and 'frustrated' but then realise: "Shouldn't it be their words? We're not being us."

New list from Alexander: hate, beating down, tying up.

New list from me: scorn, dismissive, using, pretending, fake.

Fake is good. We both like fake.

"Gonna be a cheery thing, isn't it?" comments Lexi, then asking to see the kind of choreography we're going to be doing.

Alexander's initial moves are a bit of a shock because he's so obviously pretending to be Mr. Zolotov, a particularly arrogant and vain version of Mr. Zolotov, and Mr. Zolotov isn't his devil. Is he? I'm not sure Lexi's noticed; he seems to be focusing on matching the music to the style of dance, so I say nothing and add some choreographic dysfunction of my own.

I can be Maxine, tottering here, teetering there, laughing and pointing, slapping and stabbing, with an imaginary knife and also just with my hands, prodding and pushing. Mr. Zolotov/Alexander is taken down by her/me, laid out on the floor at the end, and we both like it. We high five about it, right there on the floor.

"Right. Okay," says Lexi. "I'll work on something later, but I've got football practice now."

"You're being your dad," I say to Alexander once his younger brother is gone.

"Think Lexi knew?"

"No," I say. "But why are you doing that?"

"Dear old Dad is responsible for the lot of it," explains Alexander. "The woman who raised me, Fake Mum? She was nuts. She is nuts. And I know it's because of him; they have some weird history that no one ever talks about."

Okay. I get why he's upset, but: "Are you sure you want to play him, though?" I say, because Lexi may not have recognised who Alexander was imitating but the man himself might, and Amalphia will; I'm sure of it.

"Yeah, absolutely. What he did deserves to be shown to everyone, not hushed up like it was."

"Oh," I say, feeling there's a lot more to this story but not wanting to ask him about it. I mean why did this Fake Mum person pretend she was his mother? Why is there even a fake one and a real one? I don't really understand, but I can see it's the sort of thing that would seriously mess a person up.

Though it actually seems to me that Alexander's real devil may be his issues with his father, but mine's my mother herself. There's one week left till the auditions for the competition, so we return to concentrating on our choreography.

# 26

MY COSTUME IS FAR too nice. I mean, I love it, but my devil doesn't deserve it. But then it's me who's dancing, me who's wearing a dress so short it will most definitely 'show my bottom to the world' through the medium of national television. I'll have tights on, though, and there's a leotard-like insert too, so I won't be indecent in any way. The dance dress flows perfectly, accentuating every movement of my arms and legs. It's bright red as are my pointe shoes, and now, having begged quick, last-minute grooming help from Star and Belinda, so are my nails and the highlights in my hair. The nails are particularly impressive; Belinda found a set of fake ones, and they're like blood-red talons.

The morning auditions in the castle theatre went well; we all know *Tower* is through to the next round. The panel of judges raved about it and asked polite questions, even the famous singer who I didn't recognise but everyone else was excited about.

Justin accepted our last-minute surprise entry with more surprise than I believe he felt; our class were a bit open-mouthed about it, and perhaps not terribly pleased to have been left out of the secret.

But here we are, Alexander and me, taking up our places in the foyer, on the black-and-white floor, under the angels.

Lexi takes his seat behind us with his guitar, and I smile out at my grandmother in the audience. She smiles back. We were all allowed to invite family members or guardians, and I confided in her about this surprise piece. It was nice to have someone to tell outside of school. It was nice to have someone understand without me having to explain. She used the word 'cathartic' about the subject of our secret pas de deux, this dance that we're about to perform right now in front of all these people, all these cameras and: the Serafins!

How? Why? It's only Janet and Tomas. I scan the area around them for Jonasz, desperately seeking him, wanting him to be here so much, but he seems to be absent. Thankfully there's no time for further thinking, or looking, or anything else because: it's time to start.

We begin. The devils don't like each other, but they flirt, because that's what they do. They show off too with neat pirouettes and sharp fouetté turns. They're competing, trying to win, to best each other in this dance.

Alexander's all in black, jeans and trainers, stern and proud and laughing and pointing when I, drunken and out of control, fall over. I get him back for his laughter. I stab at him. He takes me by the neck, and we swirl and stab and strangle and struggle until we're both dead on the floor.

There's a silence – a stunned one, I think – before everyone claps.

My grandmother is smiling as we stand to curtsey and bow: she looks like she's proud of me.

Mr. Zolotov is expressionless: impassive again like the other night when he caught us in the strange glass-floored room.

Amalphia is wide-eyed and pale, staring at me: shocked and horrified. She slips back through the people, unnoticed by anyone but me – oh, and Mr. Zolotov – and the two of them head up the stairs behind the crowd.

"Everyone back through to the theatre!" shouts Justin as he comes forward and takes both of us by the arm. "Judges' decision in a moment!"

The audience obey at once and filter back into the wide passageway that leads to the theatre.

"You two," snaps Justin. "Zolotov's office now."

"Why?" says Alexander, annoyed.

"Don't start with me," says Justin. "You know why."

Alexander and I look at each other in confusion and follow the producer. It seems likely that it's the unflattering depiction of Mr. Zolotov that's the problem, but I'm sure Amalphia was looking at me, troubled by me, not by Alexander.

"Costumes your idea, I take it?" Justin fires at Alexander once we're behind the closed door of the office.

"We both did our own," Alexander tells him.

"It's what we're wearing that's the problem?" I ask, wanting to laugh as this seems so silly. I know I wasn't really 'showing my bottom.'

"You came up with this red get-up yourself?" Justin asks me. "The nails too?"

The nails are an issue? Could it be a safety, take-your-eye-out type of issue? "They were a last minute idea," I tell him. "My classmates helped."

The door flies open and Amalphia flies in, all smiles and big eyes, shampoo-advert hair flowing out behind her. "Justin, you are not to give them any grief."

Justin's eyebrows raise high. "Really, you're completely fine with this? Is Aleks?"

She doesn't answer him and turns to us. "Powerful performance. Best classical ballet we've seen today, Justin. You have to agree?"

"She's dressed like Michelle," he says.

"What?" says Alexander, staring at my clothes.

126

I really want to crawl into a bed somewhere and get changed now.

"She's not, though, is she?" says Amalphia. "When did Michelle ever wear dancewear? That we saw? For a moment there, I admit, it was as if ghosts of the castle had risen, but that's all it was, a figment: the setting, the red, Alexander looking so much like Aleks. It was actually superb. The best performances are always contentious. Now, you two get back through for the judges' comments."

"Who is Michelle?" I ask, once Alexander and I are back out in the corridor. The name is familiar, but I can't remember where from.

"My Real Mum. Never saw her wear red, though; she was always in old knitted stuff when I knew her. I'll ask Ross about it later."

~ele~

The judges loved our pas de deux; they saw nothing strange about it. But I have to change, and I have to change fast. I sprint through the woods to my cottage and swap out the dancewear for jeans and jersey, then I sprint back to the castle to the foyer where my grandmother is waiting with the Serafins. The two Serafins. Janet and Tomas. Nobody else.

It's awkward. I start to introduce everybody, but they've already introduced themselves.

"We brought Caliban, Ariel," says Janet. "He's in the car if you would like to see him."

"Oh." Caliban. My heart constricts. But this is all so weird and unexpected. I'm meant to be going out to dinner with my grandmother this evening.

"Do you want to go with these people and see your dog, Ariel?" she asks, eyeing the Serafins with what appears to be disapproval, but smiling at me.

"Yes," I say. "I won't be long."

"You were wonderful, my darling," she tells me. "The dances you were involved in were clearly the best ones." Then she goes to wait in the great hall.

"Is keeping Caliban too much trouble?" I ask the Serafins as we walk down the castle steps and across the gravel. "Shall I arrange something else for him?"

"Oh, no," exclaims Janet. "Jonasz would be furious at any such suggestion. Wouldn't he, Tomas?"

Tomas nods. "Furious."

We reach the car, and they open the back door, and Caliban leaps out at me, almost knocking me over. It's so wonderful to see him, yet so strange, so odd, like meeting a friend from an old dream, a dear supporter from a nightmare. I hug him and kiss him and try to hold him tight as he bounces around, unable to contain himself.

Janet carries on speaking. "Jonasz has been taking great care of him."

He has. Caliban's coat is softer and glossier than it's ever been.

"He really loves him, Ariel," she continues as I sit on the ground and cuddle my dog. "Takes him out in the tractor all the time. Of course, he's thrown himself into work. Out ploughing in the day, lambing at night. He's started doing a course at the local college—"

"I'm going to take Caliban for a short walk," I say over Janet's words, really not wanting to hear any more of them. Maybe it's rude not to ask if this is okay, but I don't care. Jonasz gets my dog the whole rest of time. I want him now.

I run up the hill between the tall pines with Caliban. He loves it. We dance round the ancient stones and then I sit on the flat stone, the fallen one, and cry. I sob into Caliban's fur while he licks my face.

When I hand him back to the Serafins a little later, Tomas asks: "Is there anything you would like us to tell Jonasz? Any message?"

"I said everything I had to say to Jonasz before," I say and march away from them and back to the castle. They were threatening to bring down my wall of discipline, and I can't have that. If it crumbles, so will I.

Janet calls after me, but I ignore her. It's an evening for being rude. I march straight to Mr. Zolotov's office where I don't knock; I just barge in. He's in there, at his desk, as I had a feeling he might be, and he looks up in surprise.

"Why were the Serafins here?" I demand.

He frowns. "The Serafins?"

"The people I stayed with before I stayed here? Why were they here?"

"Oh. I think they are down as your guardians in your file. They would have been automatically invited."

I should have known that. It's not like I haven't seen the file. "Well, that needs to be changed. Patti, my grandmother, she should be in there instead."

"I will change it."

"Good," I say and turn to leave.

"Are you okay, Ariel?" he asks as I open the office door.

"Yes."

"You are not. You have been crying. You know that you do not have to do anything you do not want to do? Even if it is a friend, like Alexander, who is asking you to do something?"

"I never do anything I don't want to do," I tell him and barge straight out in the same manner I came in. I only just resist slamming the door.

# 27

I KNOW WHAT I want to do, and yet, I don't want to do it just to please other people. Alexander agrees. We both want to change the pas de deux without giving in to outside pressure, not that anyone has actually said we have to change it.

"I never meant to upset anyone," I say because it's true.

"I never meant to upset Amalphia," he says, and that's precisely true. He did mean to upset Mr. Zolotov, but that's his thing. That part of the choreography is not mine, is nothing to do with me or my devil. "Michelle did used to dress in red," he tells me, "and she had long red nails too. Ross told me, said she was super glamourous back in her prime."

So, for Amalphia, it must have been like watching her husband with an old girlfriend, and I totally get that that wouldn't be comfortable. It makes me think of Katy with her big hair and her comments about Jonasz. I don't think it was true, what she said about having kissed him, but could it have become true since then? His parents were here on Saturday night. He wasn't. Maybe he was out with her. I try not to think about it.

———

After the excitement of the auditions, the choreographic mania at the castle dies down. Our class has the two pieces to work on now, and we do so in contemporary and pas de deux. The cameras are there to film sometimes; it's not daily anymore as lots more footage from various places across the country is being gathered for the Saturday shows now to make things fairer.

And I start to get used to things. I get used to the cameras; they're there, or they're not there; it's no big deal anymore. I even smile at them sometimes. I get used to living at the castle and being surrounded by many people most of the time. I get used to the minor bad feeling there has been about Alexander and I doing our own thing in the competition. It really doesn't matter. Everyone else was free to do so too, but they didn't think of it, and that's okay.

"We could keep rehearsing this version in front of everybody," suggests Alexander, about the piece. "But change it in private. Then we still have a secret, and we'll have another surprise for if we get through to the semi-final."

I like that. I like the secret. So we start changing the choreography in the evenings: in my cottage, in the stone circle, anywhere we can get to ourselves. Studios in the castle are too risky; we might be seen and the secret revealed.

My grandmother sends me some books about recovering from abusive parenting. I order some more of my own, specifically ones focused on the harm done by alcoholic parents. They're intermittently interesting and upsetting. One moment I'm all happy reading in my bed, thinking: yes, yes, yes, there's my childhood. It's all explained now. I know this bit, and I know that part; but then I'm crying, because how can I ever be fixed? I'm such a confused mess. Do I have communication problems because I was never allowed to speak my truth or express my needs? Yes. Of course I do. I couldn't tell Jonasz what I was feeling. I couldn't tell him what happened at the Young Farmers' meeting. Not really, not until he asked, and even then, not in detail.

I did tell him the big thing I felt, though, the thing that really mattered, and much good it did me. I fling the book at the wall, and wish I had Caliban to cuddle and console me.

But I know what to do with my part of the pas de deux choreography; it's all about forbidding and repressing this time. My devil will allow her dance partner to do nothing; she will try to control his every move. She will fail, of course; he's going to do whatever he's going to do regardless of her. She will wear blue next time, dark blue, the colour of a hidden bruise. Maybe it could be multi-layered? Brown and purple should be in there too, representing the different stages of recovery. My recovery, not hers. I doubt she wants to recover. Alexander could rip the skirts off as we go.

"That's good," he says on hearing the idea. "Skirt ripping; I like it."

I buy the things needed for the costume online, texting Patti afterwards to thank her again for the allowance that allowed me to do that – lots of allowing all round now – and I send her links to see it. I don't tell her the significance of the colours, so all she sees is the beauty of the dress and how much it will suit me.

Life is now very focused and very full, and that's good.

Each day: classes, rehearsal, secret rehearsal. Mr. Zolotov is still tough on me in his weekly morning class, but I'm growing to appreciate it, to like it even.

I see the difference in the mirror as the weeks go by. Somehow I am managing to make a bigger impact on the room, stretching further and longer. My legs are stronger, my core is stronger, my arms look better, more professional than they did before. I can smile at my teacher when he shouts, and the mirror shows that I'm developing a small movie-star smile of my own.

Each night: reading, reading, reading, as I try to correct the other parts, the inner invisible scars, so they can keep up with my improving arms and legs. But there's no Mr. Zolotov to stretch my mind and fix my heart in the evenings. I'm all alone with my thoughts and my memories. The nights start to grow lighter as the year quickly moves into spring, but my thoughts about the past do not lighten.

I don't want to talk about my mother's alcoholism with Amalphia in my counselling sessions yet, so we mainly discuss mundane things. I do tell her about the Serafins coming to the auditions, though, and Caliban. I miss Caliban.

And I miss Jonasz. I let myself think the thought. I let myself feel it. And it doesn't seem to have grown any easier or less painful. Isn't time meant to heal these things? Perhaps not all things. I think I'll always feel this way, and that really, this is the biggest scar of my life, the deepest wound.

We get through the next stage of *Ballerina Ballerino*; the audience vote through both first-year pieces, and we get proper costumes for *Tower*, nude-looking ones, to match our skin tones. The costume fitting is filmed, and it's then shown on the following Saturday night instalment of *Castle Dancers*, meaning that not only do my classmates see my scars, the physical ones anyway, but everybody does.

No one in the castle flinches. It's as if it's a non-issue. What happens in other people's houses across the country, I can't know. We all watch the show together in my wee home, that place of friends and laughter and happy times.

Then we stare, agog, at the two Highland dancers who are also through to the semi-final and who take up quite a bit of the programme talking about their training. We'd seen some local Highland schools at auditions, and they had been okay, but these two dancers are utterly amazing, leaping over their swords, with strong legs and perfectly pointed feet.

"Nice kilts," says Lewis. "Traditional Scottish stuff. We should've thought of that; public might go for it."

"A man in a kilt is a sexy, sexy thing," agrees Bubbles.

"We couldn't wear kilts," states Paula. "Towers are not made of tartan."

"Not usually made up of naked people either, are they?" says Alexander with a laugh.

"Most definitely not," says Paul.

"You know what is traditional up here?" says Alexander. "At Easter? And it's almost Easter." He laughs and shakes his head at various answers involving chocolate eggs and bunnies. "Dancing naked in the stone circle."

"Oh, come on," says Star. "We're not falling for that."

"Amalphia does it," Alexander tells us. "Spring Equinox; it's a real thing. She says it's empowering, and I say we need all the empowerment we can get for the semi-final. Remember: it's in London, in a great big theatre, with a bigger audience than ever. You've seen some of these dancers, and they're good. We've got real competition now."

He has gaged the mood of the room well. We are all nervous about the semi-final. It will be a scarier performance than we've ever done before. The panel is going to be super-famous, and the real-life audience? Massive. And it all takes place in two weeks' time during the Easter break.

"You know what is the best empowerment for any dance event?" says Belinda, getting up to go. We look at her, open-mouthed, thinking she's heading for the stone circle. "Practice!" she says and, laughing, leaves, as do Star and Lewis, then Clinton and the twins.

That leaves Bubbles and Henry and Alexander and me.

Alexander smiles. "Meet you at midnight in the circle?" he asks, and it's agreed.

We're doing it. This naked empowerment thing. In secret. In the stone circle. In the middle of the night. And I'm sure it's going to be fun.

## 28

WE'RE ALL GOING TO bring something to the empowerment ritual. Alexander is going to arrange the fire. He tells us that Amalphia and her classmates had a bonfire in the circle during their first term at the castle.

"It's a real thing," he insists again.

The boys leave, but Bubbles stays in my cottage to help make brownies for the event, though she doesn't actually help. She sits at the table and talks and talks, while I rake through the contents of the kitchen cupboard. Someone has placed a good selection of basic cooking ingredients in there. I make blondies too, with mini marshmallows. The brownies have chocolate chips and walnuts. They come out just the right type of chewy, despite the fact I'm not used to having company when I cook.

"Do you think we're really going to be naked tonight?" I wonder aloud, thinking that Alexander was probably just joking about that.

"Yes," replies Bubbles. "Does it bother you? I'm sure you don't have to if you don't want to."

"I know. It doesn't bother me. You all saw my scars at the costume fitting. The rest of me is pretty normal." I laugh. It's true. The parts usually hidden under a leotard are unmarked and perfectly presentable, but: "Have you ever seen a boy naked?" I ask her.

Bubbles laughs. "Of course. Haven't you?"

"No."

"But what about your boyfriend?" Her voice is incredulous. "What's his face? Farm Porn? You must have seen him. Did you do it with your clothes on? In a haystack, or something?"

"No," I say again, annoyed by her assumptions.

"Are you saying you've never done it? Never had sex?" She makes it sound like it's the most shocking revelation anyone could make about themselves. Ever.

"I wasn't saying it, but no, I haven't."

"Well, this is your night," she tells me.

"I'm not having sex with anyone tonight."

"Oh, but I think it's a hook-up situation," she says. "You and Alexander are an item now anyway, aren't you?"

"No," is fast becoming the word of the night.

"You mean he's up for grabs?"

I say nothing, because although Alexander is, as far as I know, single, I don't like the idea of anyone being 'up for grabs,' as if they have no say in the matter, and they're just available, like an item on a shop shelf.

Bubbles babbles on: "I was thinking Henry was mine, I mean Henry is cute... But if Alexander is free for the taking... Well... You see, I thought him and me... We were getting close in the first term... but then Chantal got her claws into him, and that was that. Chantal was such a complete bitch."

I look at Bubbles. I look at her more carefully than I've looked at her before. She's smiley and bright like always, but something's off. She's twitchy, fiddling her fingers together constantly. Her eyes are wide and overexcited. She's trying to hide it, but I think she's nervous, possibly even frightened.

"You don't have to have sex either," I tell her. "You don't have to get naked. We don't even have to go."

137

"Oh, don't worry," she says. "I've got the perfect thing to take with us in my cottage. Come on; let's go and get it. It'll loosen us up."

I know it won't loosen me up as soon as I see it, because I won't be touching it. I don't think Bubbles needs any more loosening up, but I know there's absolutely no point in saying anything about it. I'm on very familiar and very uncomfortable territory. I do say we shouldn't take it, but she just laughs, and the half empty bottle of vodka comes with us.

Thinking I'm changing the subject, I mention how cold it is. The weather has been bizarrely dry and hot for April, but the nights are still really chilly. "Not the best temperature to go taking our clothes off outside," I say.

"This'll warm you up," she whispers, stowing her liquid friend in her sweatshirt as we crawl under Holly's kitchen window.

Henry emerges from his cottage and hugs us both. He says nothing, perhaps saving his words for later.

We smell the fire before we see it. The smokey scent is pungent as we run up the tree-lined path. We hear sparking sounds and then see Alexander; he's poking a flaming pile with a great big stick. The fire is huge, a massive heap of boxes and wooden pallets which must have taken him ages to carry up here, and without being seen or heard too. It's impressive, and I tell him so, receiving a movie-star smile in return.

It's warm up here, in fact it's really hot if we stand too close to the fire, and so bright. The whole circle is lit with orange light that flickers and moves, making it seem like the stones are performing their own naked dance to the primal music of the flames.

I lay my brownies out on the flat stone. Everyone takes one and says they're good. Henry says it with his eyes.

Bubbles offers her contribution around. The boys take a swig from the bottle, but I shake my head.

"Don't tell me you've never done that either," says Bubbles with a laugh.

"Oh, I've done that," I tell her.

"Ariel's never seen a boy naked or done *it* before," Bubbles tells everyone.

"Nope," I say. So much for friendly confidences.

Henry points at me. "Very cool." And it means a lot. He makes this a good moment, and I get the feeling he hasn't done those things either. And that we're both very cool.

"Yeah, why wouldn't it be cool?" says Alexander, one half of his face lit by the fire. "And we only do this next part if everyone's totally okay with it."

"I'm fine with it," I say. "Both being and seeing naked. It's a lot warmer up here than I thought it would be."

We take a corner each, well not really a corner, more like a quarter section of the circle, so we're quite far apart which seems right. It's better. Less intimate and awkward. We agree to turn away to get undressed.

Giggling, I do. Top first: sweatshirt, T-shirt, bra. Onto the ground they go. The fire roars and crackles behind me as I remove: boots, jeans, socks and knickers.

"Are we ready?" I ask, as no one else is saying anything. "Are we dancing?" I don't want a standing-and-staring thing to happen. A quick dance around in a circle, with no touching, then a quick re-dress. I think that would be best.

"On three, we turn round," says Alexander. "Then we dance."

He counts so slowly: one... two... three... I think we're all laughing.

And then: woah!

Naked Henry!

Naked Alexander!

My mind registers the information that Alexander is a natural blond and Henry is not, and then I see Bubbles. She is sitting on the ground crying. She's still fully dressed.

Oh no. Oh dear. I approach her and put an arm round her. She's absolutely sobbing, taking big heaving breaths. Not looking at the boys, because laughing-naked-fun time has definitely passed, I run back round to my 'corner' and pull on my T-shirt and jeans before returning to Bubbles.

By the time I notice them again, Alexander and Henry are dressed too, and looking as worried as me. Bubbles is hugging the vodka bottle, the now empty vodka bottle, and rocking herself back and forth on the ground. Henry offers her a brownie.

"Good idea," I say to him. "Soak it up a bit."

She takes the cake and throws it at me. "What do you know, Ariel?"

"Quite a bit, actually."

"Oh no, you don't. You're just a—"

The revelation of exactly what I am is interrupted by an enormously loud whoosh and bang sound. A tree beside the circle has burst into flames, like it's a biblical burning bush or something. We all stare at it, frozen and transfixed. There's another bang, and the tree behind the first one lights up too, and then another and another.

"Oh no," shouts Alexander, over the roar of the burning trees. "That's the way I came in. Petrol drum must have dribbled."

All at once, the two lines of trees on either side of the already burning ones ignite, sending masses of giant red sparks into the air, the air that has become smokey and difficult to breathe. Clutching each other, we run away from the stones and away from the fire, through the other part of the wood, the damper part, the misty part by the pool, to the safety of Alexander's house and Amalphia and Mr. Zolotov.

# 29

"JUST KIDS HAVING A bit of fun, and it got away from them." This is the firefighter's final assessment. It comes after the longest lecture ever on forest fires and camp fires and sparks and dry weather, and even the danger of candles left unattended. The lecture took longer than it took for them to put out the fire.

I shiver. Henry takes off his fleece jacket and gives it to me which is good because I'm horribly aware that I have no bra on under my T-shirt. It's not a good look; it's a crawl-into-bed-and-get-changed-under-the-covers look. Henry's fleece is warm, and the kitchen, Amalphia's kitchen, feels like it's getting warmer as Holly bangs things about behind us.

"Aye, well. That's enough of that," says Holly, calling a halt to the lecture. "It won't happen again, not on my watch. Though how you all keep getting past me is a mystery," she says, eyeing Alexander and I sharply. "But you're all cold, and Ariel's feet are needin' attention."

I look down. There's a large smear of blood on one foot and several cuts and lots of dirt on both from the bare-footed run through the woods. We're all dirty and kind of smoked looking from that. We're greyed from the fire, though Bubbles is redder than everyone else. She quietened down during the lecture, but she hasn't actually stopped crying yet.

Holly gives us all big mugs of tomato soup and stands over us to make sure we drink them. Will comes in with a first-aid kit for my feet, and I feel like joining Bubbles in her tear-fest.

"I can do it myself," I say, embarrassed, as he opens a packet of antiseptic wipes.

"Nah, you drink your soup," he says. "Holly'll go up in flames herself if you don't."

So I drink my soup and hold Henry's hand while Will cleans and dresses my feet. Alexander has his arm round Bubbles while she keeps on crying.

Hot chocolate soon replaces soup, and Ross, Alexander's farmer cousin, comes into the kitchen to see us. It was his land that we set fire to. He shares a weird handshake with Alexander where they grab elbows before hands and then he laughs and calls us his "wee fire-starters," saying he'll know where to come if he needs rubbish from the farm burning. I decide I don't like Ross very much, but he's not going to press charges, so I guess that's good.

Bubbles finally stops crying when Mr. Zolotov comes in. We all go still and silent. Our teacher's face is grim, really grim. There's a cold, hard fire behind his eyes as we sit there waiting for it to blaze out in our direction.

Amalphia arrives and smiles at us, though it's not her shiny, movie-star smile. Unlike Mr. Zolotov, who's dressed in his usual black, she's in pink bunny pyjamas.

Justin comes into the room too, also in pink bunny pyjamas. "Brings back a few memories, this—" he starts, but even he goes silent under the glare of Mr. Zolotov.

"You will tell us all that has gone on," Mr. Zolotov says to us.

Alexander answers. "We were doing an empowerment thing in the stones."

Mr. Zolotov nods. "And it involved fire, this we know, this everyone in the surrounding community knows. What exactly were you doing?"

"We were going to dance," replies Alexander.

"Barefoot?" asks Mr. Zolotov looking at my newly bandaged feet.

"I didn't put my boots back on," I say, babbling a bit under his stare. "I just pulled on my jeans and—" I realise what I've said.

"You were undressed?" Mr. Zolotov's voice remains cool, but his anger is growing. I know it, we all know it. "You are all suspended for a week," he says.

"Aleks." Amalphia moves and puts her arm round Mr. Zolotov and looks up at him in some sort of meaningful way.

Justin coughs a bit, and I'm sure I catch the words "Hypocritical, much?" in among it. "Umm," he then says to Mr. Zolotov. "You remember our first term? Fires in the circle and drunken Ceilidhs?"

"Other things that should not have happened," says Mr. Zolotov. "But this is not the same. These are much younger students."

"But they can still go to school events despite being suspended?" Amalphia asks.

I know what she's speaking about. The whole school is being taken to the Scottish premiere of Amalphia's new film on Friday as a treat. It seems like Mr. Zolotov might be considering letting us attend when Bubbles lets out an enormous hiccup. And then another. And we all laugh because we can't help it; it's like a release of built-up tension.

"There has been drinking?" says Mr. Zolotov, and we know our fate is sealed.

"Not Ariel," says Henry, and I squeeze his hand.

So we're all suspended for a whole week, from classes, rehearsals and, yes, school events too.

The next morning, Sunday morning, on Mr. Zolotov's orders, we gather at the breakfast table in the great hall to explain to our classmates why the next week of rehearsals is now totally messed up. Well, Alexander, Henry and I gather there. We think Bubbles went home the night before. She continued crying and was not sent back to the cottages with Henry and me.

Everyone already knows about the fire, and they have no sympathy for us.

"How could you have been so stupid?" exclaims Star.

"If the wind had been blowing in a different direction, we might all have been killed," adds Paula in a serious voice.

"I don't think so," I say, because the fire had followed the line of petrol from Alexander's can, in the opposite direction from the castle. And the night had not been windy. It had been all misty and still.

"You didn't think, Ariel," inputs Belinda. "That's the problem."

"Don't let Alexander screw things up for you like he did for Chantal," advises Clinton.

Alexander is on his feet at once. "I never screwed things up for Chantal!"

"Didn't you?" says Clinton. "No one's ever said exactly what went on there."

Alexander looks annoyed. He sighs and says. "I showed her the top room of the tower—"

"Amalphia's room?" asks Belinda.

"Yeah," says Alexander. "I thought she would like the ceiling window, and the view, you know... But she went back again, after, without me." He pauses. "And she took stuff."

"What stuff?" asks Clinton.

Alexander actually appears to be a bit embarrassed now. "Underwear. She put it online and sold it. And that's why she got expelled."

"So it was actually Amalphia's knickers that got her kicked out?" says Lewis with a laugh.

Alexander glares at him, all red in the face, but says nothing.

Lewis smiles. "We should re-choreograph *Tower* so it can work without you lot in it."

I'm outraged. "You can't do that."

"No?" Now Lewis is standing too.

So am I. So is Henry. We're facing off across the table.

Clinton towers over all of us as he gets up, and this makes me want to cry. He was the first friend I made here, and I really don't want to fight with him.

"We won't do that," he says to us, then focusing on Alexander. "Not because of you, but because *Tower* is about Ariel's lost love, and I bet she didn't have much choice last night, did she? She could hardly walk out of her own house and away from you and your stupid ideas."

"Hey!" Now I'm incensed. "If I hadn't wanted to go up to the circle, I wouldn't have gone. End of. No one made me do anything." I glower at them, loathing how they all condemned us so quickly: Lewis, Paula, Star, Belinda, even Clinton, thinking they're so perfect. "Watch me now," I tell them. "I'm turning my back on all of you, and it's entirely my own choice." I swivel round to face Alexander and Henry and hug them both. "See you in a week, boys."

"Yeah, see you," says Alexander.

Henry gives me both his words: "Bye, Ariel."

Heading out of the room, I encounter the camera woman with the portable camera on her shoulder. It's pointed at me, and I have a horrible feeling that next Saturday's episode of *Castle Dancers* will have added fire and extra drama, so I pull a face into the camera for good measure.

Then it's off to the next adventure, discovery, test: is my grandmother really a Fairy Grandmother? Or is she about to pour down judgement under the stone angels? She's waiting in the foyer to take me to her house for the week of suspension.

There's a hug, a warm one, and she says: "Don't you worry, darling; we're going to have so many outings and treats, and so much fun!"

# 30

It's a week of firsts for me. Patti, definitely a Fairy Grandmother, is furious when she finds out that my feet have been hurt. The first thing she does when we get to her big house in Aberdeen is to phone Mr. Zolotov and shout at him.

"But it was my own fault," I try to tell her.

"No, Ariel, it wasn't. You are sixteen. Your school has a duty of care towards you, and that includes proper supervision. I don't know why it's the younger students that have their own cottages while the older ones stay in the main building. It's a ridiculous set-up, and I've told the head of the school that in no uncertain terms. He tried to say it's a tradition at the castle to make the first years feel special and not bottom of the pile, and that you have a matron person down there with you, but I was having none of it."

"It's so much better than what I had before," I say, thinking about it. "In London I stayed in a hostel with no supervision at all and no one to go to with problems. I have all sorts of people I can go to in the castle."

"Just because a situation is not as bad as something else, doesn't mean it doesn't need addressing, but don't worry about it, dear. Let me show you your room."

Patti's a Fairy Godmother, and I'm a Fairy Princess, in this room anyway. There's a four poster bed, though it's not like the old one in Alexander's house; this one is modern and silver

148

and twirled round with pastel fairy lights. The room is purple, pink and blue, like the highlights in my hair when I first had them done. I love it. Everything's brand new and sparkly: rugs, cushions, a dressing table with theatrical-style lights round the mirror and even a purple sofa. It's a big room. The large bay window looks out over the wide River Dee, which somehow adds to the magical feel of this, my sort of new home from home.

Or should that just be home? Things have gone so wrong between me and my new castle family. I tell Patti more about it over lunch. It's good to have a subject to move on to after the awkward moment when she offers me a glass of wine, and I tell her that Maxine is an alcoholic. We both say we should have known. We both feel bad, and the wine is put away.

"You and this Alexander certainly get up to some high jinks," comments Patti after hearing about everything.

Maybe I shouldn't have mentioned that we'd broken into Mr. Zolotov's office and read our files.

"Is he your new boyfriend?" she asks.

"No."

"New boyfriend material, though?" she says with a smile.

"I don't know."

I find I don't want to think about that; I'm not comfortable with the concept of 'new boyfriend.' I want to shout out that I will only ever love Jonasz, so how could there ever be a new boyfriend? I feel embarrassed and sad about it, a bit like I felt when Will sat down to dress my wounded feet. A wounded heart cannot be so easily fixed.

Patti chats on and through the strange moment. "He's very handsome, like his father. It was a bit of a thrill to talk to Aleksandr Zolotov on the phone this morning, even if I was shouting. Maybe, especially because I was shouting," she says thoughtfully, touching her face and neck. And then it's just funny that Patti sort of fancies Mr. Zolotov, and that she shouted at him, and we're happy again.

~ele~

The next day, Monday, we go out to get 'pampered' as Patti calls it. I've never been to a proper hairdresser before. I was never allowed. And the cut this one gives me is so shapely. It makes Star's earlier attempt look like random hacking with blunt scissors. I get highlights too, more of them, more subtle, in colours to match the new costume for the semi-final. My nails go those colours too, fingers and toes. We both get one sparkly nail. I choose the little finger on my right hand for that. It's so small and so strong; it deserves to be sparkly.

We're in the middle of buying matching make-up in the new colours when I get a text from Alexander saying that Amalphia is working on Mr. Zolotov to let us go to her film on Friday, and she usually wins these things. Patti gets really excited about this news. The whole of Aberdeen is excited about it, the premiere event. Patti buys three glamourous dresses for me which make me look like someone from a magazine.

Trying them on gives me pause. I feel myself doing exactly that: standing still and giving pause in front of the mirror, because I know what Maxine would say. It's as if she's right here in the changing room with me. Her favourite phrases run through my mind: jumped-up little madam; thinks she's somebody; what a joke! Then: 'You're nothing but a useless little trollop, Ariel! What will people think of you wearing that? Acting like you're someone that matters?' Then laughter, slurred and slow and smelling of whisky.

But she's wrong. I know that now. I've read the books. I am a valid human being in my own right, and I do not exist to validate or serve anyone else.

150

I walk out of the dressing room with my head held high and Patti applauds. She adds several pairs of high-heeled shoes to our already huge collection of shopping, and I love them.

"Dancers always walk in heels with style," says the sales assistant as I try the shoes out across the floor. She's seen the show and is treating me like a famous person.

I text Henry. I get back: "Miss you."

I text Bubbles, or as I find myself wanting to call her now, her real name, Serena. She wasn't bubbly when I last saw her. She doesn't reply, but I keep sending both her and Henry updates on the Amalphia/Mr. Zolotov/premiere situation as Alexander sends them to me.

And the texts just keep coming. Alexander tells me that Amalphia initially shouts at her husband in the house. Then, not wanting to distress their children, they decide to go to the top of the tower in the castle to fight it out, and Amalphia emerges victorious. We can go! Only to the premiere, not in the bus with the other students, but tickets are going to be sent out to us.

Patti has the brilliant idea of inviting my suspended friends to stay at her house with me for the rest of the week, so she can deliver us all to the cinema together in her car. Henry sends me his dad's number and Patti sorts it all out. Alexander tells me to give her Amalphia's number, and that's soon fixed too. Bubbles/Serena still doesn't reply. Alexander offers to break into his dad's office and get her parents' number, but I talk him out of that. We all text our missing friend to say we miss her.

We pick Henry up at the train station. He says, "Thank you," to Patti and gives both her and I chocolates.

Amalphia brings Alexander to the house. "He's promised me he'll behave, so he will," she says, giving us all one of her best movie-star smiles.

"I always behave," he replies, and everyone laughs.

"That was so exciting!" exclaims Patti, of Amalphia's visit, as the actress leaves, shampoo-advert hair flying out behind her.

We choose from a selection of take-out menus and watch movies on Patti's enormous TV until bedtime. We agree: no midnight feasts, no night-time adventures. Not here. Not tonight.

"Just me being there tomorrow is going to annoy Papa Zolotov," says Alexander, looking really pleased.

The next day, over our three-course dinner, Patti says how much she loves having a full house. Henry says thank you again, and then we all get dressed up to go out.

We look like movie stars. We feel like movie stars. I'm sure that Aberdeen has never known anything like this star-studded event, not exactly like it anyway. We drive up the narrow cobbled street where Amalphia's cinema of choice is situated. Only people with special starred tickets can take a car up to the front, and we have those special tickets.

We three climb out of the white Mercedes, and Patti tells us to have a good time and that she'll be back to collect us in three hours. We have not been permitted to attend the after-party.

There's an actual red carpet laid out in front of the cinema. I take my boys' arms to walk up it, feeling quite resplendent between the two of them so smart in their suits. I feel tall in the heels, and actually beautiful in my long blue dress that shines purple where the lights catch it.

Then everything stops. Everything stills. And I'm staring into the beautiful and perfect face of Jonasz Serafin.

# 31

THERE'S JONASZ. AND THERE'S me. Our eyes lock and I'm in that place again, that place of safety and love and everything being okay and just as it should be. There's only us. And we are forever.

There's a flash, a camera in the dark, and then another and another, and the forever moment is over. It's not just Jonasz and me; of course it's not. I'm standing on a red carpet with my new friends while he's behind a red velvet rope with a crowd of other people. He's dressed in a smart shirt and trousers. I've never seen him look like that before. He's dazzlingly perfect and, even here with all these people, I could just stand and stare at him forever. But that isn't an option.

We're ushered forwards. I'm towed like a little boat, up a red river, by Alexander and Henry. We move forward as one, and everything feels slow, unreal and strange.

There's a commotion at the side. "Ariel!" a voice shouts. It's not Jonasz; it's a woman, a girl.

I turn to see Katy from the Young Farmers, with her enormous hair. She knocks down a silver post, climbs over the fallen red rope, and grabs me. "Ariel was my best friend at school!" she shouts to everyone.

"You bullied me at school," I say because it's true, and there should be something true and real on this red current through this sea of strangers and confusion and flashing cameras. I can't see Jonasz anymore, only Katy, all aggressive and excited in my face.

Alexander's pushing her back. Henry's arms are round me. Then other men, big burly men, take hold of the big-haired girl and she's gone.

"Price of fame," says Henry. Three words.

Alexander and I are amazed, and we hug Henry, there on the carpet, in the middle of the red, red ocean. I look for Jonasz in the crowd, but he seems to have disappeared along with Katy. We're soon persuaded forwards, big burlies on each side of us now, and into the cinema we go.

It's a surprisingly small venue for such a big event. I stand in the cinema foyer with my friends, recognising people I don't know in the crowd, faces from my recent television watching. I have no names for these celebrities, having been doing normal things for too short a time, but they're not where my focus stays anyway. My thoughts are back on the red carpet outside.

Why was Katy here? There's an obvious reason which I don't want to think about, but I can't seem to think about anything else. I hold the chocolate popcorn and think about it. I hold my tall cup of cream-topped hot chocolate and think about it.

Alexander's laughing about the weird cinema food that Amalphia has obviously arranged, but all I can hear are the names in my head: Jonasz and Katy. They were here together. Did they come for a stare, a peek at the past, the dark-and-deformed past? They're not in here with us now, so where are they? What are they doing?

We walk forwards to join our classmates, and I imagine Jonasz and Katy walking arm-in-arm down a narrow street together, cobbles glinting in the moonlight beneath their feet.

Everyone's friendly here; there's smiles all round. "Sorry," is being said all over the place by our classmates. And just how friendly are Jonasz and Katy?

A large voice booms out, an American voice: "There they are! I see them!" The man seems to fill the space with his presence, sucking up all the attention, even mine, and that's a relief. He leaves no room for other thoughts, and even I know who he is. Everybody knows who he is. Crispin Truelove is the most famous actor in the world, and he's in this film too, of course he is.

The crowd parts for him, and he beams at us: Alexander, Henry and me. "The renegade teens," he says, voice still booming. "The dancers without a cause. There's never any point in playing it safe and small and staying in the background. You three are going to go far. You three have it. Star potential, that is. And now you've met me? Oysters all round! Pearls! Treasure! Come! I insist that you sit by me."

"They are to sit with their class." Mr. Zolotov speaks from behind Crispin Truelove.

Crispin moves over, and now two men compete for the attention of the room.

"Come now, Zolotov," says Crispin. "You know these are the stars of the show. I saw what went down this week."

Mr. Zolotov shakes his head. "They are not to be rewarded for their bad behaviour. They are lucky to be here at all."

"Your headmaster's very pretty," says Crispin to us, "but he can be a bit difficult. I'll see you at the after-party. I'll photobomb all your selfies, and you'll be media darlings by morning."

The castle students are now the audience at a dramatic play. Mr. Zolotov says there is to be no after-party, not for us three. Crispin is furious. He uses words like ludicrous and unthinkable. He says big personalities cannot be contained, nor should they ever be. He begins to sound almost Shakespearean, his speech peppered with words like 'thou' and 'art.' Mr. Zolotov is doing my thing from the other evening and making 'no' his word of the night.

Then Amalphia's there, and she's somehow making everything better. She extols the educational value and excellence of the film. Crispin likes that. She talks about the compromise that has already been agreed on. Mr. Zolotov nods. And it all seems a good thing: that we're here, everything fair, everything good and as it ought to be.

"Well, we'll just have to do it now," says Crispin, suddenly in among the three of us, taking photos with his phone from many directions and angles: above, below, with me, with Alexander, with Henry, and all together, faces close. Crispin calls those last pictures 'friendly full frontals' which makes us laugh. "Hashtag..." he says and thinks for a moment. "**#CrispinsDancers**. It'll be trending in a few minutes. Use it. Share it. Work it."

And he's gone. None of us, Alexander, Henry or me, spoke a word during our encounter with the actor. Not that it matters; you'd think we were actual best friends with him from the photos all over the internet. The hashtag seems to trend instantly, certainly by the time we get to our seats, and we are frogmarched straight down there by Mr. Zolotov after the 'Crispin Truelove experience.'

Henry discovers that Crispin has tagged us in various posts. Our follower numbers have gone mad. We sit and watch them grow until the cinema goes dark. Then there's no room for hashtags or photos or celebrity statuses.

Amalphia is playing a historical ballerina in the film. She did all the dancing herself and is just amazing. We are all transfixed. Crispin plays a director and producer person, a Justin of the time, but really nasty. We love and hate him all at once. He makes her, and he breaks her. We all cry, the whole cinema, and then we applaud and stand at the end for an ovation as if it was a live performance.

We're exhilarated and excited, high on Amalphia and Crispin, and brilliant acting and ballet, and numbers too large to comprehend on our social-media profiles. We fly through the foyer and out into the silvery street and jabber incoherently about it all to Patti once we're in the car. She's so happy we had such a great time.

Then we drive off, and things dull. My chest hurts and breathing hurts. Because Jonasz. Henry takes my hand, and I know he knows. He doesn't need words to convey that he understands.

Back at the house, I lie in bed unable to sleep. It's not overexcitement, nor is it overindulgence in chocolate-based snacks. It's Jonasz's eyes, Jonasz's face, his shirt, the very buttons of it, so smart, so stylish; his belt, his trousers, his shoes. I seem to have absorbed every detail of how he looked tonight. I remember every detail of how he used to look, how he looked that last time I saw him with the tractor, in the field. The landscape too: I know every furrow of the field, every tree, every cloud, every part of Jonasz's world. Or I did. I don't think I do anymore.

I understand Bubbles and her unstoppable crying better now. Maybe she had her own Jonasz.

I do stop crying, though, eventually. I eat breakfast the next morning and smile with the boys. I laugh at Crispin's glowing online comments about us, because the fact that he doesn't actually know any of us makes them stupidly ridiculous, but there's a background sadness inside. Maybe there always will be. Maybe nothing will ever be enough now. I'm never going to stop missing the old forever that could have been.

I make myself stop that: the pathetic thinking. It's part of the old Ariel, the one who everyone despised, well, almost everyone. There is so much new in my world now, so much good. I have to make it so good, so bright, that it eclipses everything else, a giant sun to burn away the past, to obliterate the dark and the sadness.

# 32

"WE'RE GOING TO PRACTISE so hard that we're going to win,"
I tell the boys after breakfast, having suggested that Henry join
us in our piece. "Seriously, every spare moment."

We start immediately. So the rest of the weekend is spent
working on the secret choreography for what was a pas de deux
but is now a pas de trois entitled *Angels and Devils*. Henry is an
angel who steps forward between the two devils. He highlights
our evil in his purity and his sobriety.

Patti is in on the secret too; her dining room transforms into a
studio, and we give ourselves class, taking turns setting exercises
for each other, using the backs of dining chairs as barres.

We do Pilates and we stretch. We're going to be the best: three
dazzling shiny stars, perfect in every way with no option but to
win.

"Crispin Truelove," says Henry, having reverted back to two
words.

He's right, of course, he's right. Our connection with Crispin
will help our plans, is already helping. We decide to start posting
things for our new followers who will also be our voters: pictures of rehearsal; movie-star smiles; my toes, shiny things all.
But we don't post our secret, not yet. The stage is the place for
big reveals.

Saturday night, the three of us sit down with Patti in her
sitting room to watch the latest episode of *Castle Dancers*, as-

suming that we won't be in it. But from the opening seconds of the programme, we know we were wrong. We're not only in it; it's all about us. In absence, our characters and actions seem to have grown larger and more dramatic.

"It's all good for our plan to win," I tell the boys as we watch scene after scene with open mouths.

The show starts with the castle's turrets and roof and driveway, aerial shots like in the very first episode. This time we fly over the trees and stop to focus on the stone circle, a circle that has been blackened by fire. We see the burnt stumps of trees, an empty vodka bottle and my discarded socks. There's no bra to be seen, though I find myself searching the screen for it a bit fearfully, a bit show-your-bottom-to-the-world and crawl-into-bed-to-get-changed fearfully.

Smoke, artificially added-in smoke, wafts across the circle as the voiceover begins. I can tell that Justin put a lot of work into the script.

Voiceover man explains that the week started with flames and exclusion and asks: can we guess who was involved? Who the rebels were?

We're suddenly looking at ourselves in the great hall arguing with our classmates on Sunday morning. We see everybody standing and glaring; the general anger is made clear, but the only words we hear are mine. The camera zooms in on me, and my speech has been slightly edited: "Watch me now! I'm turning my back on all of you!"

My swivel is played three times, each time in greater close up, and then the hug between us three is in slow motion with Alexander-style rousing music set over it, and the scene fades to an ad break.

We all fall about laughing. Patti reminds us that we're the stars of the show, whether we're there or not, and fetches snacks for us. I can't eat them, though. I feel too wound-up, too nervous or excited or something. My determination to win is growing. I know more is coming on the second programme tonight... something unpleasant, something undefined... As soon as the ad break is finished, it's obvious what it is.

Our classmates have rearranged *Tower* so it can be done without us, for six dancers, not ten. Belinda is being thrown up through the middle of the tower. Clinton is dancing with her.

"Your choreography," says Henry.

"Yeah," says Alexander. "They can't do that, can they?"

Apparently, they can't do it without my permission; the narrator tells us so, but wonders if I'll allow the piece to be done this way? Maybe we'll all reconcile? I take my boys hands and feel myself hardening.

The show moves on to Amalphia's event and away from us, or so we think. There she is, looking stunning, holding the arms of both Mr. Zolotov and Will on the red carpet. And then there I am, looking stunned, staring at Jonasz, and holding the arms of both Alexander and Henry.

"We look awesome," says Alexander.

They show Katy accosting me, but her face has been blocked out by little squares, all rainbow-like. Jonasz is in the background. Jonasz is looking horrified. He's shouting something but the camera and voiceover do not focus on him; I don't think the programme makers knew who he was.

Crispin Truelove dominates the remainder of the show, but he shares his glory with us – his rebellious three – by saying that he sees great things in our futures and reminding everyone of his hashtag. It lights up on the screen as he speaks, and smoke blows across the stone circle again.

Voiceover guy wonders what the next week will bring. We wonder what the next week will bring.

"Well, I'm very excited for the next instalment," says Patti.

"Me too," I agree. "Let's get on with making it."

160

I'm the queen of practising on my own, though I'm not on my own now, but without teachers, all the same. We have to have our own discipline, our own resolve.

We have our own hashtag, and we use it. We tell our new followers that we have great things to show the world, but not till the semi-final. Everything is secret until then.

But then, that's only one week away, the semi-final. And we know it's going to be one week of slog, one week of choreography, one week of deepening friendships, between us three anyway. And friendships lost?

Yes. We know it the moment we walk back into the castle in time for Sunday dinner in the great hall. Our classmates have decided that it's best we don't join them in *Tower*, in case anything else happens, and we are excluded again.

It's Star that gives us this information, as if she expects us to be happy and accepting of the situation. She presents it as if they're doing us a favour.

I look straight at her. "You can't use my choreography."

"We can. You just have to sign a form."

"I don't have to do anything," I say, not liking that she seems to be telling me what to do, not asking permission in any way at all.

"Betrayal," says Henry.

"Betrayal?" repeats Lewis, as if mocking Henry. "Everything's different here since you lot had your nudey ritual up at the stones. No boys in girls' cottages. No girls in boys' cottages. And we're all locked in at night."

"Not locked in," corrects Paula.

"The cottages are alarmed after eight o' clock," explains Paul. "Both doors and windows. For curfew."

I feel strong. I feel calm. "Strange you didn't mention any of this on Friday night," I say. "I remember a lot of smiling and saying sorry."

"We were behaving well," says Belinda. "For Amalphia's event."

"You were being two-faced, more like," says Alexander, cross. "Pretending to be good little students in front of the cameras. And all the time you were intending to plagiarise Ariel's work."

"Ariel's choreography is nothing special," says Lewis. "She pulled the disabled card to get public sympathy. That's why they like her now, but it won't fool 'em forever."

"Disappointed," says Henry, shaking his head, pointing his finger at Lewis and then round all the others too. It's sort of like a curse.

"Ooh, Henry, we're really scared," snaps Lewis. "Got a word or two to add to that?"

Alexander swears at him.

Clinton says, "Enough already," at Lewis, and then: "I hate this," to us three where we sit together at the table in our own little group.

"Don't worry, Clinton," I say, then looking at Lewis and directing my words at him. "The three of us have gone through stuff that would have you crying into your mashed potatoes like a little baby." He does appear to be eating an enormous plate of mashed potatoes. I hope he doesn't throw them at me, but if he does? "There's nothing you can do or say to us that we can't deal with. Come on, boys; we've work to do."

Henry, Alexander and I get up and flounce away, passing the lurking camera woman at the door. I stop and movie-star smile into her camera. "Our pas de deux became a pas de trois while we were away, but the choreography is secret until the semi-final. Okay?"

"No problem," she replies.

Upstairs, in the studio, working on our three-way lifts, I realise I have no idea what stuff Henry's been through, but I somehow know my dinner-time speech was true. I also know we're going to win. There is simply no other acceptable scenario.

# 33

I LOVE THE FEELING of lifting Henry high above our heads and making sure he's safe as we carry him. That's not the motivation of my character, though, of our characters. The devils try to rid themselves of the angelic presence by transporting him away or by abusing him.

We practice stage slaps on each other, and I apologise after each one. I can't help it. I hate even the pretence of an act of violence, though I do love that it's in our choreography now, terrible, raw and true. The angel isn't hurt as he falls to the ground. He can't really be harmed, not the inner parts of him. Evil can't touch those.

"Power," says Henry.

We agree and continue practising on the mats. The truth of the past powers our creation, to be shown to the world in all its cruel ugliness. It powers my strength to deal with other things too, like the awkward and strange situation that has arisen between us and the rest of our class.

"Ariel, about what I said yesterday," says Lewis at Monday morning breakfast.

"Don't worry, Lewis," says Alexander. "You spoke really clearly; I'm sure it'll make it onto tonight's show."

"Tonight's show?" At least three people say this. Not Henry and I; Alexander's already told us what he learned at home.

He repeats it in less detail for everyone else: "Short instalments every evening now, twenty minutes, each night till Saturday's semi-final which is now going to be shown live."

It's easy to see that everyone is panicked. They're looking at each other, all worried. I feel a pang of sorrow as my eyes meet Clinton's.

"Lewis does have something to say to you," the first friend I made here tells me, "regardless of the show."

I look at Lewis.

"Aye," he says. "I'm sorry if you got upset about what I said."

I wait a moment, to be fair, to give him a chance to say more. He stays quiet, waiting for me to say it's all right, I think.

"Nicely done," I say. "It's not as accomplished as 'I'm sorry you made me do that,' but it's a great non-apology all the same." I have the attention of the room, all eyes on me. "I was wrong, though," I say. "To mention my hand like I did to the cameras. I wanted to be the one to bring up the issue, but I was really trying to show what great friends I'd made here."

"You have," says Henry, who was not even offered a pretend apology.

"Yes, I have," I agree, and the three of us head upstairs to warm up early before class, to be extra ready, to gain the maximum benefit from Mr. Zolotov's strict teaching.

Mr. Zolotov is to take our class every day this week, because it's the Easter holidays and the older students, none of them still in the competition, have gone home. He gives a little speech at the beginning of class, which is annoying because he's wasting a lot of time that could be spent working on technique.

He talks about how the castle is a small school, and everything can seem larger than it really is in such an exclusive environment. "Now, it is smaller yet," he reminds us. "Nine students only this week. And with the current media presence, we are become like a goldfish bowl, the world peering in on us."

"So, we're to behave, right?" says Alexander.

"This is a given at all times," Mr. Zolotov replies. "I am telling you that everything is augmented at the current time. Concentrate on your works. If other problems become too great, seek help. I am here all day, every day this week; my office is open to all of you. Amalphia is free too. She has already suggested to me that group counselling might be a good idea with how things are in the school just now, and she will be popping in throughout the week to see how things are going."

"Is Serena coming back?" I ask, because no member of staff has mentioned her since the fire, and even now it's only in this roundabout way of stating that there are nine students left.

"Yes," says Mr. Zolotov, "but we don't know when."

"What's wrong with her?" asks Lewis.

"She is unwell," our teacher tells us. "Now: first position at the barre."

We obey, but Lewis keeps prodding. "What sort of unwell?"

Mr. Zolotov tells Lewis his focus needs to be on his turnout and marks through a plié combination, and we get going. And it's brilliant: class is hard, class is good, and class is extra-long, taking up the whole morning and then, after a lunch with three students at one end of the long table and six at the other, we go into separate studios to work.

Justin interrupts our group half-way through. "Looks interesting," he says as we lower Henry carefully to the mat. "But there's been a development, darlings. Your backstory has been splashed about the tabloids this morning, Ariel."

"My backstory?" I ask.

"Yes. Good as this is for the show, we were not responsible for the leaking of it. The girl who attacked you at the premiere? Katherine something-or-other? She started it all by speaking to one of the papers. Others dug around. Then there was the footage of you saying she bullied you at school, but things about your mother have come out in more detail than before."

I shrug. I don't actually care.

"Anyway," he says. "Long and short of it is, we're now working with a charity that helps abused young people and homeless young people; they'll get a donation from every phone vote, and it's good publicity all round."

He wants us to say a bit about the charity for tonight's show. We're given leaflets about the cause to read in preparation, but I don't know what I can say. What's left to tell about me that the papers didn't already cover? And then I realise there is one thing; it might seem a small thing, but it's not. The books in my bedroom have all spoken about it, the importance of it, but I don't know if I can say it. I know I don't want to, but maybe I should, it being the thing that saved me, after all. I felt it on the night of the premiere. It was a big reminder that: yes, I lived through badness, but there was good back then too. There was love.

I sit below three pointed windows between Alexander and Henry, on a soft seat in one of the tower rooms with soft lighting and three cameras.

Alexander goes first: "I didn't really have a place that felt like home till I was eight years old and came here to live with Amalphia and her family," he says into one of the cameras. "Before that I lived in a house with someone that hated me. I intended to run away first chance I got, and I guess I would have been homeless if I'd managed to do that. If our dancing can help anyone else in that situation, I would love it. It would be the best."

Justin's eyes grow misty. "I know," he says, reaching over and squeezing Alexander's hand. "I know, sweetheart."

It's my turn, and I know I have to be completely honest too: "I did run away when I was twelve. I fell into a farmer's threshing machine, an old one, and it somehow got switched on." Up goes the hand. Lewis will love it. "But in a way, that was the best thing that ever happened to me, because I met the family who lived there, and my contact with them showed me that there were other ways to live. I became really close with one of them, someone I don't see anymore, but without that closeness I don't think I would be able to form normal relationships, or have friendships now. I don't know if a charity can provide circumstances like those, but it may be the only chance some kids have."

"Oh, darling," says Justin, accepting a tissue from Nigel. "The three of you are such stars. In so many ways. Now, Henry, you don't have to say anything if you don't want to."

Henry shouts "Go!" followed by the name of the charity, and we're done.

Justin is delighted with us. "The others choreographed a little house/home thing instead of speaking for the cameras," he whispers. "Massive disaster. We won't be showing it. I think they thought it would go well with *Tower*, but it doesn't. What was your glorious pas de dix is now a crumbling wreck, sweetie, a pick-and-mix of all the bits you three didn't think up."

I feel a bit sad sitting in my cottage watching the show that night. I'm alone because of the new curfew. There we are on the screen. There's all the drama. Alexander was right about Lewis's put-downs being aired, and the fact that they are shown right after our charity speeches only makes what he says seem even worse. And *Tower* does look a shambles. And that's sad too.

My request for secrecy about our choreography ends the show and is spoken over the image of the door to our studio, open just enough to offer the smallest glimpse of us: three friends, three pairs of feet. Mine rise so slowly en pointe between the two boys, I suspect slow motion to have been used. The door closes and the credits roll.

# 34

**#TeamAriel #TeamTower**

So we are divided.

**#TeamAriel** trends all the time on social media, mainly with supportive stuff, some weird things and a small minority of haters. We have a lot of fangirls and fanboys.

**#TeamTower** never trends, and the hashtag is almost exclusively populated by derogatory comments, many of them openly abusive.

I hate it. I mean, I hate how Lewis spoke to us too, but I didn't want this.

Alexander finds the whole thing amusing until he actually reads a few of the posts and threads. He looks up from his phone, sickened. I can guess what he's seen. There's been some sexual talk, reminiscent of things I used to have said to me at school.

Henry's advice is the best: "No looking."

I nod. "We concentrate on *Angel and Devils*. It's what matters."

So we do. It's not hard; the choreography flows so easily, it's almost as if it's making itself up. We literally fall into it sometimes, realising that mistakes work; spontaneous tripping can be good. It's so organic, the stream of movement, so natural, that we just know we've got something awesome.

Saturday will be good, Saturday will be great, and we are going to win!

**#TeamTower** do not share our attitude. They look sadder every day. Lewis looks angrier, his cheeks bonier than ever. They didn't hear Henry's advice about not looking; it was only said to **#TeamAriel**. I know what it's like to be spoken about like that; I know how it hurts and how you can pretend you don't care, but really you do. Words can be worse than violence, sometimes anyway. They take longer to heal, sometimes. But I don't know how to help this situation. Anything I think of saying sounds patronising and fake, and I can't speak it because I won't do that to them. It would be shown as me being great and glorious in the night-time show, and I'm fed up of that too.

"How's your piece going?" I ask Star at dinner one night when, for a moment, it's only her and me at the table.

"Nightmare," she replies.

I want to say: it's okay, you can use my choreography, but that would basically be like saying their thing can't be good without my input, so I just pull what I hope is a sympathetic face.

"Yours?" she asks.

"Really good," I say, because it's the truth.

"Of course," she says and turns away to chat to the rest of **#TeamTower**, newly arrived with their trays.

She comes off as a total bitch on the show that night. I dread to think what the hashtags are doing, but I don't look. No looking.

**#TeamTower** have been looking; it's obvious. The next day they have turned-down mouths, bags under their eyes, and they look so exhausted that I'm not sure they've slept at all.

Amalphia joins us all at breakfast to chat about the fake nature of celebrity culture and how we should try not to let it distract us from the actual work. "You are all so talented," she tells us. "You wouldn't be here if you weren't. And you are all

170

winners. You're in the semi-final. You're being flown to London to dance in one of the most famous theatres in the world, and you're going to be staying in one of the best hotels. Turn your heads away from the rest. The next few days should be fun and exciting, not a great big fight."

"No looking," says Henry, smiling.

"That's what we've been doing," I add. "Not looking."

"Aye, well, it's easy for you lot," says Lewis. "Everybody loves you."

"That's never the case," Amalphia tells him. "No one is universally loved. Wherever there's success, there will be jealousy and envy and even obsession."

"And I suppose you know all about that?" he says, voice loud and aggressive.

"I know some," she says, quiet and calm.

"You're lying," he snaps. "Media loves you, even though you're a slut."

Mr. Zolotov and Alexander move in perfect tandem, though from two different directions, Alexander from his place beside me, Mr. Zolotov from the staff table. Mr. Zolotov's hand blocks Alexander's hand, so no one gets punched. Lewis's bony face remains intact, but he is marched quickly away to Mr. Zolotov's office.

Amalphia smiles round the table. "We all have detractors. They have their own sad reasons for being the way they are and saying what they say. The trick is never to believe what they say. Don't take it on as part of your truth."

"That's one classy lady," says Clinton when Amalphia's gone, and we all agree, united in this at least.

I'm glad to see that moment get aired. But the rest? I can't believe what Lewis said to Amalphia is shown. I thought Justin would draw the line there, being her friend. Maybe she said it was okay? I don't know. It's all confusing and upsetting, and I wish it wasn't happening.

The show closes with Alexander's after-breakfast advice to **#TeamTower**: "Get ready to re-choreograph for five."

I have to look. I have to know. There's new hashtags: **#GetLewisOut** and **#LewisIsRight** and there's nothing good around either of them.

Neither right nor out, Lewis is still with us. He was missing from one day's class and, I assume, some *Tower* rehearsals, but he's back for our last full day of work before the semi-final. He's quiet, subdued really. That was never a good sign with Maxine, and I feel the same undercurrent of trouble here, a storm about to break.

At lunch, Lewis eats a pile of bread, one white slice after the other, and nothing else. I wish Holly would make her tomato soup for him. He needs calming and nurturing, but she's angry with him like everyone else. She was stony-faced as he took his bread ahead of me at the canteen window. There were no friendly suggestions for him, no extra slices of cake or pie like she gave Alexander, Henry and me.

I feel nervous. I keep glancing over at Lewis, waiting for something to happen, for him to explode. I rationalise it in my head. He said some stupid stuff, some nasty stuff. He tried to apologise to me, and I knocked him back. Amalphia's attempt to smooth things over went wrong. I decide I'm going to try and make things better here. If I can.

"Would anyone like some hot chocolate?" I ask, getting up to fetch some for myself. If anything can break the ice or lighten the mood, surely it's hot chocolate. "Lewis?"

He snorts. "From your filthy hands? No thanks."

I freeze. I've been called filthy before, but not here. Never here. The others are saying stuff, saying he shouldn't have said that, 'leave Ariel alone' type stuff.

"You've gone too far!" Clinton shouts at him. "I'm not doing *Tower* if you're in it!"

"Good!" yells Lewis. "Go join that bunch of freaks!" He points at us three. He calls Alexander a spoilt little Daddy's boy. He calls Henry a retard. He says that I'm a scorpion, poisonous and ugly, pinching his hands in the air to make his point. "And you're just a stinking darkie boy," he yells at Clinton. "I don't want you touching me anyway!"

**#GetLewisOut**? Lewis is gone.

# 35

It's no surprise that Lewis isn't at dinner. Paul lays out the school rules for us, and explains what will have gone down. "He'll have got one strike for what he said to Henry and Ariel, another for Amalphia, and expelled for the latest outburst. The castle has a zero tolerance policy for racism or hate of any kind."

"Should have been expelled earlier then, shouldn't he?" says Alexander.

"They have to give a certain number of warnings before they do that," Paula tells us. "It's the law."

"But did he really mean all that stuff he came out with?" I wonder aloud. "Or was he just trying to hurt us?"

"Oh, I knew he was a racist," says Clinton. "He never said anything before, but you get a feeling sometimes, you know? The way someone looks at you when you speak? Like you have no right being there, let alone talking? And I'm the only one that was stinking."

Stinking. The word summons an afternoon where I was called that too. It was dark, the middle of winter. I'd returned from school to a quiet house. I'd listened, so carefully, trying to work out exactly what the situation was. The more information I had, the safer I'd be. Both cars had been in the driveway so: she was definitely in the house. There was an empty glass beside an empty bottle in the kitchen so: she was sleeping it off. I'd crept across the hall from my bedroom to practise in the bigger living room, and I'd woken her. How dare I put myself ahead of her? I, who was just— Stinking was one of the many words she'd used to describe me. Lewis had used another of her favourites.

"It's not the same," I say, because it's not, racism being its own unique and disgusting thing. "But he said I was filthy."

"Sister!" says Clinton and high fives me over the table, which is at once a return to our old friendliness and a bit ridiculous given the context, so we all laugh.

"He wasn't bigoted against me from the beginning, though," I say. "He wanted to partner me in pas de deux, but then he said, 'What Alexander wants, Alexander gets.' He resented you from the start, Alexander. I mean, you're the furthest away from being a Daddy's boy that anyone could be, so he knew you would hate being called that."

"Maybe," says Alexander.

"None of what he said was valid in any way," I stress, desperately wanting to lessen the hurt caused by Lewis. I know this stuff. I've read the books.

"He was obsessed with the hashtags," says Belinda. "Never off his phone, joining in, getting into fights online."

"Bet he still is," says Clinton, and people reach for their phones.

"No looking," advises Henry, but **#TeamTower** don't listen.

Somewhat surprisingly, Lewis isn't on the final instalment of this week's *Castle Dancers*. Nor is there any mention of what happened. Clinton's high five with me is shown but not the conversation that led up to it.

Alexander texts with information gleaned at home just as I'm getting into my soft and purple bed. There's an ugly force gathering around **#LewisIsRight**, and the programme makers are determined not to feed it in any way. It's one of the reasons that Lewis's name and face are not going to be aired again.

I want to look, but I don't. I want to sleep, but I can't. Lewis's outbursts have called back feelings I haven't felt for a while. Words and sayings float through my mind, seemingly unstoppable: stinking, filthy, worthless; useless, unable to do anything right. Talent? What a joke! Your ballet teacher says her other advanced girl is much better than you. Your ballet teacher says you don't smile, and don't speak. How dare you behave like that? How dare you show me up?

In my newly changed life, none of these things have felt valid, until now. I made friends, but half of them are now not really my friends anymore; I've been excluded in more ways than one. I've choreographed some new stuff, and no one in any position of authority here has seen it, but the whole world's about to watch it.

We're flying to London tomorrow. How has this crept up so fast? And what, exactly, is the world going to see? **#LewisIsRight**? **#TeamAriel**? **#TeamTower**? The hashtags jumble around in my head all night as I drift in and out of sleep.

Morning comes and Holly visits as she does every morning and evening now, since the fire in the circle. "Post for you this morning, Ariel," she says, leaving a pink envelope on my kitchen table.

It's a fan letter from someone who's seen the show. It's a bit odd. These usually go to the production company, and they open them and show us samples, no doubt protecting us from nasties. But this isn't nasty. The writer of the letter, a Miss Ethel Taylor, tells me how great I am and how much she enjoys watching me on television. I get the feeling she's an old lady. She says she did ballet when she was young. She's included another pink envelope, fatter than mine, folded in two, for Alexander. I put it in my carry-on bag for London, intending to give it to him as soon as I see him, but then forget about it till we're on the plane.

The plane is a really exciting experience. Henry and Alexander let me sit by the window, but then I insist on taking turns, so it's like musical chairs on the seats. Sitting down by the aisle, I see the corner of the pink letter jutting out of my bag and tell them about the fan mail. Alexander rips his envelope open, withdraws a bent card with flowers and cats on it and swears.

"Oh no, is it nasty?" I ask.

"Could say that," he says, reading a bit more of the letter in the card. "It's from Fake Mum. Simone. Let's see: how hard it was to be a single mother, blah, blah, how badly behaved I was. I might be now, but back then when I lived with her? I was a pathetic little kid. Did everything I was told."

I put my hand on his arm. Henry does the same at the other side, and Alexander reads on.

"Oh, get this: I'm to stop haranguing; is that even a word? Whatever, I'm to stop doing it to dear old Dad. Stop using the show to hurt him, or she'll come and deal with me herself." He stops speaking and goes quiet.

"You've got to show it to Amalphia," I say, knowing he won't want to show it to his father.

But it turns out I'm wrong about that. We walk back up the aisle to Alexander's family, and it's Mr. Zolotov he hands the card to. "Love letter for you," he says.

Mr. Zolotov looks sort of grey as he reads the contents of the card. Amalphia, leaning over to see, goes white. I explain how I came to have it. Mr. Zolotov asks how the outer envelope was addressed. I remember: my name, cottage number 7, the castle... I get it. She knew where I was staying, exactly where I was staying. No information of that type has ever been given out on the show.

As soon as we land, the police are called, and other authorities too. Amalphia and Mr. Zolotov and Will seem to be on the phone to many people at once, all the while keeping their family very close.

But it's all okay. They assure us that Fake Mum is still somewhere secure. How she managed this stunt, they don't know, but she's not coming to deal with anyone, and Amalphia has requested that she doesn't get to watch the show again.

"I'm so sorry," I tell Alexander in the car on the way to the hotel, Henry and I travelling with him and Amalphia in a taxi.

"No," he says. "I'm sorry she used you like this, that you were dragged into her nasty little games."

"You need to put it out of your minds," Amalphia tells us. "Don't let her spoil your fun. She'd love that, to ruin your special occasion. So..." She waves her hands in front of us all. "Erased. Now, look to the left. See the beautiful glass tower that is the Gherkin, sparkling in the sun? That's where your grand reception is being held tonight!"

# 36

THE GRAND RECEPTION FOR the semi-finalists is going to be the most glamourous event I've ever experienced, and I'm saying that as someone who has attended an Amalphia Treadwell premiere. And I'm staying in what must be the poshest hotel in the world. It seems unreal that any of this can be true, but it is.

The fun of the hotel is slightly spoiled by the recentness of the scary letter incident and the fact that I'm roommates with Paula, but she's being perfectly friendly; we share in the excitement of chocolates on our pillows, golden bottles of toiletries in the bathroom, fluffy bathrobes, cushiony slippers and a minibar stocked with various chocolate items.

"Amalphia," we both say at once and laugh.

Amalphia's staying here too, everyone is. The castle people take up a large section of this floor of the hotel. Paula and I are next door to the second year teacher Aileen on one side and Alexander's family on the other, then there's Alexander and Clinton, then Guy, adults in between the students all the way along the hall.

We get dressed in our finery. The castle provided evening wear for everyone, but I wanted to wear one of Patti's dresses: the brown one that shines purple as it moves in the light. It sort of matches the costume for tomorrow. I do matching make-up. I help Paula do hers too. I have become a person who helps others with make-up? I have, and we both look great. Wait, I look great? I can think those words without hearing Maxine's voice saying something different? Almost. And we head off to the reception.

~*elle*~

We are announced like lords and ladies as we reach the large event space at, as it feels, the top of the world. I stand between Alexander and Henry, and we step in to the big room together to loud cheers. That's a surprise. I mean, we're all in competition against each other. But the friendliness is good. The whole occasion is nothing like I expected at all.

Madame, the head of the college that I attended last year, is here. She hugs me and does air kisses either side of my face as if we'd been friends, which we most definitely had not. I'm not sure she even knew my name back then. She must have noticed me more than I thought, though, as she takes off her large spectacles that have little pink flowers all round the rims and says: "Ariel! Gloves off, I see. You've come out of your shell at the castle, and I'm glad to see it, dear."

I look at my hands, astonished at what a non-issue they've become. Shame and mockery were such an integral part of my life for years, how is it possible that I could have forgotten so quickly? Someone shouts "**#TeamAriel**!" and I forget again.

The other participants are super welcoming, asking all about Lewis and what he said and did that wasn't shown on TV.

"We're **#TeamKilt**," says a tall boy, indeed in a kilt, accompanied by a girl wearing a white dress with a tartan sash.

"Oh, you're the Highland dancers," I say, recognising them from the show. "You're really good. I loved the sword dancing."

This delights them; I get the feeling they expected us to be snobby ballet people, or something, and the boy, Callum, promises to let me play with his swords the next day in the theatre. I laugh, not sure if the innuendo was intended, and also not wanting to think about the next day.

But it's too late; I'm thinking about it now. I'm staring out windows, glass walls really, at the beautiful city below, and all I can think of is tomorrow's timetable. Morning: class. Afternoon: rehearsals on stage. Evening: real thing on stage for the whole world to see.

Then Crispin Truelove descends, and all other thoughts and sights fly away. He creates a small drama by insisting that Henry, Alexander and I sit beside him at the grandest dinner table.

"You mustn't show such obvious bias, Crispin," chides Amalphia.

"Why not?" he demands. "It's allowed. Each judge chooses who to promote, and who to support."

She shakes her head. "You haven't even seen their piece yet, and you're separating them from the other students at a time when we're trying to mend that sort of division."

He doesn't listen. Crispin Truelove gets what Crispin Truelove wants. All three of us can't sit right by him at once, so we take turns with the seats like on the plane. We change places with each course of dinner which confuses the waiting staff, but they hide their annoyance well. Social media goes mad with images again. Crispin sees to that. They love us. We're stars! We're going to win!

I dance with Crispin Truelove, or, as is more accurate, I get marched round the dance floor by him. The taking of photos is welcome at this event – phones are out everywhere – and it's that picture that reigns supreme across the internet. It's like something out of an old film: me in Crispin's arms, gazing up at him as we dance.

Taking a break from everything in the posh toilets, I gaze at the small screen of my phone and see that someone I used to know at school has liked the Crispin picture. I just happen to see the boy's name in among the other notifications. He's not even someone I knew well; I don't think we ever spoke to one another. He didn't bully me, but his name is enough to take me back to the time when I still wore the gloves. I remember the isolation, the cruelty and despair, the frustration and hopelessness.

I look up and see my stylish surroundings. I hear beautiful music wafting through from the beautiful event I am attending. This is my life now, my fairy-tale life. I dance in a pink castle every day. I live in magical woods beside that castle. I run amok among ancient stones. I'm one of the stars of a television show. I'm a semi-finalist. I have a Fairy Grandmother. I have friends, and I have a goody bag from this event that is filled with little chocolate dancers.

But I don't have Jonasz. That's the thought I take to the posh hotel bed with me. I have everything else, but not him. Maybe you can't have everything; maybe life doesn't work like that. I had nothing back then, when I lived in Maxine's house, and the universe sent him my way.

I cry, and then hate myself for it. I'm so lucky with everything else right now that crying seems so self-indulgent. I text Patti, sending her some photos from tonight because I know she will love to see it all, but it's really Jonasz I want to text, Jonasz I want to tell about all this. His number isn't in my phone, but I remember it. Of course I do. But I don't let myself use it. I cry into my pillow so as not to disturb Paula who has definitely cooled since the grand occasion at the top of the world and Crispin's obvious favouritism.

Sleep is not an improvement. I dream of Alexander's letter, the cutesy card with the flowers and cats, but in the dream it's not Fake Mum that sent it, it's Maxine. Maxine is angry and coming to deal with me herself. This actually helps me a bit because I wake up filled with determination to interpret Maxine perfectly on the stage tonight. Each inflection and movement will be hers, not mine, and people will see her for what she is, and then that will be her dealt with!

—ee—

"First position, at the barre." So says Mr. Zolotov in the massive hotel ballroom to at least fifty dancers who are all thrilled to have him teach them, starstruck even. To dancers, he is as famous as Crispin Truelove is to everyone else. Well, perhaps not to the Highland dancers who have great difficulty with the ballet class.

They do well at the barre – they have strong legs and good feet as we've seen on the show – but the amalgamations in the centre are too different from what they're used to. We are divided into groups to take turns across the room. I demonstrate more slowly for **#TeamKilt** but their coupé, chassé, pas be bourée combination into a pirouette is still a shambles.

However, another friendship has begun to form. Alexander, Henry and I sit by the Highland dancers, Callum and Morag, at lunch and stand with them in the wings of the theatre to watch the other acts, aware that the cameras could be on us, so we're careful to only look impressed. Until it comes to *Tower*. I can't pretend to be impressed with *Tower*.

I find myself thinking the word 'disgrace,' something Maxine used to call me, so I don't usually use the word, but it is a disgrace. It's awful. It doesn't even look like a tower; it's more like a rock or a squashed toadstool. A clump of people come together for no good reason, then do some mediocre pas de deux, then come back together, toss Belinda up into the air and finish.

I can't look at them as they come off stage, I feel so angry. They threw us out of this piece and destroyed it.

**#TeamKilt** are great, though. I love **#TeamKilt**. I love having a go at the sword dancing behind the closed curtain of the theatre; I love the intricate and precise foot placements required to work around the two crossed weapons, sharp and dangerous as they are.

The cameras love us. Voiceover man is there, and we get to meet him. Reading from a piece of paper, he asks who, apart from ourselves, we advise people to vote for.

"Team Kilt," I say.

"Tower too," says Henry, and I look at him in surprise.

"Oh, yeah," says Alexander, looking directly into the camera. "If you want to see us fight it out for another term, you have to keep them in."

"The boy gets it!" booms Crispin Truelove, approaching fast from the dressing room area. "Showbiz, that is."

Alexander looks at me. "Also gives them a chance to fix it. We can't leave it like that," he says, proving that he does get it; he gets it in a solution-based way that I didn't. *Tower* can be made beautiful again. It has to be.

# 37

OUR PIECE IS PERFECT, clean and new and pristine and shiny. No one else has seen it, well, apart from the stage hands and Justin and Crispin Truelove and the lighting director. To the audience in the enormous theatre and at home in front of their televisions, it is entirely new. Even our fellow competitors were cleared from the theatre before we rehearsed in the afternoon.

I am vile. I am a dancing bruise, leaping around en pointe, sharp pointes, dangerous pointes like swords, revelling in the causing of pain. Alexander is brash, laughing off all attempts to hurt him. Henry is the new and shiny one among us. He is pure and perfect, like the best part of all of us, the part that stays undamaged in bad times, the part that stays strong.

He choreographed his own solo, and I watch it as I lie wounded and finished, upstage, legs and arms tangled with Alexander's. Henry is love, I realise, as we then try to deny him, carry him away, to banish him from our lives, but he can't be diminished.

I have tears in my eyes at the end, and it's not from the heavy make-up or the hot lights. They're not really that hot; everything is on such a large scale here that the lights are quite far away.

The judges love us, well, all except one of them. The famous singer who came to the castle auditions doesn't like the tearing off of skirts and says we should lose that part. It's not a problem as we change our choreography every time anyway, but we don't mention that; we just stand and listen politely.

We become **#CrispinsDarlings** as we top the vote, and eleven acts get through to the final. *Tower* is the eleventh one, and I can't help feel that Justin created an extra place for them for the drama, or good telly, of it all.

I feel really hungry at dinner in the big restaurant of the hotel. Halfway through my tomato soup, I tell Clinton and the others that they can use my old choreography if they want. "Or make it your own. Cut it right back and start again."

"It is more of a smoking ruin than a tower at the moment," admits Star. "I can't believe we got through. Did you hear what that singer guy said to us?"

He'd said kicking **#TeamAriel** out of the piece was like taking a wrecking ball to it, and then he'd sung a little song with wrecking-ball lyrics, which I thought only made him look like a show-off.

"You have a whole term to work on it," I remind Star and the others.

"You should have seen some of the looks we were getting from dancers with better stuff when we got through and they didn't," says Clinton. "Henry, you were stellar, by the way."

"I know," says Henry, and we all laugh.

Tomorrow we are all heading home, away from London and the castle, for the rest of the Easter holidays. I'm going to Patti's. I'm looking forward to it. I'm anticipating a week of gentle fun as I get into the plush hotel bed for my final night in London and eat the sweet pillow chocolate.

There's a knock on the door.

"Who is it?" asks Paula, suspicious.

"Only the greatest actor in the world!"

"Crispin?" I say, using the peephole in the door to look at him.

"The one and only! Here to invite **#CrispinsDarlings** to a party!"

"Give us ten minutes," I call, already reaching for the dress I wore to the reception.

"Only you, darling," specifies Crispin. "This invitation is for **#TeamAriel**, no one else."

"Oh," I say, looking at Paula to see how she feels about this.

"As if I would have gone anyway," she says. "And you mustn't go either. We were strictly told to stay in our rooms until Holly comes round in the morning."

Okay. I turn away from being told what to do and remember that I have two dresses. The green one with lace panels is the third dress that Patti bought me, so, dropping the brown one from the other night, I pull it on fast, scrabbling around for make-up to go with it.

"Ariel," says Paula. "Are you listening to me?"

"No," I admit, though I am aware that she's been talking all the while I've been getting ready. I bless Patti for the green heels that complement the grand gown, and I exit the room.

The boys have readied themselves faster than me. Crispin, Alexander and Henry stand in the hallway, also in their posh clothes, though maybe all Crispin's clothes are posh; I find it hard to imagine him lounging around in trackies or jeans, somehow.

We're whisked away through the hotel but warned to be quiet. Off we go in a golden limo that transports us through the streets of London to what looks like a narrow white-painted townhouse but is actually some sort of palace.

"My little London house," Crispin tells us.

It's feels like it's so much bigger on the inside. Our actor friend obviously owns several of the houses in the street and has knocked them together into this one glorious space. The whole place is lit with a magical golden light – even the music feels golden – and there's famous people everywhere. At least I think they're famous people; they behave like I should know them, so I just act like I do.

There's a lot of waistcoats and open-necked shirts among the men, lots of white and cream. Some people are dressed in period costumes from other times and places in the world. Some even look otherworldly. One woman has a costume involving silver antennae attached to her forehead and a silvery spacesuit. There's ancient Egyptians in the lobby, Shakespearean actors with neck ruffs enunciating speeches on the stairs, and room after room of happy, beautiful people.

"My friends, stars all, timeless like me," says Crispin as he ushers us upwards to the roof to look at actual stars. The people on the roof applaud us. We are part of the gang now, admitted to the inner sanctum of Crispin's... life? Heart? World?

"Is Amalphia here?" I ask, thinking that she's the most famous person I know, and surely she must be here.

"No." Crispin laughs. "She could be, of course, but she has let herself be taken up with earthly pursuits. Her love is not concentrated on the stars." He points upwards, and we all stare into the heavens as several shooting stars fly past. "You could be in danger of that too, honey," Crispin says to me. "You have a romantic heart, but you can choose stardom. That is clear. You, my lovelies," he says to the boys. "You are safe enough for now, though both a little too beautiful for your own good. Don't let it lead you astray."

We lie on soft beds on the roof and stare at the stars and listen to celestial music. We drink fizzy something; it seems to be filled with stars too. For a moment I panic, and the golden light of the evening fades.

"Is this alcohol?" I ask, horrified.

A woman in a medieval-looking gown laughs and touches my face. "Not here," she tells me. "Never here, pretty maiden."

Good. The children of alcoholics are statistically more likely to become alcoholics themselves, and I know I must never go that way. But it's okay, everything is okay, and disturbing thoughts fade into the ether as I gaze into the heavens once more.

People waft by, majestic people, special people, people in robes and togas and ball gowns.

We zoom off in the golden Limo again, without Crispin this time, and waft upwards in the lift of the hotel.

Mr. Zolotov is in the hall by our rooms, and he is furious. He doesn't shout, but he nearly does. Stars fall to the floor all around us as we return to the real world and try to explain ourselves.

"Crispin doesn't have a townhouse," says Amalphia. "And he flew back to the States earlier this evening."

"He does, and he didn't," I insist, but they don't believe me and are unwilling to wake Paula for verification that Crispin was at the door.

Will says something about Crispin being rumoured to run some sort of secret society for starlets, but they don't believe that can be true, because why wouldn't Amalphia be in it?

And then there's that word again; nobody says it, but it's in my head: disgrace. We are in it. We are of it, but somehow, it doesn't seem to matter that much. We didn't realise we'd been out for most of the night, but we know we were somewhere special, whatever anyone else thinks, and we know it was an achievement just to be admitted there.

So we tolerate the ill-tempered looks and silent treatment from our fellow dancers at breakfast with good grace.

And then we sit, a select three, a golden three, on the plane as we fly back to our lives.

"Mr. Zolotov was really worried about you," I tell Alexander, seeing that truth as a golden truth, as something shiny and

189

important that should be mentioned. "That's why he was so angry this morning."

"Nah, your head's still in the stars from last night," he says.

"It is," I admit.

"But it's true," says Henry as we fly over the clouds and home to Scotland.

# 38

THE NEW TERM, THE summer term, gets off to a sunny start, and things calm down at the castle. Preparations for *Ballerina Ballerino* are no longer taking up too much of our time, not the majority of it anyway. There's first year exams to be studied for. Aileen, the second years' morning ballet teacher, takes us for those classes, and none of us like her. Our class is united in this one thing at least: our dislike and disapproval of Aileen.

Sunlight streams through the windows onto the old-fashioned wooden floor of the upstairs dance studio. It creates a golden light which is almost magical, though not quite, but it's enough to make me remember that golden night at Crispin's house. I recall the atmosphere of the large townhouse and the party, the diversity of people and the stars.

"Ariel! There's nothing whatever for you to be smiling about," snaps Aileen, whose teaching method is very different from both relaxed Guy and intense Mr. Zolotov. "Your turnout is terrible, and the positioning of your hands is not what it should be at all. I don't think you should even be entered into this exam. You're nowhere near ready. You should be made to repeat the first year if you're allowed to remain at all."

"What a bitch," murmurs Clinton beside me.

Aileen swings round so fast that her blonde ponytail hits her in the face, and Clinton is sent to Mr. Zolotov's office.

"You remind me of my mother," I say to her, which is the worst thing I could ever say to anyone, but she doesn't know Maxine, so I explain: "You enjoy being cruel."

I am sent to Mr. Zolotov's office where I am lectured on the importance of being respectful to teachers. I tell him that Aileen is not respectful. "She said I'm not good enough to be here."

"You are absolutely good enough to be here," he says, brow furrowed.

"Okay then," I say and walk out to find Clinton and see how he got on.

"It was fair enough really," he says. "I was told not to call teachers, or any women, bitches."

I watch Aileen's usual students, the second years, at dinner. I've never really noticed them much before. They're quiet, actually subdued looking, unlike the third years who are about to set off on their tour and don't look nervous in any way; they're lively and laughing and loud. Excited, I think.

"They're the ones who survived Aileen," says Alexander, when I mention it to him. "There's always a lot of changeover, second year. She must be my dad's way of weeding out the weak and the stragglers."

"That's wrong, Alexander," says Paula. "Aileen knows the exam syllabus inside out and guarantees a hundred percent pass rate for the school every year. That's why Mr. Zolotov employs her."

"She could be our project next year," suggests Alexander. "Hashtag: Get Aileen Out!"

We all laugh, but we also all know what the current projects are, and that they leave little time for much effort against Aileen's cruelty. There's the competition: lots of choreography ahead. There's the exam, the passing of which will involve Aileen, and then there's the main objective of most of the staff at the castle: to end any remaining division among the first year students.

It's to this end that we all find ourselves in wellies on Saturday afternoon, cleaning various types of animal poo out of various types of outbuildings on Ross's farm. Animal Assisted Therapy is supposedly going to help us mend those broken bonds. And the idea turns out to have some validity: when you've done your best to make a disgusting job faster and funnier, feelings do warm. Clinton and I make short work of a donkey's stable and get given a 'funcy piece' and a 'fly cup,' or chocolate biscuit and cup of tea, by Ross's mum in her big square kitchen.

Clinton can't understand anything Ross's mum says; I translate, and all three of us find the situation amusing. She tells us we can go and watch the sheep shearing which has just begun, so up the track we head, the others still ankle deep in poo. We sit on a craggy cement-free wall – a dry stane dyke – to watch the sheep having their coats removed. I see the blue tractor again, up on the hill, raking up the ploughed ground.

"Jonasz wanted to get a tractor just like that," I tell Clinton. "First week I was here, we went to a tractor shop together and looked at one."

"You haven't spoken about him for a while," says Clinton

"I suppose not."

"He's what's missing from *Tower*. Or your feelings about him."

"I suppose so," I say, gazing at the tractor as it turns and starts another length of the field.

"Can we try and put that aspect back in?" asks Clinton. "Would you mind?"

"I don't mind," I tell him, but I've had enough of looking at the blue tractor. The figurative wall that I built up between Jonasz and me doesn't feel as strong as it once did. Unlike the sturdy structure beneath me, it could crumble at any time. "Let's go help the others with their poo shovelling."

The month of May zooms by. It's filled with classes, choreography, rehearsals, exam practice, Aileen being snarky but not bad enough for an official complaint, and me talking to Amalphia about Jonasz, possibly more than is necessary. It all just pours out. My wall of discipline has, indeed, crumbled and fallen away. I need to tell someone about that awful last weekend at the Serafins' house because I can't stop thinking about it.

Amalphia doesn't usually butt in and give her own opinion on things, but this time she does. "When something terrible happens to a person," she says, "it's not only that person who is traumatised. The people who care about them are too. So, sometimes, at the worst times in your life, the most important people in your circle are not functioning at their best."

Taking advantage of this more chatty Amalphia, I tell her about Jonasz showing up at the premiere. "Why do you think he came?" I ask.

"To see you."

"But why?"

That, she can't tell me, and I do try to stop wondering about it, but then, at the end of the month, it's my birthday. I'm seventeen which means Jonasz is now eighteen. He's been eighteen for over a month. We are the ages when we said we would 'do it,' as Bubbles would say. Have sex, as I would say. We thought we'd be mature enough so it wouldn't damage our relationship, our closeness, our forever, but, of course, now, we won't. Or he might, but it won't be with me. It will never be with me.

I try to walk away from the thought, away from the past, always intruding as it does. I need cake, and I need my friends, so I head to the great hall.

# 39

"A BONNY QUINE LIKE you should be smiling on your birth-day," says Holly, laying down an enormous chocolate cake on the table in the great hall. "But if cake's not enough to cheer you up, dinna worry; you're all being taken on a picnic this afternoon. We do it every summer. Whole school, down to the beach. So, look out yer dookers!"

I eat my cake and then go to my cottage to look out my dookers, or swimsuit. I climb into the bus with the others and feel a small stab of excitement. The trip reminds me of primary school outings, but without the meanness that accompanied those. Here, we're all, if not exactly friends, compadres, all in it together, all needing a break from the daily slog.

The sun's shining. There's hampers and hampers of food, and I know the beach we're going to, or at least I've heard of it. I've been near it that once with Alexander in the Deil's Lum. This is a little further round the coast from that dark cave, but it'll be nice to see the topside, the sunny side, the sea and the surf.

It's beautiful. It's stunning. It's like a page from a holiday brochure. En masse, we run along the grass, past an ancient well and down onto the sandy part of the beach. We dump our stuff on mats and run back along to the stones and into the sea which is completely freezing. We knew it would be, but the temperature is still a shock. We scream with the cold and the thrill of it. We splash and swim and shiver. We run back up the beach to Amalphia and Mr. Zolotov and Will and Holly and Aileen in her tiny shorts and high heels combo. We wrap ourselves up in big towels and are given hot chocolate and little cakes, and we begin to feel warm again.

"The ocean should never be that cold," says Guy, chilled in a different way from usual. "I'll never get used to Scotland's climate."

"It's warmer over in the next bay," Alexander tells me. "Wanna go?"

"No going into the caves," warns Amalphia when she hears where we're going. "Who knows when there could be rock falls? Stay on the path, and then stay on the beach."

"I'll go with them," says our chilled Australian ballet teacher. "See if this warmer thing is true."

I get the feeling Alexander doesn't want Guy to come, but we all head up the narrow coastal path and over the top of the cliffs.

Again, it's so beautiful. There are flowers everywhere in the grass: soft yellow vetch and springy pink thrift. When we reach the top, we look down at the next bay where the sea is brilliantly blue, the water clean and clear and surrounded by dark pink rocks.

"It does look more sheltered," says Guy. "See you down there." And he marches off down the path, quickly disappearing between the dunes.

"It's nice along here," says Alexander, pointing the way to what looks like a grassy cliff edge. "We could watch Guy, see if it looks cold."

We sit down at the top of what is not a sheer cliff but more of sloping hill. There's a steep path down to the bay from it. We see Guy run into the blue sea, give a double thumbs up to the sky, dive gracefully under the water and swim off, right out into the bay.

"He looks a bit like a dolphin," I say, laughing.

"I'm glad you're not scared to sit on a cliff with me again," says Alexander.

I look round at him, his hair drying in the sun, and it's a bit like that last time we sat on a precipice, just before the edge crumbled. There's his dark eyes, and his smile. Alexander this close up in a non pas de deux way is intoxicating.

And then we're kissing. Really kissing. His mouth kissing mine. Mine kissing him back. His fingers through my hair like before. I touch his shampoo-advert hair. It's wet. Everything feels all tingly and I pull back. I look at him, this most beautiful of boys, and then I lean forward and kiss him again.

I may be kissing Alexander, but it's not where my attention is. I can hear a tractor, and I know that Jonasz would know exactly what make and model it is just from the sound. He's so clever like that. So in tune with the things he loves. I pull back again.

"Alexander, I'm in love with someone else."

"I know," he says, and touches my hair again. "So am I. You and me are messed up in a lot of the same ways. Doesn't mean we can't..."

He leans in again, but I shake my head.

"It does," I tell him. "For me, it does."

"Bummer," he says, but he smiles. "We're still best friends, though?"

"Of course. But think about it: if we got involved and it all went wrong, we'd lose it all, our friendship and everything. And I don't want that to happen, not again."

We lean foreheads together, and I know we're okay, closer than before maybe because a question that was hanging over us has been answered and let go.

The tractor is definitely closer than before; it's actually really loud. I look round and see it in the sloping field behind the beach, just sitting there, being loud.

"It's your cousin's blue tractor again," I say. "It's like it's haunting me."

"That's not one of Ross's. It is his land, though, so it must be a hire. You up for a warmer swim?"

We take the path through the long grasses as the tractor turns and trundles away up the field. Then we wade into cold but not freezing shallows; lots of tiny silver fish dart around our legs. And then, like dolphins, we swim out into the bay and back again. We walk up over the hill hand-in-hand, fingers locked. It feels nice, like our friendship has become more childish and innocent, yet all at once deeper and more grown-up.

Back at the beach with the others, I creep into a cave that has a really low roof to change out of my swimsuit; Paula shows me where to go and holds a towel up to ensure maximum privacy.

When we come out, Alexander's little sister, the one with all the blonde curls, Faye, is standing there looking quite formidable.

"Were you and Alexander doing kissing on each other?" she asks me.

"I'll leave you to it," says Paula, heading back to the others, a smile in her voice.

The little girl continues looking at me, hands on hips, waiting for her question to be answered.

"We were," I tell her. "But we've decided to stay friends, not be girlfriend and boyfriend."

"There's a sea slug in that rock pool over there," she tells me, pointing across at a rocky plateau then taking my hand.

We walk over the flat pink rocks, avoiding all the pointy limpets with our bare feet, and gaze into a seaweed-filled pool. Faye locates the rippling blue-and-green slug, and we watch its progress across the pool floor.

"It's good you're going to be friends," says Faye. "Alexander needs friends. Chantal just wanted him for kissing."

"Really?"

She nods. "Chantal wasn't nice."

I feel like I've passed a test. I think Faye likes me. She offers me a plate of cakes once we're back up on the sand with the others.

"You and Alexander?" asks Henry, looking up from his phone as I sit down beside him on a blanket. He looks terribly serious, actually quite down in the mouth.

"Friends," I snap, fed up of everyone being so nosey, and then I feel bad because Henry is my friend too. "We kissed, but then decided to stay friends, not anything else."

Henry's smile is also a loud outbreath like he's relieved, and I'm not sure why. There's no vibe between him and me, I'm sure of it. Maybe it's Alexander he likes? But I've never picked up anything like that either, and we've all worked so closely together. He goes back to his phone as I lay back and gaze at the blue sky and feel the warmth of the sun and the peace and the friendship all around me.

# 40

FAST FORWARD TO MONDAY morning. Fast forward to the day of the exam. I look back fondly to Faye's test at the beach, the one I passed, as Aileen repeats her belief that I shouldn't have been entered into this one, that there is no way I'll pass, that it is, in fact, just a massive waste of her and everyone else's time to even be trying to get me through it.

I grit my teeth and say nothing. Because I don't know. Maybe she's right? Maybe Maxine was right? Maybe I am useless and a joke and a disgrace and stinking and filthy.

"Hey," says Henry, hand on my shoulder.

"Don't let her get to you," advises Alexander, before I go in with the other girls. "We'll put an end to her balletic terrorism next year, I promise you."

I feel slightly better. I know all the exercises so well, and the exam itself doesn't feel too hard. But my hand? Here in the castle, it's easy to forget the disfigurement, but Aileen's earlier words about my hands must have been about that hand. Does it mean I'll never look right, never have the right positioning? Never be good enough? I try to be objective: I think I'm as good as Paula and Star and Belinda. My legs go up like theirs. My feet are strong en pointe. But how can I tell? How can I really know? And what happens if I do fail? Am I gone from the castle next year?

A panicking spiral happens as I glide across the room in a glissade and beat my legs in a cabriole. I mess up the steps and have to start again, so is that it? An automatic fail? The examiner, an old lady, smiles and tells me not to worry, but is she just being nice in the moment? Like, don't worry, it's not the end of the world, but here: fail!

"It'll be the end of summer till we get the results," says Belinda at lunch.

"No, it won't," says Alexander.

"It always takes two or three months, I think," says Paul, who's usually up on these sorts of things.

"Not here," Alexander insists with a movie-star smile. "You wait, you'll see. Bet we know by the end of next class."

He's right. Amalphia interrupts pas de deux with Mr. Timms in the dungeon and asks to speak to us all.

"Ah, the girl with the beautiful line," says Mr. Timms about Amalphia, before retreating to the front of the room and leaving her alone with us students.

The actress stage whispers: "You all passed with distinction."

"All of us?" says Paula.

"Yes."

"Even me?" I ask, because maybe she's wrong. How can she even know?

"Of course, even you. I read all the extra notes and everything. Yours were very complimentary, Ariel, but I'll leave those details for when you get your official notification."

She exits the studio with no further explanation. I look at Alexander, confused.

"She takes the examiner out to lunch at the pub," he explains. "Reads their notes when they go to the toilet. She asks the owner to keep them talking in the hall, or if they leave their stuff here, Will goes and photographs it all for her. She'll do it again with dinner tonight to get the second year results."

"Distinction's the top mark, isn't it?" I ask, still not quite believing what's happened.

"You're distinction all the way, baby," he says, and we both fall about laughing and find it hard to keep straight faces during the rest of pas de deux.

I like our newly deepened friendship. I like the extra relaxedness there is between us now. We're close and cuddly and warm, and it's good.

In fact, so many aspects of my life are good now. It's different. I'm different. I find that I can look back at some things that happened and feel differently about them now too. From this new place. From this better time.

And, though everything feels good and warm now, I know I wasn't always warm to everyone. Sometimes I was cold and rude. I'm thinking about the Serafins again: that week I lived with them, that last weekend in their house, and their visit here to the castle. They brought Caliban to see me. That was so thoughtful, and I behaved like an entitled brat. I could have spoken to them. In their home and here. I could have explained how I felt. I could have expressed gratitude rather than all the flouncing off I recall doing. I think I did say thank you to Janet when I was moving out of her house that morning, but not properly. I'd felt distinctly unfriendly towards her then. And what had she done but express concern for her children, surely a natural and good thing for a parent to do. And she did try to look after me too.

"You never had a parent who wasn't all about them," Amalphia says, when I tell her my thoughts in our next counselling session. "Which basically means you never had a parent. Everything you were dealing with that week was entirely new to you, on top of the most horrific trauma. You did incredibly well, Ariel. You are doing incredibly well. Don't take guilt on board; it only messes you up."

So: I've to try and feel no guilt. I'm not sure how to manage that. But maybe a little healing could be arranged? Or at least a thank you. In my next counselling session, after we've covered stories such as: Maxine and the perfect cup of tea, having to perform for Maxine's friends, and Maxine and the bottle of whisky, I ask Amalphia: "Could I send the Serafins tickets to the final of the competition here at the castle? As well as Patti? They were so good to me, that family, not just at the end, but over the years, and I want to thank them. It feels like something I should do."

So I write a card, no flowers or cats on the front, just a farming landscape, and I thank the family who helped me. I try to write from the heart without gushing or being weird. I enclose five tickets, though I doubt they'll want to come. It's the thank you that's most important. As I seal the envelope, it feels like the end of a chapter, or perhaps even a whole story. I stick a stamp on and drop the card in the outgoing castle mail tray to be posted.

I almost want to cry but I stop myself; I almost want to curt-sey like at the end of class or performance. Révérence. Closure. Finis!

# 41

"Too cuddly," complains Henry of our choreography.

He's right. We're supposed to be expressing raw, naked anger this time, not Henry of course, not our angel, but the devils are to unleash their deepest, innermost rage for all to see on the stage. But the way the choreography almost wrote itself before? That's still happening, but not to plan this time. It seems keen to display our friendship, and we struggle to keep it in check.

I stamp my foot. I am determined to be Maxine. I list aspects of her and perform a posé turn for every bullet point, stepping turns that travel round the room, or edge of the stage as it will be.

- Cruel at every opportunity. Turn.

- Violent sometimes, especially when drunk. Turn.

- Dismissive. Turn.

- Angry, angry, angry! Three turns.

- Full of hate. I go for a triple pirouette for that one and manage to turn for five. Score!

- Empty of love. No love at all. Five turns: no love, no love, no love, no love.

Alexander joins in and we end up in perfect sync, finishing with a beautiful supported arabesque, laughing up and down at one another.

Obviously, we just have to practise harder. So, every evening we go to an upstairs studio in the castle, and every Sunday we have lunch at Alexander's house and use the studio there.

Alexander asks for Will's help, but Will is actually no help with our particular, friendly problem. All the renowned choreographer says is: "If that's the way it's taking you, go with it, change it out."

We don't want to go with it or change it out. We want to be angry, but we're not which is in itself is a bit angering.

We try our choreography out in the stone circle on a sunny Sunday evening. Maybe some ancient magic will help? The sky reddens up as we dance, lighting our faces with such a perfect colour for the devils, but we're still laughing and smiling and forgetting to be angry a lot of the time. Still, we decide to request red lighting for the final.

"Yes," says Justin, agreeing at once when we ask him about it. "A fiery light for my agitators. I like it."

We decide to wear white to enhance the effect of the lighting: jeans and trainers, no flouncy skirts, no fancy costumes, just us, and our anger, and the lights.

The final is replacing the usual end-of-year performance at the castle. Mr. Zolotov expresses both relief and worry about this, at one of the family Sunday dinners Henry and I are invited to.

"Is great to have a break from the organisation of the normal event," he explains. "But I have concern for the second and third years; they are to be left out, and it is demoralising for them."

"We can do some extra stuff," suggests Justin. "Acts between competition pieces, maybe. How's that sound?" He looks at

Alexander, Henry and me. "I want to save these three revolutionaries till last."

It's arranged. The second years are to do a contemporary composition, and the third years something classical from their tour, and everybody is happy, or happier, even us, and we're supposed to be angry.

The Saturday television shows run throughout June, and they showcase our cosiness which is a bit embarrassing. We do look ridiculously cuddly. We actually look—

"You two are together now, aren't you?" says Star at lunch, looking at Alexander and I intently with her colourfully made-up eyes.

"No," says Alexander.

"No," says me.

"They're not," says Henry.

"Oh, come on," says Clinton. "Look at you."

We look at each other and the way we're sitting. Okay. Alexander and I are leant against one another at the table. But it's not like that. It's more like being siblings, not that I've ever known what that's like.

"This is just how real dancers are," Alexander tells the table. "So get to it. Snuggle up, you melts!"

It's all terribly funny and does not help one bit with our anger development. We even find the new hashtag that's appeared – **#ArielAndAlexanderForever** – hilarious. We try to start another: **#AndHenryToo**, but it doesn't take off.

Then yet another tag starts to trend. And it's not good. Paul and Paula tell us about it at lunch in the great hall one day, and out come the phones.

**#CastleRejects** is all about Lewis and Chantal. They've met up and made a video together. Apparently Chantal did lots of vlogs while she was here at the castle too, mainly make-up tutorials and beauty guides.

Paul expresses the opinion that she focused too much on making her videos and not enough on her class work. "And the knickers, of course," he adds seriously.

Today she's putting black nail varnish on Lewis as he talks about favouritism at the castle. She nods as he says: "Some get away with everything. Rest of us, one foot wrong and we're out."

I look at Chantal with her pink sparkly make-up and perfectly straightened hair, and then I look at Alexander's face. It's pale. Red patches have appeared on his cheeks. And I think I know who he's still in love with, but all he says is: "*Tower*'s looking a bit different these days," and the conversation moves on.

We've seen the *Tower* rehearsals on the show, sitting curfewed and alone in our cottages on Saturday nights, and the piece is different; it's better but not great. It's got no chance of winning, and everybody knows it. And that makes me momentarily sad. But not angry, so it's not helpful for our composition, and I try to rid my mind of the sadness, to replace it with other thoughts and feelings. But thoughts of the person that I'm still in love with appear in my head as I push the tower to the side. I force myself to think about the final, the performance, the judges, and the Highland dancers that we will be up against. It works. For my mind. But not for my heart. That's a far more difficult space to clear or distract, a deeper place, and an altogether more painful place.

# 42

THE WEEK OF THE final soon arrives. It's the last week of term, but no one cares about that because we can't see past Saturday, and our performances.

The other dancers start to arrive for the event. Some stay at the castle, others at hotels, but they all attend morning classes in the upstairs studios with the three years of castle students.

**#TeamKilt** stay with us in our cottages: Morag with me, and Callum with Paul.

It's nice to have some company in my wee house, though it means I have to open the door to the second bedroom, and I haven't done that since the day I moved in. I shut the past away in there back then, and now I have to face it in a very practical and, it feels, visceral way.

I have to move the 'murder clothes' as I've been thinking of the things I had on that terrible night, the night before I started here. It's a bit weird. I hope that looking at the clothes, touching them, might fuel my anger for the performance, but it actually just makes me feel sad again. As does seeing Jonasz's old phone in the drawer, all uncharged and dead. I hold it in my hands and remember all sorts of things. Him giving me the phone. How happy I was that he would think of doing such a thing, and how I loved him, how I love him. Oh. I found a happy moment from the past. But, somehow, it just makes me even sadder.

Amalphia wants me to go to grief counselling; she says I've got to grieve the parents I never had, the life I could have had, and who I could have been without the abuse. And in grieving, I'll take steps towards it: that better, more whole version of me.

But really, apart from the odd weird moment like this, and the one lingering sadness that is not about abuse or my parents, I am mainly happy, happy, happy in my life now. I touch the dried blood on the neck of the old sweatshirt and realise: what a good thing it was that I could run so fast. Ballet training saves lives! I wonder if anyone has ever thought to market ballet classes that way, and things are a bit happier again as I stuff the clothes into the bottom of a bin bag. The phone, I put at the back of a drawer in my bedroom. I can't bring myself to throw it away.

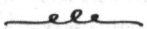

The morning of the final dawns sunny and bright. Morag comes into my bedroom with a cup of tea for me.

"No one's ever done this for me before," I tell her of the tea.

"Seriously?" she says. "What about your mum?"

And I realise she doesn't know about all that which is so refreshing. I don't enlighten her, but I do tell her something, another truth. "I learned to make tea for her when I was seven years old. She was very particular about the way she liked it. I was punished if I got it wrong."

"Aye," says Morag with a shake of her head. "Some folks are not made to be parents."

"No," I agree and sip the tea that someone brought to me in bed, before we head to the castle and the rest of the exciting day.

Class is a huge gathering in the dungeon today, with all three years of students and the visiting competitors taking part. The studio is filled with people for once, portable barres lining the centre of the massive room. Then there's a mid-morning brunch thing in the great hall, and then filming begins in the theatre.

The programme is going out in two instalments. The first is to be two hours long and showcase all the finalists; the second is going to be a bit shorter and include the extra non-competitive performances and then the results. Of course, the results.

Our piece is being shot last, around dinnertime, but we get our things ready early in the large swimming-pool changing rooms along with everyone else. The smaller theatre changing rooms are being kept just for whoever is on next. We change into our white gear, agreeing that we will have to be mega careful not to spill anything on ourselves or lean against anything dirty.

I can only find one of my shoes. It's infuriating. I know I packed it in my bag this morning. Morag was there, and she says she remembers seeing me do it.

So, maybe it fell out. Feeling a bit stupid in my skinny white jeans and big black boots, I head back to the cottages, searching all along the path for the missing white trainer. I see it as I approach my cottage. It's been shoved into my letterbox and is sticking out as if to mock me. This is even more infuriating, because, who did that? Didn't they know it's the show today? They obviously knew it was my shoe, or they wouldn't have—

There's a pink envelope shoved in there too. I stand looking at it, shoe in one hand, pink envelope in the other. I recognise the writing from before: it's from Alexander's Fake Mum, the one who survived, the one who said she would come to deal with him herself. This time there's no address, no stamp, just my name: Ariel. This time it was hand delivered.

My heart starts to pound as I rip open the envelope, and then it's like reading lines from a bad film, or a joke. It must be a joke, surely? If only. The letter, written within a cat-and-flower-covered card again, tells me to come to the Deil's Lum cave by way of the underground tunnel from the castle. It tells me to tell no one. It tells me that if I ever want to see Alexander alive again, I will obey this instruction about telling no one. I will bring no one and nothing with me, not even my phone.

But Alexander was just up at the castle in the dressing rooms with the rest of us, and I can run fast. Ballet training saves lives! I crash into various people as I make my way through the passageway and kitchens, across the great hall and down the corridor to the swimming pool. I find Henry but not Alexander. I can't see Alexander anywhere.

"Where's Alexander?" I shout across the pool and then into the dressing rooms. "Has anyone seen him?"

"He was here a minute ago," Callum tells me. "He found a letter at the bottom of his bag."

"He ran off," says Henry, frowning, knowing something's wrong.

Maybe it's not too late to catch him, to prevent him meeting Fake Mum at the cliff edge!

# 43

I RACE. I RUN. I dodge people; there's slow-moving people everywhere, and they're slowing me down. I race up the kitchen passageway and locate the place where we did our first 'research.' The door to the strange room with the green lights and the glass floor is unlocked, the glass door in the floor standing up and open.

"Alexander!" I shout down into the space with the bottles and barrels, hoping he'll hear me and come back.

There's no reply, not from the hole in the floor anyway.

"Ariel, what's wrong?" says Henry from behind me.

I'm crying now. It's hard to speak, and I know I can't obey the letter, not completely. I hand the horrible card to Henry and say: "If I'm not back in an hour, call the police. And tell Mr. Zolotov. Don't come yourself!" I shout as he steps toward me, eyes wide and face pale. "I have to go alone!"

I turn and climb down the steps as fast as I can. How far can Alexander have got? Far enough not to hear me shout, that's for sure. I've brought my phone in spite of the instructions – how will Fake Mum know, anyway? – and at first I'm glad because it lights the way into the inkily dark tunnel. But I was told not to bring it. By a devil. Will I be searched for it? Will Fake Mum pat me down like a police officer searching for weapons? And if she finds it? What then? I swear like Alexander does sometimes, but decide to take the phone most of the way anyway. I can hide it behind a stone or something nearer the cave.

A strong draft in the tunnel carries the smell of the sea to me. It's cold down here and I shiver. I shake. My head is full of half formed plans. Alexander and I will be two to her one, and surely we can deal with her instead of her dealing with us? We're dancers. We're strong. Ballet training saves lives!

I arrive at that weird boulder, the chamber door, and stop in spite of my desperation to get to Alexander. The big stone is all lit up round the edges with an orangey light which is really weird. Is the light connected to what's happening? I touch the stone then push on it. It doesn't shift, doesn't acknowledge my hand at all.

There's no point to this delay; I am wasting precious time. On I go, glad of the light of the phone as the walls and floor get rougher. The world slopes downwards, down to the sea, but not to a nice day out at the beach, not with cake and kisses and a blue tractor. I wipe away a tear, this being no place for that sort of thing, and keep going.

The fishy smell in the place is not quite so bad this time. The breeze is more like proper wind now, clearing the air a bit. I can hear roaring: the sea.

I come to the cave itself, and step out onto the plateau under the high craggy dome of the roof. There's nobody here, so I'll have to go round the corner to where Alexander said it all happened before, to where Fake Mum took him, to where she nearly killed him.

Got to think clearly, Ariel.

Got to be clever, Ariel.

I silence the phone and place it in a little crevice above me. I can come back to it. We will come back to it and have Fake Mum arrested. If she's even here. Maybe it was all a hoax, some bizarre trick that I've fallen for like an idiot. The stink of lies is detectable, all mixed together with the smell of rotten seaweed and fish and seagull guano, decaying, disgusting and abhorrent. But I have to go on, investigate and find out the truth, and save my friend if he is here.

I creep along the dark pink rock wall, straining to pick up any little sound, any little clue. I want to discover anything that might help. I know from experience that the more information you have in an encounter with an abuser, the better. The more clarity, the better. It's why I always seek it: clarity, clarity, clarity.

Best of all, of course, would be if this is all a big, fat lie. No Fake Mum. No danger. No Alexander, Alexander being back up at the castle, all safe and sound.

I reach the edge of the rocky wall and peer round: nobody, nothing. Well, not nothing. The sea is incredibly rough down below the cliff edge. Waves are crashing, raging against the rocks, even sloshing right up onto the ledge here. There are wet patches on the floor of the cave, darkened pink splotches. They look a bit like blood. I shudder with the thought, the image, and the whole situation, the whole stupid situation.

I step round the corner to the place I sat with Alexander that night, and I discover that it was all a big, fat lie. Of course it was. There's no Fake Mum here. No Alexander.

There's just me: me staring at the double-barrelled end of an old rifle, the dangerous end, the end that should never be pointed at anyone. I remember the rifle, at least I think it's the one I think it is, but my thinking has become jumbled, mixed up and fixated on those two round barrels. My father used to shoot rabbits in the field with that gun, in the Serafins' field. He made me do it too. I hated it. I missed deliberately and got beaten for it. Poor rabbits. Poor me. What sad and sorry little creatures.

I force my focus to widen, force my eyes to extend their gaze beyond the two big metal eyes of the weapon, and look directly into the two bloodshot eyes of the devil. The eyes are angry but the mouth is smiling, pretending to be nice, even here, even like this, pretending to be nice.

"Hello, Ariel," says my devil, my mother, Maxine.

# 44

IT SEEMS LIKE WE stand there for a long time. There's a long pause in the activities of the day.

There's the devil with her leering pink-lipstick grin and her perfectly in-place, blow-dried, hair-sprayed hair, the smell of it so familiar and so vile.

There's the little-girl/frightened-rabbit thing that I've become, like I've instantly travelled back in time to a different era of my life.

Gone are the castle and friends, and doing well and passing exams, and votes in my favour, and parties imbued with golden light. This is me. This is her. Back at the beginning. Or the end. Perform a curtsey. Take a bow. Discharge a firearm.

"So," she says, and I hate her voice so much, hate the tone. That one word expresses the constant derision of my childhood in all its sadness. "So," she says again. "It is the little bism."

Bism. Bism. What is a bism? It's like I should know. I think it's a Scottish word, and it sounds wrong in the posh English accent of Maxine. Whatever. Fitever. She's calling me it, so it's a bad thing.

She clarifies: "Trollope. Harpy. Giving it up for anyone. It's one way of getting on in the world, I suppose!" The laugh of the devil echoes all around the cave, bouncing back at us from the roof and laughing all over again. "I bet you've been at it with all of them," remarks Maxine. "That boy, Alexander? Why else would he be interested in a little freak like you? And his father. The whole lot of that family, all mingled in together, aren't they?!"

It's this that pulls me forward in time, not all the way, but a step up from being a tiny child cowering in front of a monster. "They're good people," I say. "They're nothing like you."

"What do you mean?" she asks, and I realise that my words have shifted her attitude a little. There's a hint of the sorry-for-herself Maxine in her voice now.

"I mean they're nothing like you," I repeat, knowing I have to be very careful. She's still pointing the rifle at me, and in one second she could shift from someone who once tried to kill her daughter to someone who actually did.

"Oh, what would a bism like you know?" she scoffs. "You never were very bright. Parents' evenings at school were so unpleasant and such a lot of work. Running from one room to the next at the whim of all those teachers. They all had so much to say. Thinking they were important."

"You only went once," I remember. I also smell whisky, very real and present, not just a memory.

Be careful, Ariel.

Be clever, Ariel.

She's drunk and a bit sorry for herself, and she hates hard work. I have years of training for this.

"That must be very heavy," I say of the gun, then experiencing a flicker of fear that I'm making a mistake, that she might just shoot me to have done with it. So, I go quickly on: "It's a shame we're not somewhere that I could cook you a nice meal."

This confuses her. "Oh," she says and looks around briefly. "Well, Simone said this would be the place to get you on your own."

Simone. Fake Mum's name. "Is she here too?" I ask. "Simone?"

"No. I got her to write the letters for me today – one for you and one for him – and she told me all about the place. Daddy got your address for her that time, so she owed me."

I go cold. Alexander got a letter too. Where did it send him?

"So she wrote a letter to Alexander today as well," I say.

"Oof, a piece of nonsense, but it got him out of the way."

"So, he isn't somewhere down here?"

"Why would I want to see that pompous little arse? I saw enough of him on TV. Thinking so much of himself. And you thinking he's your boyfriend." The laughter happens again, much louder this time, creating bigger echoes round and round, and back and forth, over the stormy sea below.

I relax again, relatively speaking obviously; I am still being held at gunpoint by a drunken devil. It's time to do submissive; it often worked in volatile moments before.

So, gentle tones, sad tones, knowing-I'm-useless tones: "I don't think that," I say. "He's not my boyfriend."

"Well, of course he's not. Who would want you? The two of you telling all those lies together, though, and on television for all to hear. You both came from loving homes, but now people believe the rubbish you spouted. You enjoyed that, didn't you?" She jabs in my direction with the gun. "Making people feel sorry for you? Forgetting to mention what a good mother I was?"

The 'good mother' presses the gun into my chin, and I do the only thing I can: I pretend the gun isn't there and try to speak to her love of good food and being taken care of: "Eggs with Hollandaise sauce. I would love to make that for you, like I used to."

I've got her interest. She cocks her head to one side, thinking. The gun lowers a little. I bet institutional food has not been good. She's probably been eating stuff that resembles school dinners recently.

"Beef olives with mint jelly; roast potatoes and gravy," I say, the retro mixture being a favourite of hers. "I have my own cottage here with my own kitchen; no one else would be around."

"It's a long time since I've had proper roast potatoes," she says, all dreamy and drunk. "And I've had such a difficult day. I had to take a bus, and then I took Daddy's car. Do you think he'll mind?"

"Only if you damaged it," I say, thinking aloud, then stopping myself from saying the rest of the thought, the part about how he won't mind what she's doing now. But the car? That matters to him.

She starts issuing orders, strictly, clearly, as if to a stupid person: "The potatoes will have to be par-boiled for seven minutes, roasted in pre-heated oil with rosemary and garlic for exactly forty-seven minutes, and they must not be allowed to cool before serving."

"I can do that. I've done it many times."

The sea roars as she considers. A big wave splashes up, showering us with droplets, perhaps sobering one of us up a little.

"Do you think I'm stupid?" she shouts, and the cave shouts it back. "I didn't come here to eat roast potatoes! I came here to rid the world of you. End the job that the thresher began. It sliced away some of your foulness; I'm going to blast away the rest. Ariel needs to be released into the ether like the spirit from Shakespeare's play. Gone completely. How sorry everyone's going to be for me. Crazy Ariel going mad with a gun and being washed out to sea. Poor Maxine being lured to a place like this by her evil, lying bism of a daughter. I'll be famous, properly famous, not like you with your stupid little show. It'll be in all the papers, on all the news programmes. They'll say: what that poor woman must have been through over the years..."

And I wonder if she really believes this. Is she actually mad? Or just drunk?

She fumbles with the back of the gun, not knowing how to use it. But then I hear the click. She's ready to shoot, ready to kill.

I close my eyes and prepare to die.

# 45

"ARIEL, WATCH OUT! THE SEA!" It's Henry. Henry shouting lots of words. Henry, here, like a miracle.

His words grow and repeat as they bounce round the cave, and he's with us, me and Maxine, as we are all thrown back by a wave so powerful it knocks us off our feet. It pushes us to the back of the cave, like bits of seaweed. The three of us are flotsam and jetsam, shocked and bruised debris washed up by the ocean.

It's quiet. It's still. The sea slides back from us, a retreating tide, a line of wet shapes left in its wake: a boy, a girl, a devil and a gun. The gun's just lying there, not held by anyone.

I reach for it. She reaches for it. We both grab it. We wrestle with a fully locked-and-loaded rifle there on the rocky plateau. The only sounds are those of exertion as we compete to be the victor, the one pointing the gun. We're soaked and we're slimy which makes it hard to get a firm grip on the deadly prize. Henry joins the tussle, and then we're surrounded by people and noise.

For a moment, it feels almost intrusive, a quiet murderous moment barged in on and interrupted, but it's good, so very good, because it's our class, our whole class.

Clinton is sitting on the devil, holding her arm behind her back. Paul joins him by sitting on her legs as she struggles and complains. What she's saying is not clear. It's slurred and fast, but I think it might be: 'get off me' which is surprisingly sensible given her predicament. Bism is in there too, of course. Her drinking-session rants often contained a much repeated word or phrase. Today, it's bism.

I take hold of the gun and stand up. I point the gun at her head.

"It's all right, Ariel," says Clinton. "We got her."

"She was going to kill me," I tell him.

"Don't listen to her!" shrieks Maxine. "She was the one that had me. Look at her. She's insane. That Lewis boy was right. I liked him."

Clinton twists her arm further round her back. "Could break it if I wanted to," he says. "So quiet down."

She quiets down and just stares at me. It's her 'I'm going to get you later when all these people aren't around' look, easy to read despite her face being pressed into a wet, pink rock floor, lipstick smudged, hair-do undone.

Star and Paula and Belinda are saying things like: "Oh my God, Ariel. Are you okay?" and "What is this place, anyway? It's crazy." Their words all morph into one long incredulous speech.

Henry's words are clear though. "You're not like her," he says, putting his hand on my arm, my gun-holding arm.

Slowly, I lower the gun and point it at the cave floor. It reminds me of a camera pointed at a studio floor, a piece of equipment taken out of use and prevented from doing harm. I look at Clinton and Paul and know that there's no way she can escape them. I remove the cartridges from the rifle and briefly consider tossing them over the edge and into the sea, but they're live so that would be irresponsible. I push them into the front pocket of my white jeans which are white no more. I touch the large grey and brown stains on my legs, like scars, scars on clothes that were supposed to stay clean.

"I must have leant on something dirty," I say.

"Don't just stand there, you lot," Clinton orders, and I jump. "Give Ariel your warm-ups; I think she's going into shock."

I'm in the process of being wrapped up in layers of knitwear when Mr. Zolotov and Alexander and Will arrive. There's lots of talking, but I can't take it in.

I hug Alexander and don't want to let him go. I'm so glad he's safe. I tell him what happened. Sort of. I think. He tells me about his letter. He'd run across the fields to that old cottage where he used to live and then gone down into the underground chamber to find me, or her, or somebody, actually nobody. Then he ran back and went straight to his father.

Mr. Zolotov is in charge, the commander of this shipwreck on the shore, or the ledge of a shore, wherever we are. But he's gentle too; he speaks kindly to me. Will goes outside to call the police. He climbs through the roof of the cave, the real Deil's Lum part, to the hillside to get phone reception.

They come, the police, two of them, a man and a woman, and they take Maxine away. She tells them that I'm the one they should be taking, that it's me that's in the wrong, and that it always was.

"Enough!" shouts Mr. Zolotov, and I listen to the echo. It's right and he's right: enough of this now, enough of this forever.

We go up the tunnel together, a little crowd. Will thinks he should carry me, but I say: no. I am not a pathetic little girl. I can walk. I remember my phone in its little crevice and retrieve it.

"I got a text from you," I tell Alexander as I see the notification on the screen.

He hugs me. So does Henry. And we walk on and up towards the light as an entwined three.

Then there's an ambulance, and paramedics, and more police, and so much talking, talking, talking. But I'm okay. We're all okay. We're all unharmed. And everyone's so sorry. I'm so sorry. It's a sorry, sorry day.

# 46

PATTI'S THERE IN THE hospital, and she's so sorry too. She cries, and I cry. I feel as if I'm just joining in with what everyone else says and does, like I did with the choreography at the castle right back at the beginning of this year.

It's amazing what a cup of really sweet tea can do. Will makes it in a patients' area with two tea bags and five sugars. I watch him and am reminded of another boy from what seems like very long ago, a boy who was always there for me when I needed him. The feeling leaks out and I cry some more.

But this is now: I am a girl with lots of friends, and they're all right here, in the hospital with me. Mr. Zolotov insisted that they were all checked for harm too.

"I don't want to be like her, my mother, Maxine," I tell Alexander and Henry.

"You're not," says Henry, a little croaky, rubbing his throat. The others have told me what a lot of speaking he did earlier to explain to them why they had to come down under the castle.

"Not in any way, ever," I clarify. "Not in our piece, our choreography. I want to do what it was turning into. Just be us. Friends."

"You have much time to think about this," says Mr. Zolotov. "You will get to do your entry another day once you are rested and recovered."

"No," I almost shout. "She wanted to sabotage the show; I know that's why she chose to come today. And we're doing it today." I look at the big clock in the waiting room. It's four o' clock. "There's still time, surely? Or has the whole thing been cancelled? Or am I being selfish?" Like her. "None of you have to do it. Of course you don't."

The whole thing has not been cancelled, and there is still time, and everyone wants to do it. On this we all agree. We shall not be stopped by drunken psychos in caves. I laugh when I say this. I called Maxine a psycho. She would be so furious.

So, we are doing this, but not the same this. Another this. A different thing. I have a much better idea, and I detail it to my friends, wanting all of them to be involved.

"But will it even work?" asks Paula. "And are you sure you feel well enough?"

It will work, and I do feel well enough. I have a few bruises, but I'm not in shock now.

Everyone loves the idea. Clinton 'whoop whoops' about it. I love Clinton. He's trained in martial arts, and his dad's a paramedic who has shared a lot of knowledge with Clinton over the years which helped today. Clinton's like a super-hero.

"Never been called that before," he says, and I realise I have been speaking my thoughts out loud. But that's okay. Some things should be said out loud.

When we arrive back at the castle, Justin is all for the idea of our changed piece too, though he fusses over us in what feels to me like a motherly way, how mothers should be, which is weird and not really quite like the Justin I've come to know.

Amalphia's there too, a mother to us all, making sure we're warm and fed before any performance is considered. She hugs us, Alexander and me longer than the others. She inspects our faces super carefully. I try to look unshocked and un-bruised in case she says we can't go on.

I hear her on the phone to someone, my social worker who I've yet to meet, I think. Amalphia is scary when angry, but then it is terrible how no one noticed that two women who had committed crimes and had a link like this on the outside were living in the same building and regularly socialising together. I nod along as Amalphia rants down the phone, and then feel myself relax a little when she tells me that Maxine is now going to be housed somewhere with much higher security and is going to be assessed again to see if she can stand trial and be sent to actual prison.

"That whole subterranean hell down there needs to be filled in with concrete," Justin tells Amalphia now. "I couldn't believe it when I heard what had happened."

"It's a historical site, so it can't be interfered with," she says. "You know that."

"Yeah, the whole castle's historical," says Justin. "Yet they built the new theatre extension. And the swimming pool. Things can be arranged, Phi. You'll have to look into it..."

We leave them to their discussion and hurry through to the backstage area of the theatre. Justin soon follows and insists on hair and make-up being done, but we get to keep our own clothes on. I'm wearing the new jeans and top that Patti brought into the hospital for me. Everyone else is casual too, in their everyday clothes. There was a lot of running about and changing when we got back here.

And there in the wings is Bubbles. Serena. Alexander swings her round, high in the air, and then there's a group hug. We meet her two sisters, one older, one younger, and she tells us how great they are. I know there's some kind of pretence here, not the same as Maxine's, but this family are nice on the outside and not quite the same on the inside. I recognise that in them.

Serena can't believe what's happened. None of us can really believe it either, so it's easier to think about this thing that we're doing right now, and I want Serena to be in it, if she wants to be.

"But I don't know the choreography," she says.

"Neither do we," says Star. "It's all changing again, as of now."

"Well, I would love to be a part of it," says Serena, sounding a bit more like her old bubbly self. "But, what about a costume?"

"It's just our own clothes now," I say, gesturing at all of us, and on to the stage we go.

# 47

IT'S BOTH BEAUTIFUL AND a shambles. We are completely unrehearsed in our return to *Tower* in its original form. And there are nine of us, so, on the spur of the moment; we decide to turn the pas de deux section into three sets of three dancers instead. With no practice. At all.

I love twisting upwards in the spiralling form that our combined bodies make. This is how the great tower was meant to be; it's about friendship and love. It's perfect, all of us together like this, together in raucous harmony, in random alignments all over the stage. I love dancing with Henry and Alexander; we naturally return to our recent cuddly choreography and somehow Lexi, pulled into this at the last minute by his brother, manages to make guitar music to suit everybody in a jumbled sort of way.

There are mistakes and confusion all over the place, of course, and I know we're not perfect in any conventional sense. Maxine would say it's a 'pig's breakfast' of a performance. I smile at that thought as I lean across Henry's leg and hold Alexander's arm for balance. A pig's breakfast can be a wonderful thing; it just depends on what's being served.

I'm thrown upwards, up high above the stage and the audience and the day, and when I fall, when gravity has its way with me, I don't crash down onto a hard floor. My friends are right there to catch me.

The audience in the small castle theatre go wild for us, regardless of any mistakes or confusion. They cheer and clap and stand and shout, feeling the magic of the moment. We all hold hands and bow. Clinton curtseys and the cheers grow louder.

There's so much happiness and laughter at the end of this strange day, though it's not actually the end; it doesn't have to be.

"You can all go home right now if you want to," Amalphia tells us after the performance, Mr. Zolotov nodding alongside her. "If you want to stay for the after-party, you can go upstairs and get dressed up. But only if you want to." She keeps stressing this last bit, with much examining of our faces in between her words.

We all want to stay. We don't want to let go of each other. This is our last night as first years at the castle, and we want to make it count. The television show will be aired at the after-party on a large screen in the theatre, and we want to watch that together, like we did back at the beginning, in my cottage.

So upstairs we go to one of the studios, and there's more hair and make-up and dresses, so many dresses. I don't want to be the colour of a bruise or red like that first pas de deux that Alexander and I did where I looked like his Real Mum. So what is left for me? A brilliant blue dress, that's what. It makes me think of summer skies between white clouds, the sea on a clear day and a bright blue tractor. It's a good memory that one, that day in the tractor shop, and I let myself feel it properly for a moment. I realise there's no metaphorical wall left there at all now, and that's okay.

Amalphia tells us there is a great spread of food downstairs, and that we're all to make sure to eat plenty to ground us. And if we're tired? We can go home or go to our cottages, but we must tell her or Mr. Zolotov or Holly where we're going. They're jumpier than we are today, the teachers and staff; they're certainly more shocked looking than we are.

The truth is that we're okay. Me and my class. Me and my friends. Maybe there will be more emotional fallout. I remember that. It comes later. But for today, tonight, we're a shiny, happy group of first years, of dancers and friends.

Bubbles gets dressed up too. She's back, properly back, she tells us. "I'm sorry about before, Ariel," she says in a lowered voice at the side of the room. "When I was starting to become ill. I hope I'll be better at recognising the signs in myself from now on and not take it out on other people."

"It's all right," I tell her, noticing how much weight she's lost since I saw her last, and wondering about all she's been through. "And if you want to talk about it anytime, I'm here for you. I really mean it. Not just saying it."

The day just gets huggier and huggier. Bubbles, as she actually prefers to be called – I checked – looks really feminine and gentle all in lilac. Belinda is glamorous in dark pink. Star is golden, as she should be, and Paula is regal in purple. We're offered tiaras, which at first seems so stupid, but once we try them on is actually totally awesome. We're fairy princesses in our pink fairy-tale castle, all ready for the ball!

The boys, in a mixture of bright shirts and ties and suits, meet us in the corridor and we meander towards the stairs together, stopping to look at the pictures on the walls. Famous faces look back at us, most of them well known to me now. Amalphia features heavily in the photographic gallery of the first-floor corridor. Justin's there too, and Will, and even Crispin Truelove in a picture taken at some ceremony where he's handing Amalphia an award. He doesn't look as happy and golden in that photo as he usually does.

Down the stairs we go, arm-in-arm. Henry and Alexander and I lead the way towards the foyer with its familiar black-and-white floor and stone angels above.

There's a lot of noise from the great hall, a buzz of people talking and eating and clinking glasses, but there's only one person in the foyer: a man, a man in a kilt. He's in full Highland dress, proper black jacket and bow tie and sporran and everything. Jonasz Serafin is looking up at me, because he's got down on one knee, in his kilt, and he's holding out a small box.

The other people seem to fade away. And it's just him and me in this moment, like we've moved into our own separate time or dimension. The past? The future? I don't know. I just stare at him and he looks back at me. And that's all there is.

# 48

JONASZ LOOKS LIKE HE'S going to speak, but he doesn't. I walk forward to look at him more closely. I see his short brown hair and his tan from the fields. I see his perfect face, so well known, yet wearing a new expression that I've never seen before. I can't make it out; it's almost smiling, almost desperate, almost hopeful.

"I love you, Ariel." That's what Jonasz says first, and then he starts saying lots more, his words pouring out in a rush: "I always did. And I wanted you to ken that, in case you didna ken, because I never said it, and I realised I never said it, and I'm so sorry I never said it. I want us to have our forever. If you want it too, of course. I want to marry you."

He opens the box, and something inside it sparkles, but I can't stop looking at Jonasz's face.

"I always wanted that," he says. "And I know you probably don't, but I wanted you to ken that's how it was in case you thought it was some other way that it wasn't, and I want you to remember how it really was. To know that I love you. Always did. Always will."

His words are a jumble. My heart and mind are a jumble too. There's so many feelings here, and I don't know how to unravel them.

Someone walks out of the great hall, and my awareness that we're not alone returns. Sometimes, like earlier in the theatre, it's great to have an audience. This is not one of those times. There's everyone behind us, friends, of course, but still an audience. There's people at the door of the great hall; without looking away from Jonasz, I suspect that one of them is Justin's assistant Nigel, and that the cameras and Justin will appear any minute.

I put my hands out and close the small box in Jonasz's hands. He blinks, nervous about what this means, I think.

"Come with me," I say to him, taking his hand and pulling him across the foyer.

We run down the passageway to the kitchens and on past many, many rooms to the back door of the castle. I start up some sort of running commentary as we go.

"This is the back door of the castle," I tell him, letting go of his hand to open said door.

Much of what I say is just stating the obvious, but it's like I need this clarifying moment, this pause in what is happening. We both need it. It normalises the evening, a bit, as far as such an evening can be normalised.

"This is the path to the first-year cottages," I say as we start to walk along it. "Those little lights come on when it gets dark."

"Solar powered with light sensors," says Jonasz, nodding.

Then I tell him which cottage is which, who stays in each one, and then we come to mine, and we go in, and I ask him to sit, and he sits on the sofa, and everything starts to feel really strange, unreal and like things need to be clarified again.

Jonasz is here in my sitting room. "You're here in my sitting room," I say, but it doesn't make it feel any more normal.

"Aye," he says, and I sit down on a chair across from him.

I can see him better like this. This situation, him being here, is all too new and peculiar, and I need to adjust before anything else can happen, before I can even think about any of what he said back there in the foyer.

"This place was never on TV," he says, looking around at everything.

"You watched the show?" I ask, amazed.

"Course. Voted for you every week."

"Really?" I laugh.

It seems bizarre and impossible. Jonasz is from another world, another life; his reaching into this one, having been in it in some small way all along is a difficult concept to accept.

He takes my laughter the wrong way. "Do you want me to go, Ariel? I ken this must seem like some cheek, me showing up after all this time—"

"No." I stop him before he says more, more that I'm not quite ready to hear. "But I need to get used to you being here. I'm going to make sweet tea."

I get up and go through to the kitchen. I put on the blue light-up kettle and get mugs out, one with a painted mermaid, the other with a seal. I put lots of sugar in the tea. I know he's there behind me. He's followed but is staying by the door, hanging back, unsure.

I turn and look at him. Jonasz. Tears prick at the back of my eyes. I'm looking at the most beautiful sight I have ever seen. I can see his knees. Between the top of the cream-coloured kilt socks and the kilt itself I can see Jonasz Serafin's knees. I now know that Jonasz Serafin's legs are a bit hairy and entirely beautiful. He's almost too gorgeous to cope with in the kilt.

"You've even got the proper shoes," I say, which doesn't express what I'm feeling at all.

Or maybe it does because he says: "Is it too much?"

I shake my head, and then I rush at him and grab on, hugging him tight, and I'm hugged back. A Jonasz hug. I've known these since I was twelve years old, and nothing has changed. It's only safe and good. I feel his warm breath in my hair, and it's everything I need. He's everything I need. There's a 'new shirt and soap' smell about him but also that fresh-air wonderful-ness that is Jonasz.

"She tried to kill me again today," I tell him because in this safe place I can voice things I find hard to think about. "Or do you know that already? Does everybody know that?"

"Fit?" he says, holding me back to look at me. "Your mither? Maxine?"

"Maxine," I say, thinking that the word mither or mother has to be earned, and that's not what she is to me.

"Are you okay?" He's examining me for harm now.

"Just a little bruised. That's from when the wave hit and washed us to the back of the cave." And then, I tell him the rest of the day's story.

"But she's locked up properly now?" he says, properly angry.

I nod. "Amalphia says she's going to be put somewhere with better security and may have to stand trial now."

"Good!" he exclaims. "They did say something today in the theatre. They said you and your class weren't going to perform, but they couldn't say why for legal reasons, but then there you all were, and I thought everything must be fine."

"You watched today's performance?" This seems amazing to me, and so unexpected.

"You invited us."

"I didn't think you'd actually come."

"You ask me to be somewhere, I'm gonna be there. I came to the premiere, hoping you might see me and ken I was on your side. Always. No matter what."

It's almost a kissing moment – he's looking down at me; I'm gazing up at him – but it's not, because an unpleasant thought has appeared.

"Did you bring Katy with you this time too? Is she here tonight?"

237

"Katy? No. Ariel, I didna bring her to the premiere. She heard I was going and she showed up to try and get in on your fame and success."

"My fame and success?"

"Aye," he says, sounding a bit defensive. "That's not why I'm here, if that's what you're thinking."

I walk over to the tea. I hand him his. I walk back through to the sitting room and sit in the armchair that only one person can sit in. He sits on the sofa again.

Boundaries in place again, I say: "Why don't we discuss your Katy thing?"

"What Katy thing? There's no Katy thing."

I take a drink of tea and close my eyes, really not wanting to say what I'm about to say but unable to stop myself. "Three slow dances. At Christmas. Then you really knew what you were doing."

He's looking at me blankly when I open my eyes.

"She talked about it at that Young Farmers' meeting."

"Well, she was talking shite. There's only ever been you, Ariel."

"Really?" I'm doing Amalphia's face-studying thing, searching for any hint of deception in him. I find none. He's looking right back at me, honest and cross and agitated.

"I ken it's not the same for you," he says. "I ken about Alexander. I mean, it's okay." He says this like it's really not okay. "You'd every right. And I ken Henry said it wisna what it looked like, but I ken fit I seen."

I raise my eyebrows high, not deliberately; they just jump up there into some sort of astonished expression because this is a lot of information, a lot of odd information.

"It seems you ken a lot of things, and I ken very little," I say. "Start with Henry," I request.

# 49

I THINK THE RIGHT word is: gobsmacked. It's not the word of the night; there's another word hanging around in the air between us wanting to be said, despite the current astonishment, but gobsmacked is the word of the moment, and I want to stay with gobsmacked for a while.

Jonasz has been talking to Henry all this time. There's been lots and lots of talking. How? By text. Henry only ever sent one or two words by text to me when I was at Patti's. Not so to Jonasz.

It's my turn to be cross and agitated. "You met him at Ross's farm," I say, having just learned this. "And then you got him to spy on me?"

"No. Ariel, it wasn't like that. I told him I was worried about you. I told him how I felt about you. I told him I'd never told you, and I didn't know what to do about it. He said he'd let me know how you were doing. He'd let me know if you ever said anything that suggested you might want to see me again."

"Spying," I repeat, staying strong, not letting myself visit any emotional word-of-the-night type place. More clarity is needed first. "And why were you there, anyway? At Ross's farm?"

"I work there at weekends; I'm qualified in tractor mechanics now, so—"

"The blue tractor. That's been you, hasn't it?"

"Aye, I went back and bought it with Dad. Be paying it off forever, but it's paying for itself really—"

"You really do have some cheek, Jonasz Serafin."

"I reckoned showing some cheek was the only chance I had to get you back."

"So you stalked me in your fancy new tractor?"

"No. I was working. I liked the idea of being near to you, though."

"Stalker."

"No," he says again. "I didna do anything like that. I wanted to walk Caliban in the woods here, thought he would like that, thought we might even meet you and get a chance to talk. But that would mean passing right by your wee house here, and I didna do it. I just went the places Ross sent me. So it just happened I was up on the hill that day you were all at the beach."

The day at the beach. The tractor. "You were in my head, that's where you were," I tell him. "I could hear the tractor, and I knew you would know what type it was just from the sound because you're so clever like that. But it wasn't because you're clever; it was because you were in it! Oh! This is so infuriating!"

It's far too infuriating to continue sitting calmly in a chair. I need some sort of physical outlet. I need to run up steps, lots and lots of spiralling steps, but I'm not beside a tower, so my own short flight of stairs to the cottage bedrooms has to do. It's not enough, but I don't know what else to do. So I sit on my bed and listen to Jonasz walk up the stairs.

He stops on the landing and looks into the bedroom. "Was that when you were kissing Alexander that you were thinking that stuff about the tractor?" he asks, as if there's been no interruption to our conversation at all, no change of venue even. This is also infuriating.

"Yes," I say, cross.

"And?"

"What do you mean, and? There is no and. I told him I was still in love with someone else, and we decided to remain friends, and we've been really close ever since. We have a lot of the same or similar crap in our pasts. We get each other. But we're friends, and it's quite annoying that people keep thinking other stuff about us."

"Are you still?"

"Friends? Of course we—"

"No. Are you still in love with someone else?"

"Oh." I look right at him and the real word of the night gets spoken. "Yes."

"Can I come in?" he says at the threshold. "I mean, is it okay?"

"Oh. Yes," I say again and gesture towards the other end of the bed for him to sit.

He sits. He looks sort of too big for the small room with its sloping ceilings. He has to bend a little to sit on the bed.

"And is it with me?" he asks.

"Oh. Yes." Seriously. These may be the only words I can say now.

His mouth does a quick twitchy smile, and he looks down at the carpet, relieved or in shock or something, I'm not sure. He reaches inside his jacket.

"I don't know if you're considering this," he says, small box in hand again. "Or if you think it's a stupid idea."

"Yes," I say, dropping the 'oh' this time.

"Stupid idea?" he asks.

"No."

"Considering it?"

"No." I provide the needed clarification: "Yes. I'm saying yes."

"For real?" His eyes are wide as he looks at me.

"For real," I echo.

# 50

"ARIEL. I— ARIEL." I'VE never seen Jonasz all stuttery like this. He was prepared to be sent away or to be told this was a stupid idea. He wasn't prepared for yes. "You should totally see the ring," he says as if grasping for something to say. "It's really valuable – there's something about carats and purity – it was my grandmother's. But we could get a new one if you want. If that's better."

His hands are shaking as he takes it out of the box and holds it out to me.

I take the ring in one hand, and his hand in the other. "Are you frightened, Jonasz Serafin?"

"No. I stopped being frightened the moment you said yes."

I lean back, holding the ring up towards the window to see it. The diamond is big and shiny; it glints as the last sunlight of the day hits it.

"Wow," I say, lying back onto my pillow. "How did you get your grandmother's ring?"

"Mum gave it to me when I told her I was going to do this."

"Really?" I feel a bit incredulous. Janet approved of this idea?

"Yeah," he says sliding himself up between me and the wall, lying down and leaning up on one elbow on the bed.

We used to lie together like this at the top of the tower sometimes in what feels like the olden days, a long time before now anyway. Jonasz put cushions up there, and we'd lay facing each other and talk and talk. And snuggle. And that's what happens again, now, here in the new, in the now.

He tells me how bad his mum feels about what I overheard. She didn't even mean it, not how I must have picked it up. She was concerned for us both, but she didn't tell him about it until recently, and then he was so angry that he moved out of the house.

He touches the ring. He puts the ring on my finger, that finger, the proper one. It makes me glad that it was the other hand that got damaged and not this one. The ring feels strange, but right, absolutely right, as if this was always going to happen, all along. This is where we were heading. All along. I lay my head down on the pillow and look at the ring and then back at Jonasz, who's busy filling in detail after detail for me.

"I couldn't believe you thought I might go away to university. You know I was no good at school; I'm not clever like you."

"Jonasz," I say with some firmness because I hate it when he says things like this. "You are the cleverest person I know."

"You're the only person thinks that," he says, laughing. "But. Okay. I love you. And I love farming. Surely it's the clever choice to do the things you love?"

"So you're going to do me?"

He flushes. His cheeks go really dark red. That's new. I reach out and feel the warmth with my palm.

"Not what I meant," he says, covering my hand with his. "But it made me think," he says. "When Mum told me what you heard. You know, that that was why you finished it with me and not because you didn't want me?"

"How could you have thought I didn't want you?"

"You broke up with me, Ariel. I thought I wasn't good enough for you. I always kind of thought that."

"Jonasz!" This is so awful. "You were everything to me. Everything good in my life."

"And you to me."

We're both crying now. He kisses my forehead and then my nose, but not my mouth. We don't go there yet. Not a triple kiss. Not yet.

"But your family," I say, because Jonasz has a lovely family. I was not everything good in his life. "They're lovely."

"Janek so brainy? Jack so sweet? Then there's stupid little Jonasz; just stick him outside to play."

"Really? That's how it was for you?"

"Oh aye. It's not dramatic. It's not on the level of what you went through. It's nothing to that. I'm not trying to say it is. They dinna even mean to do it. But losing you? I couldn't cope with it, Ariel, couldn't see straight. Drove the old tractor into a dyke right after you left. It's why we had to buy another one."

I kiss his forehead. I kiss his nose. I linger by his mouth but then just hold on to him. Tightly.

"But then there was the show," he says. "Things you said on there made me think. You did that reaching deep inside thing with the choreographer guy, and you came out with *Tower*. Your lost love," he says. "And then I was absolutely" – he swears like Alexander, and it's a shock, because I've never heard Jonasz swear – "fizzing when they kicked you out of the piece. It was yours. No one else had any right."

I love listening to him. I could listen to him forever. In fact, I will.

"Well," I explain. "We got everyone into trouble with what we did in the stone circle. There's a curfew now."

"When you set fire to the forest, aye?"

"We didn't mean to. We were doing a naked empowerment thing—"

"Naked?"

I smile. "Did Henry not mention that we'd seen each other naked?"

244

"He did not." Jonasz's tone has gone all clipped and tight. He sounds like I felt when I thought things about Katy, and I love him for his crossness.

I love him so much. I lean across the bed and kiss him on the mouth.

When I kissed Alexander on the cliff, it felt all tingly. When I used to kiss Jonasz, it was different, but we were children to begin with, and then it did get tingly as we grew, and then more, more than tingly. It was secret and just ours and special for being that, but this is different, totally different.

The moment my mouth touches his, something explodes in me and everything goes a bit wild like some sort of rampant force has been set free. We're kissing and kissing, rougher than we were before, like we're trying to consume each other. My heart doesn't pound. It thumps. I feel like I've run up lots and lots of steps, and I press my ear to Jonasz's chest to hear if his heart is the same, and it is. I listen to it and catch my breath, and then I look at him again, and it's too much, far too much.

I'm kissing him, and I understand more of why he was cross. About the nakedness, I mean. I've never seen him, not all of him, and I try to undo his shirt to at least see his chest or to kiss more of him. The bow tie is a problem. He unhooks it. I undo more buttons and uncover a **#TeamAriel** T-shirt under the smart shirt.

It's so funny, I laugh. He laughs too, and the energy in the room calms down a bit. We calm down a bit. I lay my head on his chest over **#TeamAriel**, knowing this is not quite the time for more to happen. Not that. Not yet.

Though: "I am seventeen now."

"Old enough to learn to drive," he says, and that's funny too because I know he knows what I really meant.

There's a terrible banging from downstairs, no, more than a banging: a crashing like another disaster is underway. It's a furious thumping, but not of hearts, and then we hear someone unlock my front door and burst into the cottage.

"Stay back," says Jonasz, leaping up from the bed. "Stay here."

We're both thinking the same thing, I know it. Is it her? Has she escaped again? Come for me again? There's no way I'm staying up here and letting Jonasz face her alone. I'm the one that knows her. I know how to pacify and calm an angry alcoholic. I can make her the perfect cup of tea. I could offer her food like I did before. Holly keeps our fridges extremely well stocked since the curfew.

I'm menu planning at speed as we descend the stairs slowly to meet a murderer. There's cheese in the fridge. There's bread and eggs. I could do Welsh rarebit. The meal of cheese on toast topped with egg is great hangover food, drunk food, good for both states of being.

A voice from below shouts: "Ariel!" It's a man's voice. The voice shouts again: "Ariel! Are you here?"

The voice has a Ukrainian accent. I see Mr. Zolotov looking all wild haired and wild eyed in my sitting room as Jonasz and I reach the bottom of the stairs.

"Ariel, are you okay?" says my teacher, coming forward, inspecting me for harm like everyone has been doing today. He's also eyeing Jonasz suspiciously.

"I'm fine," I say, taking hold of Jonasz's arm to steady myself as the brief state of terror fades. I introduce them. "Jonasz, my boyfriend. Mr. Zolotov, my teacher."

They shake hands.

"Fiancée," corrects Jonasz.

"We just got engaged," I tell Mr. Zolotov, holding out my hand with the ring on it for him to see.

"Oh. Well. This, it is very nice. But everyone is terribly worried." He speed dials someone on his phone. "She is here," he says into the phone. "Yes, she is well. We are coming back up to the castle now."

"Oh, but I'm still talking to Jonasz," I tell Mr. Zolotov, knowing that Jonasz and I still have so much more to say to each other.

"I will wait outside for you," says my teacher then exiting and standing, hands in pockets, right in front of the sitting room window. I get it. Nothing else is going to happen to me on his watch. Nothing else.

"He seems kinda wired," says Jonasz.

"Well, a lot has happened at his school today. Maybe we should just go."

So we do, and it's actually rather nice, like it's what I need, this walk through the tall green trees with these two men, in the soft breeze and the gentle twilight glow of the world. The solar-powered lights switch on as we walk by, and Mr. Zolotov tells us that he is happy for us.

I am too. Happy for us. Happy forever. Happy for everything.

# 51

As soon as we step into the great hall, we are surrounded by the previously worried people, and it's all a bit much. I want to be on my own with Jonasz again. Patti holds me very tightly, and I feel bad for not realising people would be concerned when I skipped off out of the castle. Janet's there too, and I get the feeling that she and Patti have been talking.

"Does this mean what I think it means?" Janet says, smiling, taking my hand and looking at the ring.

It's so strange. Janet is happy about the engagement, and Patti isn't. I mean, Patti is smiling, and acting pleased to meet my boyfriend, my fiancé, but I can tell this is actually another worry to her. But it won't be, not when she gets to know Jonasz.

She tells him he must come to dinner soon. He says thank you and that he'd like that. It's oddly formal and wrong somehow.

Then there's Tomas and Janek and Jack, all: happy, happy, happy.

There's my class, all over-excited and telling me I've missed the first TV show and that our piece was a worse mess than we thought at the time, and then, before I can introduce them all to Jonasz, there's a mass exodus out of the hall and back through to the theatre where the second show is about to be shown on a big screen.

I pull Jonasz along with me to sit with my class in the theatre, and people notice the ring.

"No way," says Alexander in astonishment, but then he adds, with a genuine and not too movie-star-ish smile: "That's totally awesome, Ariel."

He shakes hands with Jonasz and congratulates him.

"I really wanted you to be gay," Jonasz tells him, and Alexander looks like he doesn't know what to say, but we're saved by the dark and the hush that falls over everyone in the theatre as the second show begins.

It's a bit of a shock, the show, at least the opening scene of it. Crispin Truelove sits beside the glass door in that floor, in that odd room, by the start of that tunnel that leads to the underground places.

"It's a shocking thing," he says, face lit-up green from below. "This place has known terror in the dark, walls tumbling down, and people being crushed."

There's movement at the front of the theatre. Amalphia stands up and says, "Where are they? Crispin? And Justin?"

Crispin speaks from the screen as if to calm her down, even performing a sort of soft patting gesture with his hand. "Rumours all, don't worry, gentle viewers. The castle is a mysterious place, with many deep, dark secrets." The camera pans down to the wooden steps and the barrels. "And only today," Crispin goes on, "there have been misadventures. Events of which we must not speak, for legal reasons, and yet..." He pauses.

Amalphia is still standing, silhouetted against the screen, hands on hips, super cross.

Crispin speaks again: "These events, were we allowed to detail them, would explain much that has happened on our own little show today. The delays. The changes in schedule... but see for yourselves..."

There's a quick montage of clips of dark places in the castle accompanied by dark and mysterious music. The castle images are interspersed with parts of our group performance, which all look a bit sinister with the music – I think that's the intention – but our smiles cancel out the dark, somehow. To me they do, anyway.

Crispin's booming voice fills the auditorium again. "**#TeamAriel** and **#TeamTower** are reconciled under this old roof." There's a quick blast of an older aerial shot of the castle, highlighting the roof with its many turrets. "But have the audience gone for it? Is this what the adoring public want?" Crispin looks sceptical. "Is that ever how show business works?"

The rest of the programme basically demonstrates that: no, that is not how show business works. Our previous fans are dismayed. They enjoyed the drama of the fight, the competition, the tension of friendships destroyed. I can't blame anyone for not being impressed by our impromptu performance, but we're in tenth place. At first I think that's not last, as there were eleven finalists, but, of course: we combined our two. We are last, and the internet is not a happy place.

"Don't look," advises Henry, and everybody takes the advice this time. There's too much else to be happy about.

After the show, I locate **#TeamKilt** – the winners of the competition – to congratulate them and introduce them to Jonasz. They're not looking too happy, despite holding a shiny trophy.

I know they just overheard Justin expressing horror and disbelief that it was Highland dancers that won, but then we all watch as Amalphia takes Justin down. She actually pins him against a wall in her fury.

"No one can control Truelove when he's on a roll," says Justin.

"You are the producer," she says in a stony voice. "You control everything."

Nigel whisks us students away from the theatre and the increasingly heated voices. He whisks us back along the corridor and across the foyer. We pass under the angels and into the great hall. It's party time at the castle.

# 52

I WALTZ ROUND THE huge room in Jonasz's arms, and it feels like a dream. Him being here. Us being together. As we sway past the buffet table, I realise it's one of those dreams where I'm really, really hungry, so we stop there. We stuff our faces with little star-shaped sandwiches and gold-topped chocolate squares and make noises of appreciation. Jonasz hadn't eaten much today either; he'd been too nervous.

Bubbles joins us and asks to look at the ring. She jumps up and down and claps her hands. "Oh, it's so lovely! So romantic! And I don't think you're too young at all. I think it's lovely."

So, someone has said we're too young. It's weird, but I've not anticipated that, and I should have. I mean, I know how old we are, or how young. It's what Patti's thinking; I know that. We are young, but then again, we're not.

We move off onto the dance floor again, and I look up at Jonasz. "I don't think we're too young," I say.

"We're not," he replies. "You had all those years being the grown-up in your house."

"And you had to be the grown-up in the tower for me. I'm sorry, Jonasz, if that put pressure on you."

"You're kidding, right?" he says, looking down to study my face. "Ariel. You're the strongest person I know." He grins. "And the hottest, and I got to make out with you in the tower. Best moments of my life."

I don't have to examine his face to know he's telling the truth. All those moments in the tower were the best, absolutely the best. So far.

"And now we can be together properly," he says. "Did I tell you I have a house now?"

He has a house now. It was part of a surprise inheritance from his grandfather. He got it when he turned eighteen, but he didn't move into it until he found out about my overhearing his parents' conversation.

Jonasz's house is made up of three old farm cottages that have been knocked into one and done up. It sounds amazing. He's put a ballet barre up in one room for me. He says he always would have kept it, even if I'd said no, even if I'd sent him away. He would have kept it because it was mine.

I can't wait to see the house. I can't wait to live in the house. I can't wait to live with Jonasz.

"Sent you lots of pics," he says. "All the stages of doing it up and stuff."

"What? When? Where?"

By text, that's how. To my old phone, that's where. I want to run and get it, to charge it up and see the house and the texts.

"No don't, Ariel, not just now. I texted you every day since we broke up, said everything I couldn't say before, told you I loved you every night."

So Jonasz's side of the story, his life, his thoughts and feelings from this last five months, wait for me in that old phone. But that's for later. In the now, the music slows and a kissing moment is reached again. The music stops.

"Who could've called this one?" booms an annoying and loud voice. "Ariel and Jonasz? Did you two just meet tonight? Or did you meet up at the farm?"

I look round to discover the source of this nonsense. It's Ross. The farmer. Alexander's cousin. He's standing with the band.

In fact he has a guitar strap slung over his shoulder, so perhaps he is part of the band. He is speaking into a microphone, hence the loudness.

"We met years ago," I shout over at him.

"In the tower!" someone else shouts. I think it's Paul, ever informative, ever factual.

"No way," continues Ross. "We could have had a thing going there: **#TeamJonasz** and **#TeamAlexander.** I would have gone for the latter, of course."

I'm furious. I take a few steps towards Ross to give him a good telling off, but it seems this is enough in itself. I must look scary, or something.

"Oh, okay, Ariel, okay! No need for... You weren't kidding; she really is like Amalphia." This last is said to Alexander, who is also approaching, I imagine with the same aim of putting an end to Ross's stupidity.

"Ignore him," advises Alexander. "He's been drinking; always gets a bit mouthy."

I get that; I know this stuff. I turn back to Jonasz who seems to be finding the whole thing quite amusing.

"I don't like Ross," I tell him.

"He can be a bit of an idiot," he agrees. "Young Farmers all supported you, you know, all voted for you."

"Really?" This seems a bit unbelievable.

"Katy's been banned for what she did to you, both at the meet and at the cinema."

That's good. That's cool.

Then Henry cuts in which is a bit of a shock on two counts. First, he says: "Can I cut in?" Word count: four. Then we realise it's Jonasz he wants to dance with, and that's not so much a shock as just funny. But I suppose the two of them are friends now, what with all the texting they've been doing.

I dance with Clinton. "And I thought you were going to marry me," he jokes.

"You look so happy," Alexander calls over to me.

I am happy. He gets it. He would be too if it were happening with his... whoever he's in love with. Seeing the way he's looking at Bubbles as they dance together, I'm no longer completely sure that it is Chantal.

Crispin appears and takes my hand as if to dance with me, and then he sees the ring. "Oh, my dear, I'm so sorry," he says and is gone, like vanished, gone.

It's strange, but I'm getting used to that with Crispin and the castle and actually with life in general, so I just laugh it off and then dance with both of #TeamKilt together. We perform an impromptu Highland fling in the middle of the floor.

Jonasz dances with Patti which I think is weird and awkward for them both, and then we all arrive back at the buffet together along with Amalphia, Justin, Mr. Zolotov and Will. Amalphia's all excited, apparently because it's raining.

"Not just raining," she says in exasperation at no one understanding her excitement. "It's torrential. A summer storm. Come on; it'll be the perfect way to end the school year."

We run up the path between the pines. It's slippy in places. Deep puddles have formed on the dry ground from the sudden rainfall. I hold Jonasz's hand and Patti's hand. We stop while Jonasz gives me his smart kilt jacket to make sure I don't get cold, and I see Patti begin to approve of him.

I smile into the rain, let go their hands and race Jonasz up to the stone circle.

And then I spin and spin, in and out and between the tall stones as they shine and shimmer yellow and green and blue in the wet. Someone brought glow sticks and dotted them around the circle. No fire tonight. The rain is magnificent as it thunders down over us all, drenching us, soaking us, but also: washing us clean. Preparing us for a fresh new start.

Jonasz looks so handsome with his hair plastered to his head. So do Alexander and Clinton and Will and Mr. Zolotov. Both the older men are dancing with Amalphia, and laughing and smiling, and it's beautiful.

Patti stands up on the low stone in her bare feet. "Your school is such a bohemian place," she tells me, laughing and happy too.

"Hey," I say to little Faye as she dances round and round with Alexander and Bubbles in the middle of the circle. "You said we would win. Back at the beginning, you said that to me."

She smiles through the rain at me. "You don't think you won?"

I hold out my hands in question, because: umm...? Then I look around. Jonasz and Patti are right beside me: my family; I love them and they love me. There's Alexander and Clinton and Bubbles and Henry: good friends, true friends. And the others, the teachers and adults in my life are all good now too: reliable, caring, helpful people.

Of course I've won.

I think back to that moment in the tower when I knew nothing would ever be the same again. I want to reach back through time and say to that sad and panicked girl: it's only good. It's only great. Nothing will ever be the same again, and it's fantastic. Nothing will ever be the same again, and it's more joyful than you can imagine.

"You're all mad!" says Justin, the first to leave the circle to seek dry clothes and warmth.

"Don't forget 'Project Aileen' next term!" Alexander calls from in the midst of a difficult looking ballet lift with Bubbles, as I make to leave with Patti and Jonasz. "Get planning. Text me."

"What is this project?" asks Mr. Zolotov.

Alexander tries to look innocent. "We're going to do the absolute best we can in her class," he tells his father, and Bubbles does jazz hands. I have to leave before I give them away with laughter.

It's the last night of term at the most prestigious dance school in Scotland, so, of course, I'm going home with my Fairy Grandmother to read several months of love texts sent to me by my handsome, kilted boyfriend, now fiancé. He's coming to lunch tomorrow, and then we're all going to drive out and see his house which will be our house. Nothing is going to be the same again, ever. Happily Ever. After all.

**Read the next title in the Castle Dancers series!**

### Bubbles: Dancing Through History

It's going to be the most boring year of her life. That's what Bubbles has decided. This, her second year at the castle school, will involve no naked dancing, or television appearances. No fires in stone circles. No meltdowns. No hospital stays. You know, not like last year.

As she walks up the tree-lined drive towards the castle, she is immediately surrounded by TV reporters. Next she encounters the enigmatic and charming new boy, American student Aiden, and finds herself in an instalove situation. Being cast as the lead in a historical documentary is altogether too exciting and fun, as are the night-time visits to caves and underground chambers.

As Bubbles navigates her difficult home life, the complexities of her mental health and various intense experiences at the castle, she struggles to maintain equilibrium.

Will she be able to find balance amidst the chaos, or will her carefully laid 'boring' plan unravel completely?

# Helpful Places

- The National Association for Children of Alcoholics: https://nacoa.org.uk/ Free (UK) Helpline: 0800 3583456

- National Association for People Abused in Childhood: https://napac.org.uk/ Free (UK) Helpline 0808 801 0331

- The blog of Dr. Glenn Doyle, who specialises in trauma recovery: https://useyourdamnskills.com/

# About the Author

AILISH SINCLAIR TRAINED AS a dancer and taught dance for many years, before working in schools to help children with special needs.

She lives in Scotland beside a loch with her husband and two children where she dances (medical conditions allowing) and writes and eats rather too much chocolate.

See the blog at ailishsinclair.com for posts about Scotland, castles, history, stone circles, dance, living with chronic illness, and writing.

# More Ailish

## Online

**www.ailishsinclair.com**

**@AilishSinclair on X/Instagram/Threads**

## Contemporary Fiction:

### A Dancer's Journey (series) (explicit content)

When dance student Amalphia Treadwell embarks on a secret relationship with her rich, handsome teacher, she has no idea of the danger that lurks in his new school in Scotland...

Titles: Tendu, Cabriole, Fouetté

# Historical Fiction:

## Sisters at the Edge of the World

From the misty hills of ancient Scotland emerges a tale of love, betrayal, and the fight for freedom. Set in the 1st century, the story includes the battle of Mons Graupius between the Romans and the Caledonian tribes. There's a neurodivergent main character and some rather complicated romance!

## The Mermaid and the Bear

Set in a castle in Aberdeenshire (yes, the same castle), Ailish's debut novel blends an often overlooked period of history, the Scottish witchcraft accusations, in particular the 1597 Aberdeen witchcraft panic, with a love story.

## Fireflies and Chocolate

Torn out of her isolated life in a Scottish castle, Elizabeth embarks on a determined quest to return home. Exhilarating adventures unfold on the high seas, love blossoms, and the chocolate, purchased in Benjamin Franklin's printing shop, is delicious!